SHROUDED

Shrouded is first published in English the United Kingdom in 2024 by Corylus Books Ltd, and was originally published in Icelandic as *Miðillinn* in 2023 by Salka.

Copyright © Sólveig Pálsdóttir, 2023
Translation copyright © Quentin Bates, 2023

Sólveig Pálsdóttir has asserted her moral right to be identified as the author of this work in accordance with the Copyright, Designs and Patents Act, 1988.

All rights reserved. No part of this publication may be reproduced in any form or by any means without the written permission of the publisher.

All characters and events portrayed in this publication, other than those clearly in the public domain, are fictitious and any resemblance to real persons, living or not, is purely coincidental.

Published by arrangement with Salka, Iceland.

www.salka.is

This book has been translated with a financial support from:

Corylus Books Ltd

corylusbooks.com

ISBN: 978-1-7392989-6-8

SHROUDED

Sólveig Pálsdóttir

Translated by Quentin Bates

Published by Corylus Books Ltd

1

Are you the genius we're looking for?

Arnhildur put her coffee cup aside, her eyes fixed on the newspaper. It was a full-page advert, with heavy pink letters overlaid on a picture that wasn't easily made out. She hunched over the table, squinting in the hope of seeing it more clearly. There were fairly clear outlines, but she couldn't discern the faces. It was a group of people, somehow jumbled one on top of another, almost as if they merged into each other. They all appeared youthful, although there could well be a middle-aged figure or two hiding among them. Arnhildur sat up and sipped her coffee. It was cold by now, and bitter. Why was she fooling herself? Of course the picture didn't mean anything. These were just some people or other, who could more than likely have been brought in by an advertising agency, she muttered to herself.

She resolved to not think about the picture, but she read the text again. What was this genius supposed to do? Was this person expected to be someone young – or could it be someone already past middle age? Were there any education or skills requirements, apart from simply being a genius? Was it possible that this presumed *he* could be a *she*, heading for the third stage of life, as the retirement years were referred to these days?

Arnhildur had difficulty making out the fine print. A mist

obscured the letters and she could only hazard a guess at this or that word. She got slowly to her feet, as these days the stiffness in her joints affected her in the mornings when the weather was cold. Her new glasses were on top of the refrigerator and she felt the ache in her shoulders as she stretched to reach for them. Even though she knew perfectly well that the delicate frames were strong, she picked the spectacles up carefully, as she had been taught as a child to treat belongings with respect, especially in the case of something new, or on the expensive side. Glasses were both. She felt a pang of guilt at her own profligacy, as well as a flutter of pleasure deep inside. The frames were dark red, with the upper corners broadening and curving slightly upwards.

'Your face has just the right contour for cat-eye glasses,' the amiable man in the shop had assured her with a winning smile. 'There aren't many people who can carry off this look as well as you,' he added with a wink that made her heart beat faster. The day became brighter, her worries flew away for a moment and she gave in to indulgence.

The lenses were grubby now and she went across to the sink. She leaned a hand against the cold steel so that a tight row of lines formed on the back of her hand. A drop of detergent on each lens and she rubbed them carefully before turning on the tap to wash the soap off. The amiable man had given her two cloths to polish the lenses, but she wouldn't use those right away. They might get dirty and she wasn't sure if they were washable. It was best to leave them pristine in the spectacle case, at least for the moment.

'Genius,' she said out loud, shaking her head. It went without saying that this wasn't going to lead to a job for her, any more than any of the other job ads would. Her knowledge and skills were of no account – nobody was going to employ a woman who was past seventy. She wasn't in demand, and maybe she never had been. But she wasn't going to give up. She'd keep fighting, find a way through it and rid herself of this wretched misfortune. All the same, Arnhildur knew that it would call for a stroke of genius to extricate herself from the difficulties that so tightly enmeshed her, like an unfortunate fly trapped in a delicate but strong spider's web.

She took a cloth from its hook and polished her glasses with the soft material. There, that's better. Now she'd be able to see clearly. She glanced at the window and wondered whether it might be time to take down the Christmas lights and maybe run a duster over the furniture, but she couldn't summon the energy – no more than she had been able to yesterday, or the day before, or during the weeks before that. She had no desire to do anything useful. Her thoughts were all of how to find a way out of the terrible misfortune she faced and what she would have to do to make this happen. A foul feeling of nausea swirled inside her at the thought of tonight's meeting. She sat down again at the kitchen table and stared at the newspaper. Now she could see the text clearly, but wasn't able to concentrate.

2

There were six of them in the little hall and each of them had left an envelope containing a contribution in a basket on the table by the door. Arnhildur could sense from the heavy, dust-filled atmosphere that the place hadn't been aired properly for days, even weeks. That's to say, if it had ever been. The walls were hung with black drapes and it didn't look as if there was a window anywhere that could be opened. In the centre of the room was a small table, and on it stood a three-armed candelabra. She glanced around discreetly, taking care to not stare too long at any of the others. It was quite likely that these people harboured the same inner feeling as she did, a discomfort at being present in this place. Other people could be similarly inclined and she didn't want to make anyone uncomfortable. She wasn't that sort of person.

All the same, she could also sense an expectation, even a spark of excitement in the air as the doors opened and closed again as if by themselves. She shivered and for a moment considered going out to the row of hooks to collect her coat, but decided against it just as a short, bony man took the floor. This was the medium, and she avoided catching his eye. He raised one hand and gestured towards a rack of stacked chairs in one corner.

'Welcome, dear friends,' he said quietly, running his fingers first through his mousy hair and then down one pale cheek. 'Please take your seats in a circle, but not too close to each other.'

SHROUDED

Arnhildur placed her chair between a young woman with tattooed eyebrows and a colourful scarf covering her hairless head, and an older man wearing a blue woollen cardigan with large, black buttons of pressed leather that caught her eye. She adjusted her glasses on her nose and caught sight as she did so of the man's thick moustache and deep blue eyes. He looks lovely, she thought as she patted her grey hair into place. He gave her a faint smile as he shifted his chair a little to make it easier for her to join the circle. The young woman who didn't look to be a day older than twenty made no move, merely stared as if hypnotised at the carpeted floor in front of her.

She must have cancer, poor thing, Arnhildur thought. *She must be going through chemotherapy, or have recently been through it.*

She felt a wave of sympathy for the young woman, and wanted to give her an encouraging pat on the shoulder, but didn't. Instead, she adjusted her skirt and shifted to make herself comfortable. Her ankle-high snow boots were still damp from the walk through the wet snow, and even though she had carefully wiped her feet on the mat by the door, she was disturbed to notice a dirty splash on her thick tights. She discreetly rubbed the stain, but it did no good, simply spreading the mud more widely. She was annoyed at having mud-stained calves now that she had finally gone out to meet people, but reconciled herself with the thought that nobody here in this hall would be paying the slightest attention. Their thoughts were firmly on other things. Arnhildur sighed and furtively sneaked a glance at those present. They included a good-looking couple she guessed to be somewhere between thirty and forty. They held hands and appeared apprehensive. Arnhildur had seen none of these people before, and this was a relief to her.

The clatter of chairs being moved gradually faded away, replaced by an expectant atmosphere. The medium lit the three candles and used a remote control to dim the lights. In a low voice he asked those present to join hands and to focus their thoughts on a collective prayer. He reminded them that he was merely an instrument; a link between two worlds, and once he had entered a trance, he would have no control over what came next.

The man with the handsome eyes and the moustache grasped Arnhildur's hand. His palm was damp and cold. She reached out a hand to the young woman, who extended her own hand in return. Arnhildur squeezed gently, as if to send her an instinctive message of support, but there was no response. She was about to turn and say something pleasant to the young woman when the medium began to speak. His voice was almost robotic and his prominent Adam's apple bobbed up and down in his scrawny throat. He said that this evening had brought together a remarkably good and receptive group, which would help open the channels. He repeated that he was merely an unwitting and humble conduit. Then he made a plea for all good spirits to be with them, to protect them all and give them strength. Finally, he asked that the powers channel messages between the worlds. Arnhildur felt an inner warmth; despite the discomfort in her belly, she felt this to be a beautiful moment.

A long time passed before anything more happened. The medium sat completely still, staring at the flickering candles. He finally closed his eyes and his head dropped forward onto his chest. Arnhildur felt her heart beat faster and her trepidation grew.

The medium emitted a short, hoarse groan. His body jerked a few times, and then relaxed completely. For a while he made no movement as he sat, until his head lifted, in an almost dramatic manner, his eyes opened and his back straightened. He seemed to swell, becoming more upright and graver than before. The man who now appeared to the people in the hall was very different to the

SHROUDED

one who had addressed them earlier, and a shiver passed through her.

3

Arnhildur carefully adjusted the Japanese silk scarf, a retirement present from her colleagues, before putting on her coat and gloves. She tried not to let it show that she was deeply affected, but then most of those present were in a similar state. Some had been on the verge of tears, some had wept, while the young woman with the headscarf who had sat beside her was no longer downcast, but looked around with a broad smile as she zipped up her brightly coloured down anorak. She had been brought hope that everything would turn out well, and simply seeing her expression made Arnhildur feel better.

The couple who had lost their sick little boy after his bitter struggle for life had ended had been told that he no longer felt pain, that he was healthy and his beautiful soul awaited an opportunity to return to earth. They had laughed and wept at the same time. It did her heart good to see them and that sick young woman. All the same, her heart hammered erratically, and she felt out of sorts. The grey-haired man who had sat beside her came over.

'That was amazing. Yes, just unbelievable,' he said, his index finger forming a hook as he stroked his moustache.

'It certainly was,' Arnhildur replied distantly, tightening the belt of her woollen coat. The man opened the door for her with a gentlemanly gesture that under other circumstances she might have appreciated, and they went side by side out into the winter evening. It had snowed hard while the meeting was taking place, and instead of the slush that had left muddy stains on her tights, a thick white layer had settled on the city.

'If anyone with doubts had been there, an experience like that would have changed their opinion,' the man said brightly as he turned up the collar of his dark overcoat.

'You think so?' she replied, just so as to say something, and hoped that the man's route home would take him some other way. On any other day she would have been glad of the company, but not tonight. She needed time to settle her nerves and his presence was almost oppressive.

'Is it a long time since you lost your husband?' he asked.

She shook her head quickly, without looking up, giving the impression that she was watching her steps.

The man dug his hands deep into his pockets and shivered.

'It's hellish cold tonight. We can expect the frost to harden now that it's snowed again.'

Arnhildur muttered something to indicate agreement. This pushy man had to have a car parked somewhere, considering he was so poorly dressed for a cold night. He wasn't even wearing gloves.

'It's four years since I lost my wife,' the man said, offering the information without having been asked. 'The sorrow is always there. It's become a constant companion.'

'What has?'

'The sorrow.'

'Oh, of course. I'm so sorry,' Arnhildur apologised.

'Only to be expected that you've things on your mind, after this evening's events,' the man said, looking at her intently.

'It wasn't easy,' Arnhildur said, her voice low, looking into his eyes. That was true enough.

'I'd have never believed in anything like this, but sorrow sends you in unexpected directions,' the man continued. 'My children would be demanding I see shrink if they knew

I'd been to a séance. We're a family of rationalists. Zero tolerance for bullshit!' He laughed apologetically, as if embarrassed by his own foolishness. 'But I suppose there has to be something in all this, considering what we witnessed.... As they say, it's about keeping an open mind.' He laughed again, awkwardly. 'Surely you're in no doubt, after your experience this evening?' he added, and Arnhildur felt a shiver of cold discomfort run down her back. Why couldn't this man just go away?

She pursed her lips, said nothing, and walked faster. He did the same. Unbelievable how intrusive this man could be!

'Was that your grandmother who appeared? The old lady ranting about what became of the silver decoration on her national dress?' he asked.

'Yes,' Arnhildur mumbled.

'She must have passed away quite some years ago,' the man continued, with no let-up in his persistence.

'Yes.'

'It's remarkable that folk should still take an interest in this earthly existence after such a long time. It must be pretty dull over there on the other side,' he said, his laugh tinged with sarcasm.

What was this boor insinuating? If he didn't go his own way before long, she would take another route home. She silently counted the steps to the next corner, but before she reached it, the man suddenly said good-bye and turned to walk along a side street. Arnhildur was relieved and sighed out loud as he disappeared from sight. She stood still for a moment as her heartbeat settled. Then she set off again.

The frost nipped at her face and the street lights cast a dim glow into the darkness. There were few people about this late on a Tuesday evening in early February as she crossed Lækjargata, heading for the bridge crossing the lake. The sudden appearance of a bus from the darkness startled her.

SHROUDED

'These wretched electric buses sneak up on you without making a sound,' she muttered to herself. 'The old buses were better. At least you could hear them coming and you could pay your fare with money or a ticket, instead of some idiotic phone app that nobody understands.'

As far as she could make out, there was nobody on the bus other than the driver. It went without saying that she couldn't be the only one who failed to adapt to new ways of doing things. She focused her thoughts on all the things that had been so much easier in the old days, as a way of avoiding thinking about what had taken place at the meeting. That would have to wait until tomorrow, otherwise she wouldn't sleep a wink tonight.

Arnhildur walked along Skothúsvegur and saw a young man locking a car before taking the steps leading up to a large white house on Tjarnargata at a run. She heard the light sound of his footsteps and the muffled click as the door closed behind him. It was again silent and Arnhildur had the feeling of being alone in the world, just like Palle waking up in a deserted world in the stories every child knew so well. She again felt her own rapid heartbeat and her breath came with difficulty. The events of the evening had certainly been distressing enough to upset her and she felt a deep fatigue that settled on her whole body. Every step was an effort and the snow that clung to her boots seemed to be as heavy as lead. After making her way along Suðurgata, she had no choice but to pause and lean against the graveyard wall. She felt faint, could barely breathe and the weight in her chest was increasing. What was wrong with her? Was this a heart attack? Shouldn't she feel her arm tingling? Or was this a stroke, but wasn't a terrible headache a warning of what was to come? Arnhildur pulled off a glove and felt in her pocket for her old-fashioned phone. She was frightened but didn't know who to call. Now she had the feeling that a brick had been placed on her chest. Terrified, she tried to think of anyone she could call for help, but nobody came to mind. She'd have to call an ambulance. She tried to punch in the emergency number but wasn't sure if she was finding the right buttons. Now she couldn't see clearly, and tried to feel for the buttons, but arthritis had robbed her fingertips of any sensitivity. Something crunched in the snow behind her. Now someone would undoubtedly come to her aid. She looked over the graveyard wall, peering among the gravestones and the bare branches, but saw nothing there but darkness. She glanced around, but the street was as deserted as before. Once again, she heard the clear crunch of footsteps coming her way. Someone was coming through the graveyard.

'Hello? Anyone there?' she called out as loudly as she could. There was no response and she couldn't be sure that her voice was audible. 'Will you help me? Hello? Help, please.' Her voice was faint but she hoped it would carry through the winter silence.

There was no response, but she could hear and sense more clearly that someone was approaching.

'I need help...' She hesitated at the sound of something breaking, a tree branch broken off. What was going on? She pressed herself against the graveyard wall, knowing that she had to support herself while the world spun around her. The sound of panting breaths drew closer, and then there was a voice that said something she was unable to make out clearly.

'Who's there?' The weight in her chest was increasing. 'Hello!'

There was nothing to be seen across the street, not even the pavement, just the dim glow of lights from houses and along the street by the lake.

'Who are you?' Arnhildur whispered, her voice feeble. She was faint and she heard a sound, almost like the howl of a dog, but couldn't be sure if it came from her or someone else. Was she suffering an attack that distorted her senses? She summoned the last of her energy to ask again for assistance.

'Could you help me? I can't see the buttons...'

Before she could say any more, she felt a heavy blow to her head and shards of pain flashed through her nerves. She dropped to her knees. Heavy breaths and gasps could be heard, someone swearing.

This was a voice she'd heard before and she tried to see who was speaking, but saw nothing even though she felt that her eyes were open. Now she sensed that hands were grasping her under the arms and she was being dragged. There was an indistinct scraping sound, panting and her body bumped across the uneven ground, but she no longer felt anything. Then there was another blow, and the ice-cold snow settled to cover her.

4

A gale had blown through Wednesday night, accompanied by a downpour. The weather's fury was mostly spent by the time Guðgeir and Elsa Guðrún from Reykjavík CID drove early in the morning through the city to the oldest part of its western district. Unusually, Elsa Guðrún, the one who was habitually cheerful and positive, was under a cloud of gloom that refused to lift. She'd been late for work after a struggle with her twin boys who hadn't wanted to go to school, on top of which her car was booked for a service. It needed work ahead of its annual inspection, and she hoped fervently that another year of life could be squeezed out of the old rattletrap. She would have preferred to be rid of the expense that went with running a car, but her circumstances were such that a carless lifestyle – as it was referred to these days –wasn't an option for the family as long as they were living here in the capital region.

Elsa Guðrún had confided in Guðgeir that she doubted it was good for the twin boys to be living alone with her, far from their father, grandparents and a host of other relatives in the north of the country. These days the boys spent two weekends a month during the winter with their dad, and it always took a couple of days for them to return to normal after having been relentlessly spoiled by their relatives in the north.

'Always dark here in Reykjavík,' Elsa Guðrún sighed,

gazing blankly at the wet tarmac dotted with puddles rippled by the wind.

'It's still February,' Guðgeir replied, peering into the gloom. 'And now most of the snow's been melted by that rainstorm, and that means there's even less light.'

'Sure. I mean, it's so dark,' she replied. A scowl appeared on her broad face. 'My boys go to school in the dark, and it's dark again by the time they come home.'

'People have taken their Christmas lights down. That has an effect as well,' Guðgeir said in a tone meant to lift the mood.

'It's never this dark in Akureyri,' Elsa Guðrún assured him, a hair tie between her teeth as she pulled her brown hair back into a ponytail.

'Really?' Guðgeir grinned. This north country pride that some would describe as conceit had always amused him. 'All the same, it's a good way further north than Reykjavík.'

Elsa Guðrún wasn't going to accept Guðgeir's straightforward geographical point. She extracted an unwanted hair caught between her lips, and shook her head doggedly.

'Makes no difference. The weather's simply better in Akureyri than it is down south. There isn't this endless howling gale that you get here.'

'Absolutely, I'll believe you,' Guðgeir replied. There was a stronger note of sarcasm in his words than he had intended, and generally he enjoyed the north country attitude that everything there was biggest and best. He could never be entirely sure if she was being serious or making fun of him. 'There's a bit of a breeze blowing now, but it's not a gale. That's a pleasanter word,' he said with a smile. 'Words have characters of their own and that affects our mood. Try saying it slowly.'

'Shit's still shit,' Elsa Guðrún muttered sourly. 'Even if we call it poop.'

'Well, it seems to me that you need to spend some time

up north, Elsa Guðrún. You're obviously suffering from incurable homesickness,' he said amiably. She sighed and nodded.

'More than likely I'm just tired of this endless stress and constantly being in a rush,' she said. 'But that'll sort itself out, like it always does,' she added with more warmth in her voice.

No more words passed between them for the rest of the short journey. During Guðgeir's years in the police force, this was how going to the scene of a death had always been. There would be a conversation about something inconsequential for the first few minutes, followed by silence. Everyday chatter wasn't only an instinctive way of calming nerves, but it provided a contrast to a scene at their destination that could be overwhelming. They drove along Suðurgata and pulled up next to a patrol car parked across the street at the graveyard end.

'Time to get to work,' Guðgeir said, serious now, as he killed the engine and opened the door.

'How old is she?' Elsa Guðrún asked.

'I think she's around twenty. Her name's Embla and she's a student at technical college. She was on her way home from her work experience placement at a hairdressing salon somewhere nearby and took a shortcut through the graveyard, as a lot of people do. Her first week at a new place and she stumbles across a body,' Guðgeir said.

'There are a few of them there,' Elsa Guðrún muttered, her voice so low as to be almost inaudible.

'What was that?'

'Bodies in a graveyard,' she replied.

'Well, certainly.' Guðgeir pretended not to notice the black humour. 'But most of them are long since part of the ground and it's rare that anyone's buried in this old graveyard these days. If it happens, it's normally an urn of ashes in a family plot.'

'Earth to earth, in the certain hope of resurrection. Isn't that what the priest says when he drops a handful of earth on the coffin?' Elsa Guðrún asked, not expecting an answer.

'As far as I remember,' Guðgeir said absently. 'Forensics are here.' He nodded in the direction of two vans that had been parked on the pavement on Kirkjugarðsstígur.

Leifur stood with the girl at the graveyard gate. As usual, his overcoat was unbuttoned so that his checked shirt could be seen, as well as a blue tie that lay crookedly across a mighty belly that was close to reaching its former size. Leifur had adhered for a whole year to a strict diet, which had undoubtedly been good for his heart, but not for his temper. Now his disposition had improved and he was more like his old self, although its effects on his health were debatable.

The girl had obviously made an effort to be presentable for work, but her carefully done hair was now wind-blown and a short fake fur coat over her green work clothes provided little protection from the cold. The girl had her arms wrapped around herself and she shivered.

'What's the old fool thinking?' Elsa Guðrún snapped, and turned around on the spot. 'I'll get a blanket for the girl. There should be one in the car.'

'Of course,' Guðgeir said. The same thought had occurred to him – a fraction of a second behind Elsa Guðrún. Leifur waved them over. He was a solid character in every way, a gentle man and very good at his job, but when it came to equality and issues of the day, he was very much at home in the last decade of the previous century.

The girl was grateful for the blanket that Elsa Guðrún placed over her shoulders. Her slim, heavily ringed fingers clasped the corners. Her nose was red with cold and there were smudges of mascara under her deep-blue eyes.

'Thanks,' she said, sniffing and squeezing out a grateful smile. 'I'm freezing. It's so cold.'

'That'll be the shock,' Leifur said thoughtfully and took

a woollen hat from his pocket and pulled it down over his balding head. He had finally got round to reading an article about the psychological effects of shock that Særós, the head of CID, had sent him months before.

'More likely it's just this lousy cold,' Elsa Guðrún snapped, shaking her head.

'Hello, Embla. My name's Guðgeir Fransson. Won't you sit in the car where it's warmer?'

'I should be at work by now.' Her teeth chattered. 'Can't I go there now? The salon's just round the corner.'

'Unfortunately not. I have to ask you to sit in the car with Berglind.' Guðgeir pointed to a patrol car. 'She'll take you there, or she'll call your workplace and let them know the situation and that you can't come right away. You'll have to go with her to the station and give a statement,' he continued, and Elsa Guðrún gave the girl an encouraging smile.

'Do I have to?' There was a bewildered look on her face. 'Can't we just do this now? Look, I was just walking through the middle of the graveyard, y'know, where the path is widest, and I saw a foot … a snow boot by a gravestone a little way away. I thought it was some junkie getting a hit and I was going to keep going,' she carried on quickly in the hope of escaping this terrible situation as soon as possible. 'But I thought it was so cold outdoors that I ought to check in case it was some homeless person who didn't have anywhere to go, but I was a bit frightened and wanted to be quick … It's my first day. It's really hard to get a placement at a salon and I didn't want to be late, but I checked anyway …. Waited to see if the foot was going to move and when it didn't I called out hello a few times to try and wake the person up and of course I didn't know whose foot it was. So I thought I'd better take a closer look. I went around the back of the gravestone and she was lying there, just a really ordinary woman. Could have been my granny.' Embla's eyes were wide with the shock she had experienced. 'She was lying there in the mud, poor thing. It was so horrible to see her.'

The girl burst into sudden tears and sobs shook her frame.

'There, you've had a bad shock. I'll take you to the car,' Elsa Guðrún said. She put an arm around Embla's shoulders and led her away. 'You could make yourself ill if you're out here in the cold for too long.'

Guðgeir and Leifur watched them, and not a word was said until Elsa Guðrún returned.

'Was that closed when you got here?' Guðgeir asked, pushing the graveyard's black iron gate. Its rusty hinges squealed in protest, and they went in single file along the narrow, rutted path that snaked between gravestones and the bare trees.

'Yes,' Leifur replied. He was breathless and stared down to watch his step. The ground was wet and slippery, with scattered patches of ice here and there that the rain hadn't managed to finish off. 'Not that it makes much difference. To be honest, I'm not sure we'll find anything here in the graveyard that's going to tell us much, considering what the weather's been like and that the body's been there more than twenty-four hours. I'd guess the woman lost her life two or even three days ago, judging by the state of rigor mortis and the colour. There are also indications that the body has been moved.'

'Any CCTV around here?' Guðgeir asked.

'The nearest one is on the corner near the hairdresser's salon, and there's another one about the same distance away in the other direction. It's possible there's nothing to be had from them, but I'm hoping both will have been in working order for the last few days,' Leifur said.

The forensic team had fenced off the area around the dead woman, and the three of them watched from a distance. They waited in the grey morning gloom as floodlights were set up, illuminating the scene. The woman lay on her side, apparently with her mouth open. A silk scarf was wound tightly around her neck and she was dressed in a brown overcoat, thick nylon tights and fur-lined ankle boots. A skirt that had been twisted and bunched beneath her could be made out. What was laid out before them in this old graveyard was a deeply disturbing sight. A twenty-four-hour downpour had melted a covering of snow that had made walking through the city a challenge, and had left the ground waterlogged.

'Any visible traces?' Guðgeir asked with foreboding.

'We've only just started, but it looks like a blow to the back of the head,' Leifur replied. 'The scarf is wrapped tight around her throat, so that could have restricted her airway. It'll all be clear before long.'

'This is neither suicide nor death by natural causes,' Guðgeir said, and Leifur nodded, a serious look on his face.

'Doesn't look like it,' he agreed with a sigh. 'All the indications are murder.'

'She's lying not far from the Watchful Woman, and that's no bad thing,' Elsa Guðrún murmured, with a meaningful look in her deep-blue eyes as she glanced up at Guðgeir. He looked back at her in surprise. 'Her name was Guðrún, like me, and she was the first person who was buried in this graveyard. There was a superstition that she would watch over all those who would come after her, but people were still frightened of her and didn't want to be buried too close. That's something I find odd, as she was undoubtedly a good woman who endured a great deal. That's her grave there, I think.'

Elsa Guðrún pointed a large black iron cross.

'Thanks for the history lesson, but maybe we ought to keep our minds on the job in hand,' Leifur said drily. 'But why are you telling us this, Elsa Guðrún?' he added in a warmer tone.

'Ach. It just occurred to me. I hope this poor woman lying

here had a better life than the Watchful Woman did,' Elsa Guðrún said, her eyes on the body.

'Whatever kind of life she had, it certainly didn't end happily,' Guðgeir said, beating some warmth into his hands.

The icy morning breeze nipped at him and he shivered with a cold chill of foreboding.

5

The newest recruit to the forensic team came over to them. Helgi Már Bragason held a brown handbag that looked tiny in the hands of such a well-built man.

'Let's see if things are starting to look clearer,' he said. 'There's a good chance that this bag belonged to the victim and either she or someone else dropped it or threw it away. She was lying behind one of the graves not far from the large gate that opens onto Ljósvallagata. We'll need to knock on the door of every house in the district and ask if anyone noticed anything unusual over the last few days.'

'I'll get that going,' Guðgeir said, took out his phone and took a few steps away from the others while he called Særós, their superior officer. By the time he returned, Helgi had opened the handbag to reveal an old-fashioned keypad phone and a spectacle case. A zipped pocket yielded a set of house keys and a lipstick.

'If this was a robbery, then the thief didn't come away with much. A few notes, at most,' Helgi said. 'Who kills for small change?'

'It wouldn't be the first time,' Guðgeir said with a sigh.

'The perpetrator could have been after something other than money. It could have been something that's gone from the woman's bag,' Elsa Guðrún said.

'Could be,' Guðgeir agreed. 'Let's bear the possibility in mind, before we jump to any conclusions. What about the phone?'

'It's a bit of an antique and fortunately there's no passcode,' Helgi said, scrolling through the last numbers called. 'You don't often see a phone like this any longer. Mostly children have them. This is the cheapest, simplest type on the market. All it lets you do is call and send text messages.'

'What's the first number that comes up?' Elsa Guðrún asked.

'The last call to this number was almost a week ago,' Helgi said, holding the phone out to her. 'Best if you do the talking and pretend you've found it.' He handed her a disposable glove and she pulled it on before taking the phone.

Guðgeir frowned, but stayed out of it.

The woman who picked up did so with a cheerful greeting.

'Well, hello Arnhildur. It's unusual not to hear from you for such a long while. Are you somewhere abr...'

'Hello. This isn't my phone. I found it and would like to find its proper owner,' Elsa Guðrún said, sounding completely natural in a way that would have done credit to any trained actor. 'Well, no. See, I was walking to work and it was just lying here on the pavement in town. Could you give me this person's address so I can return it? Did you say her name's Arnhildur? Yes, and what's her patronymic? So I'm sure I have the right person?'

The pretence played out. Elsa Guðrún repeated the information as it was given to her and Guðgeir punched the name and address into his own phone.

Now the woman in the graveyard had a name and an address. They gazed without speaking at the body and the forensic team at work around it. It was remarkable how much changed by giving the person a name. It brought the victim to life, with a personality, a career and a history.

'You'll be busy here for a while,' Guðgeir said to Leifur. 'Is it all right if Elsa Guðrún and I take ourselves off for a while? I feel we need to check Arnhildur's home and try to put together a picture of what we're dealing with before we approach relatives.'

'You know how it is with Guðgeir,' Elsa Guðrún explained helpfully. 'He always needs to get the feel of the environment and the atmosphere for himself, without any interference.'

Leifur thought to himself before giving his agreement. The look on his face told them that he desperately wanted to tell them to tread carefully, and not disturb anything that could be evidence. But he kept it to himself. If he could trust anyone, then it was this pair.

'We won't be much longer here. I'll send some of the team over once the initial investigation here is complete,' he said after a pause.

'Of course,' Guðgeir replied, already on his way.

6

Elsa Guðrún parked outside a red-painted, two-storey house built on a narrow-windowed basement in the old part of the city's western district. It was a handsome building, although it showed signs of neglect.

They had switched seats, and now Guðgeir sat on the passenger side, engrossed in finding out what he could about the deceased. He slipped his phone back into his pocket, reached for his work bag on the back seat, and as he did so, noticed a youthful face in the window of the next house along. Curious eyes stared at him from under a set of light-coloured blinds. They followed as he got out of the car and walked the short distance to the house. Their path through the neat garden to the door was lined by trees in pots, hung with multi-coloured lights.

'See, not everyone's taken their Christmas lights down. Some people hang on as long as they can,' Elsa Guðrún said.

'Quite right, and there's a decoration up there as well,' Guðgeir said, nodding in the direction of the upstairs window and an illuminated Christmas star made from gold-coloured paper.

'Arnhildur Drífa Friðthjófsdóttir,' Elsa Guðrún read out from the little silver plaque next to the doorbell. 'She's unlikely to have a partner, considering her disappearance hasn't been reported.' She crouched down, opened her bag and took out protective suits, gloves and shoe covers. 'We should take all the precautions, shouldn't we?'

'Of course. And we'll have to tread carefully. Did you check who answered the phone earlier?' Guðgeir asked, leaning against the rail leading to the door as he pulled on the white suit.

'Yes. The number's registered to an assisted living place in Árbær that's for disabled people,' Elsa Guðrún replied as she pulled the white head covering over her brown hair and zipped up the suit.

'We'll check on that later today. There are two apartments in this house and when we've checked out Arnhildur's home, we can have a chat with the people who live downstairs,' Guðgeir said and took the dead woman's house keys from his bag.

The entrance hall was barely five square metres and included a closet for coats. There were several hanging there, a black waterproof, a longish waxed coat and a couple of jackets in dark colours. The only item of furniture was a shallow chest of drawers and a slim stool. They exchanged glances as a mutter of conversation carried from inside the flat.

'Hello! Anyone there?' Elsa Guðrún called out, pushing a door panelled in dark, patterned glass that was already half open. 'Hello!'

The entrance hall opened onto a hallway and the other rooms. The place was laid out on the conventional lines of its era, and appeared to have been left completely untouched by changing tides of style over the years since it had been built.

'Who's there?' Elsa Guðrún called out, but there was no reply. 'I'll bet that's steam radio,' she muttered as she went into a compact kitchen. A conversation about traditional Icelandic cuisine carried from a little radio high on a shelf and a soft female voice asserted that although pickled rams' testicles and shark both taste vile, their cultural importance could be in no doubt. Elsa Guðrún reached for the radio and switched it off.

'My parents have exactly the same radio at home and it has a timing setting that they've never been able to get the hang of, so it switches itself on at midday and off an hour later.'

'Not many people have these now, do they?' Guðgeir said. 'They must have stopped making them, surely?'

Elsa Guðrún shrugged.

'No idea,' she said as she looked around the room. The kitchen was tidy, apart from the dust on the shelves and windowsills. The only thing that stood out was a cup containing dregs of coffee and a newspaper open on the table. A large advertisement was spread across a full page, calling on a genius looking for work. A large, gold Christmas star hung in the window, and was connected to a socket.

'I don't get ads like this. What do these people mean?' Guðgeir muttered, glancing at the newspaper on the table as they moved on to Arnhildur's bedroom. A single bed occupied the middle of the carpeted floor. The bed had been neatly made, and the only thing that caught Guðgeir's eye was an indentation, as if someone had lain down or sat on the bedspread. A gaudy lamp stood on the bedside table and shelves above a weighty chest of drawers were filled with books and ornaments. The air was stuffy in here, as it was throughout the flat, and they longed to open windows and allow some fresh air in. Elsa Guðrún opened drawers and cupboards, while Guðgeir continued through the place, first the bathroom and then the dining room and the living room next to it. An older type of flatscreen TV occupied a space on a heavy sideboard, and motes of dust danced in the air in front of the screen in the brief brightness of the February sunshine. Everything about this flat and the way it was furnished demonstrated its owner's tidy, ordered lifestyle. Guðgeir resisted the temptation to run a hand over the surface of the dining table, an exceptionally beautiful piece of furniture that showed it had been made with a craftsman's love and not mass-produced. A large crystal bowl on the coffee table contained an advertisement from an estate agent. Guðgeir noticed that the sales rep's name and phone number had been underlined in green. He took out his phone and took a picture. There were two other rooms in the apartment, the smaller with walls lined with bookshelves, while someone had obviously lived in the larger room. It looked as if the room's inhabitant had taken a long holiday, extending even to years, as Guðgeir had the feeling it hadn't been used for a long time. Photos of a girl at different stages of life stood on a shelf. The largest of these looked to have been taken in a studio some years ago, showing a man and a woman standing each side of the girl with a pretty bow in her long, fair hair. Guðgeir assumed that these had to be the girl's parents, and that Arnhildur had to be the mother. In the picture she leaned close to her family, dressed in a bland, dark dress, her hair meticulously combed and hanging to her shoulders. Her eyes were fixed firmly on the photographer, as if concerned that he wasn't up to the job. The father, broad-shouldered and corpulent, sat straight-backed, a stiff smile on his lips.

Guðgeir took another circuit around the apartment, hoping to notice something that could shed light on what had happened to Arnhildur, but without success. Elsa Guðrún was in the entrance hall, speaking on the phone. She soundlessly mouthed Særós's name.

'I don't see a computer or any other devices,' Guðgeir said when Elsa Guðrún had finished her conversation.

'Sure. I thought the same. Arnhildur must have had a computer. She wasn't that elderly.'

'She could have put that kind of thing away in a cupboard somewhere,' Guðgeir said.

'That doesn't sound likely to me,' Elsa Guðrún said. 'I'd

have expected to see an oldish kind of computer on a desk somewhere, but we shouldn't expect people to do this or that, should we?'

'No, of course not,' Guðgeir replied. 'But there's a chance she was completely offline, there are people like that. Some people choose to do without all that stress.'

'But there's stuff in the bedside table that might tell us something,' Elsa Guðrún said.

She led him to Arnhildur's bedroom and opened a drawer. In it were a book from the Spiritualist Society, a photograph of a young woman, some packs of pills and at the bottom some sheets of paper that had been stapled together.

'This is Imovane, so at some time or other Arnhildur must have had problems sleeping,' Guðgeir said, tapping the medication packs. 'She's had something on her mind.'

Elsa Guðrún shook her head.

'I wouldn't be inclined to draw too many conclusions from this. My mother hasn't slept a whole night through since the menopause started, and that's almost twenty years ago. But look at the picture. It's the same girl as in the other room, but she's changed. You see the difference?'

Guðgeir peered at the picture. She was right. This was certainly the same person, but her appearance was not the same. She had changed. Her eyelids seemed heavier, the eyes less alert and there was a sadness behind them. Guðgeir put the picture aside and unzipped his suit. He would have to get his glasses to take a closer look. Elsa Guðrún had been quite right. Something had happened to this young woman.

'Remarkable,' he said to himself and picked up the stapled sheets. 'It's a printout of a police presentation. *What is online crime?*' he read, flipping through the pages. 'It's all here from one of our presentations.... Online abuse, fraud, catfishing, bullying, stalking. And the title is *if something can be abused, it will be.*'

'Sheesh. It stinks,' Elsa Guðrún said with a shudder. 'I hope my twins get to live in a better world than the one we have.'

7

There was no hiding the curiosity on the thin face of the young woman downstairs. She had a fair complexion and a prominent forehead, her lips were bright with lipstick and her brown eyes stared at the tall man. She had small but noticeable rings in each ear and her delicate fingers repeatedly tugged at the arms of her large, coarse-knit sweater.

'Good day. My name's Guðgeir Fransson and I'm from the city police CID. Are you Hafdís?' he asked, pointing at the name next to the doorbell.

'Yeah. I'm definitely not Skúli or Freyja.' This latter name had been added to those of Hafdís and Skúli under the bell, with a slip of paper and many layers of clear tape. Hafdís's hand went awkwardly to her mouth, as if she was unsure how to behave when faced with the police. 'Sorry. That was supposed to be funny.'

'Sure,' Guðgeir said. 'Are you home alone?'

'No. Skúli's here as well,' she replied without making any move.

'Then I'd like to speak to the pair of you together,' Guðgeir said and peered past her to see where a door led into the apartment beyond. A man who looked to be about the same age as Hafdís came towards them.

His appearance was artfully careless, designed to attract attention, with mousy hair cut short at the back, but with a bushy mop at the front, painstakingly combed forward over a low forehead. Guðgeir reflected that more than a little hair product of some kind must be needed to keep this elaborate display in place. There was a noticeably spicy aroma about this man, who was dressed in a beige sweater and sky-blue trousers that suited his spare frame.

'Hello,' Skúli said, extending a hand. He came across as more assured than Hafdís, and Guðgeir wondered what the situation was.

'It's about Arnhildur upstairs. When was it that you last saw her or were aware of her?' Guðgeir asked, and the pair exchanged questioning glances as they thought it over.

'Well .... It's been a while,' Skúli said at last. 'Has something happened to her?'

'Could be,' Guðgeir replied in a tone that discouraged further questions.

'Arnhildur is pretty much at home all the time and I've knocked on her door a few times,' Skúli said, sounding concerned. 'We have a spare key, so I went up there this morning to check on her, see if everything was OK, but there was nobody home. Could she have gone away somewhere?'

'Why did you need to speak to her?' Guðgeir asked.

'What? Who?' Skúli stuffed his hands into his pockets and fidgeted in the doorway, coming across as suddenly distant.

'Arnhildur, of course.' Guðgeir could make out the impatience in his own voice.

'Yeah. Sorry. I was just worried. I mean, the cops asking questions, has something happened that you're not telling us?' Skúli flushed slightly and looked awkward. 'Maybe I shouldn't have gone upstairs, but I really needed to talk to her about the rent. She owns this apartment.'

'Could I come in? I need to ask you a few questions.'

'Of course!' Hafdís said, apologising as she stood aside. 'Let's go into the kitchen. Would you like coffee? I've just made some.'

The downstairs apartment was smaller than the one

above, and as different as it could possibly be. Instead of the white-painted walls and strictly conventional arrangement of bland furniture, this place was painted in bright colours, and there were leafy pot plants and pictures on the walls. The different styles of heavily patterned wallpaper on two of the walls caught Guðgeir's eye. The kitchen had a homely feel to it, with the original cupboards painted green, and the implements to be seen indicated that meals were prepared here, and not bought in ready for the microwave. An imposing cat was asleep on a stool with a padded seat. Guðgeir took a seat on a bright yellow chair.

'When did you last see Arnhildur?' he asked as he unzipped his coat. He was feeling the warmth.

Hafdís and Skúli exchanged glances and appeared to be thinking it over.

'Well, I don't really remember...' Hafdís began, and got no further. 'Hey, I forgot to give you some coffee.' She stood up and poured for him into a colourful Moomin mug. 'Milk?'

'No, thanks.'

'Errr, I reckon it must have been the beginning of last week. Yes, early last week,' Skúli said. 'I was taking out some bags of rubbish as I was leaving for work. She was doing the same .... Except she wasn't going to work. She was just taking out the rubbish...'

'And you remember this?' Guðgeir asked, his attention focused on Skúli.

'Yes, because she complained that we young people – as she referred to us – couldn't be bothered to clear the snow from around the bins. She said something about us being supposed to shovel her path as well, not just ours. She seemed to think it was part of the rental agreement, which absolutely isn't the case,' Skúli said. The irritation was plain in his expression as he rolled his eyes.

'I understand. Did you notice anything unusual about her demeanour that day?' Guðgeir asked as he sipped his coffee.

'No, not really. Or yes. She seemed quite upset about this,' Skúli said and paused as he thought back. 'It's not like her to get uptight. She's the relaxed type, an old-school kind of lady and quite reserved, I think. Keeps herself to herself, as my grandmother would have put it.'

Hafdís sniggered quickly, and put her hand to her mouth. Skúli glared at her.

'Arnhildur is really very old-fashioned,' she explained hurriedly. 'She told me once that the women of today are so brassy.'

'Brassy?' Skúli broke in, as if he hadn't heard this before. 'What did she mean?'

'Y'see, it's not just that we're colourful in the way we dress, but we have opinions about everything and everyone. As if that's a bad thing! She said that young women today are unbearably pushy,' Hafdís said, eyebrows lifted. 'But Arnhildur can also be really lovely. She's just a very conservative person and thoroughly set in her ways,' she added, as if to emphasise that she wasn't talking her down. 'She's actually a lovely person...'

'Yes, understood,' Guðgeir interrupted, rubbing a thumb through his dark stubble. He decided it was time to let them know the facts. 'I'm sorry to have to tell you that Arnhildur was found dead, not far from here,' he said, watching them carefully as he spoke.

Hafdís gasped.

'What? She's dead? Is that true?'

'Unfortunately, yes. But I have to ask you to keep this to yourselves for the time being. We're in the process of tracing her family, and haven't heard that anyone has been located yet,' Guðgeir said. 'Could you help us with that?'

'Why didn't you say so before?' Hafdís demanded, almost angrily, while Skúli kept his mouth firmly shut. 'That's so sad. What on earth happened to her?'

'It's not certain, but we hope everything will become clear before long. Do you know of anyone close to her we should contact?' Guðgeir repeated.

The couple again exchanged questioning glances and shook their heads. Hafdís puffed and sighed.

'To tell you the truth, I have the feeling she was a terrible loner and I'm already feeling guilty that we didn't speak to her more often. Arnhildur asked me in once, showed me pictures of her daughter and...' Hafdís hesitated. 'It looked to me like there's something wrong with her. I think she's disabled somehow.'

'Have you been aware of any visitors?' Guðgeir asked.

'Not that I've noticed,' Skúli said with a sideways look to catch Hafdís's eye. 'Have you?'

'No... Well, yes. There was a woman who came to clean occasionally,' she replied.

'And over the last few days?' Guðgeir asked. 'Try to recall the last two to three days.'

Hafdís and Skúli looked thoughtfully at each other.

'I've been up to my ears in a large assignment with a deadline at the end of the month, so most days I'm up early to get a desk at the National Library,' Hafdís said after a moment's consideration.

'You said you were on the way to work last time you ran into Arnhildur,' Guðgeir said. 'Where do you work?'

'I'm a hairdresser,' Skúli said. 'I took the day off today, had a few things to sort out. Including this problem with the rent. Where was she found?'

'Not far from here,' Guðgeir replied quickly, avoiding mentioning the location. 'And you, Hafdís?'

'I'm studying. I'm in the first year of Leisure Studies at the University of Iceland,' she replied, dabbing at her eyes with the sleeve of her sweater.

'Do you know where Arnhildur worked before she retired?' Guðgeir asked, taking a sip from the cup that had been untouched for some time in front of him.

'She worked for some lottery. I can't remember what it was called, it's some acronym, some institution .... Or maybe it was the university lottery. It might no longer exist. Do people still buy lottery tickets?' Hafdís asked. 'Hasn't that died out?'

'I've no idea,' Guðgeir said. 'Lotteries were a big thing when I was a youngster. But you mentioned the rent, Skúli. Was that why you wanted to speak to Arnhildur?'

Skúli sighed and rolled his eyes upwards.

'Ach. It's so unpleasant,' he said with a groan. 'The thing is, Arnhildur wanted to increase the rent. She couldn't seem to take on board that we have a rental contract until the first of July, and she's not legally able to do that. Let alone such a huge increase! I tried to explain this to her, but she didn't seem to understand any of what I tried to tell her. The thing is that she was adamant that we ought to pay more rent after Freyja moved in with us, while Hafdís and I are the ones with our names on the rental contract.'

'Surely we can ask a friend to stay with us for a while?' Hafdís said, the indignation in her voice rising. 'It's a clear breach of human rights if we can't.'

Skúli glared at her in annoyance, as if her interruption was unwelcome.

'How long has she been here?' Guðgeir asked.

'Well, let me think .... Wasn't it back in the spring that she moved in properly?' Skúli asked.

'Yep, maybe March or April, something like that,' Hafdís snapped back.

'So close to a year,' Guðgeir observed.

'That's it. Freyja lost the apartment she had been living in and was in real trouble,' Hafdís continued. 'The rental market is just crazy, and we had a spare room. It's pretty small, so I was going to ask about the little studio apartment that's here in the same building. Arnhildur hasn't wanted to rent it out because there are some repairs that need to be done to it, but Freyja's happy to take that on. She's training as a joiner and is incredibly good with her hands. So for Arnhildur it would have been ideal.'

8

When Guðgeir had spoken to the tenants in the apartment downstairs, he went out to get a breath of fresh air and consider the next move, and found the forensic team had arrived. He glanced quickly up at the next house, and saw a curtain twitch, but no youthful staring eyes.

A car horn sounded and he looked around. Elsa Guðrún was behind the wheel of the car. She beckoned and he hurried across to her.

'I was getting in their way so I thought I'd best leave them to it,' she grinned. 'The new guy doesn't hang about.'

'You mean Helgi Már?'

'It seems he has some super-duper training abroad behind him.'

'He comes across as an accommodating kind of guy,' Guðgeir said mildly, moving the seat back to make space for his long legs.

'Accommodating!' Elsa Guðrún giggled. 'Who uses a word like that? Sometimes you sound like an old-fashioned dictionary.'

'I could also suggest that he's most agreeable,' Guðgeir said with a wry smile.

'That's better, but to my mind Agreeable Helgi comes across like some kind of alpha male,' Elsa Guðrún said, hesitating and a moment later she had thought again. 'Well, you know. He's nice enough, new to the job and needs to make a mark. But did you get anything out of the tenants?'

'Not much, other than that Arnhildur wanted to increase the rent, and she also wanted them to shovel the snow off her steps as well as theirs. They said there's a woman who cleans sometimes, but don't know anything more about her, and Arnhildur worked for a lottery before she retired.'

'Yes, the University Lottery,' Elsa Guðrún said. 'I already checked that, and the home help is from the city's social care programme. There was an invoice in a drawer. It looks like Arnhildur was in arrears with that, even though home assistance is subsidised, so it's not exactly expensive.'

'Which makes it understandable that she was trying to screw more out of the tenants. Retirement can mean a serious loss of income for some people.'

'That's so true. I try not to even think about it,' Elsa Guðrún said with a grimace. 'It's all somehow so lousy. I mean, getting old and living alone with no income. Not being able to afford to pay the home help, and then dying under such awful circumstances. A little time passes, and there's nobody who misses you.' Elsa Guðrún shuddered visibly and her eyes opened wide. 'It's just so tragic.'

Guðgeir nodded in agreement. For a while they looked at the red-painted house without saying anything. Guðgeir noticed the peeling paintwork, the poorly maintained basement and the worn-out gutters, all of which had escaped his notice before.

'It's very sad, but Arnhildur seems to have been better off than many others. Property prices are high, and she could easily have sold the ground floor and the basement. She could even have sold the whole house,' Guðgeir replied. 'Although she would have had to do some repairs, and that could have been expensive.'

'Of course. I'll check what mortgages there are against the house,' Elsa Guðrún said and tapped at her phone.

Guðgeir drummed his fingers against the wheel and stared at the house. His impatience to get back into Arnhildur's apartment was overwhelming.

'Any more information on the deceased?' he asked after a short silence.

'This just popped up. Arnhildur has a 32-year-old daughter called Unnur who lives in some kind of sheltered accommodation.' Elsa Guðrún looked up at Guðgeir. 'That must be the place I called earlier,' she said and continued reading. 'The father is a German national, and nothing is currently known of his whereabouts. Arnhildur has a sister called Regína, whose registered address is in Hveragerði.'

'Any other family?' Guðgeir asked.

'Well, Regína has a husband, children, children-in-law and grandchildren. There don't appear to be any other close family, but there must be a wider network of relatives.'

'It's not known where her ex lives?'

'Resident overseas, according to the National Register,' Elsa Guðrún replied.

'Where?'

'Hold on, partner. I didn't get to check everything while you were chatting to them downstairs,' Elsa Guðrún said and paused as Helgi Már approached from the house. He was clad in the standard forensic overall but had removed his shoe covers. His white suit was laced so tight that it puckered the skin of his forehead. Broad eyebrows were a strong feature of his face, and the right eyebrow half hid a narrow scar that led up to his forehead.

Guðgeir and Elsa Guðrún were out of the car almost simultaneously.

'What do you have for us?' Guðgeir asked.

'After the initial inspection, it doesn't look like there's much, but we'll go through everything,' Helgi Már said, his voice low and with a serious expression on his face. He clenched his teeth so that the tension in his jaw muscles could be seen as he stood on the pavement in front of them. 'There's no doubt that she received a heavy blow to the head, but we won't know until the autopsy if that was the cause of death. There's also trauma to the throat.' Helgi Már's voice was dark and had a scratched feel to it. 'I'll go back in now, and we have quite a bit more to work through, both here and at the graveyard. You'll hear from me or Leifur as soon as we have anything.'

Helgi Már raised a hand as he returned to the house.

'He's like an American country star,' Elsa Guðrún muttered from the corner of her mouth.

'What? How so?' Guðgeir asked, raising a questioning eyebrow.

'Well, the stance, his voice, the affectations ... Apart from the white coveralls and the Harry Potter-style scar,' Elsa Guðrún said.

'So, that's your impression,' Guðgeir said with a grin. 'Maybe not so wide of the mark now you come to mention it. But now we'll go and find Regína and Unnur.' He slapped the roof of the car for emphasis, opened the door and got in. 'We need to give them the bad news.'

'Ach. I hate having to inform people of a bereavement,' Elsa Guðrún groaned as she fastened her seat belt.

'That makes two of us,' Guðgeir agreed with a sigh. 'We'll start by paying the daughter a visit. Let's go.'

He started the car and had just pulled out of the space when Særós appeared, pulling into the next parking space. Guðgeir stopped, reversed and wound down the window.

'We're just off to inform the next of kin. That's a daughter who lives in sheltered accommodation and a sister who lives in Hveragerði. I was going to call you on the way.'

'No problem. I'll speak to you later. Go and do what you need to. Right now I'm more focused on what Leifur and his people have to say.' Særós adjusted the collar of her stiffly starched shirt, got nimbly out of the car and tightened the belt of her overcoat. 'It's a relief it's stopped raining, at last,' she added, looking to the sky before striding determinedly towards the red house.

9

Elsa Guðrún couldn't recall ever having set foot in an assisted living facility of this kind before. Now she and Guðgeir found themselves standing and waiting in the entrance hall of a very ordinary detached house in the city's eastern suburbs. The manager, Ragna, had been out shopping for the residents when they called, and the member of staff on duty said that, unfortunately, he couldn't let them in until she returned, that he wasn't authorised.

The entrance hall was unusually roomy, with linoleum on the floors, and Elsa Guðrún couldn't help noticing that all of the doors were surprisingly wide. Then the member of staff who said his name was Máni reappeared in the doorway.

'Ragna will be right with you. I'm sure that was her car I saw turning into the street when I looked out of the kitchen window just now.'

A young woman appeared behind Máni and gave a loud whoop. Elsa Guðrún was startled, and he noticed.

'Don't worry. It's exciting for her to get visitors,' Máni said, smiling at Elsa Guðrún's nervous reaction. 'We're all unique and express ourselves in different ways,' he added in a tone that came across as being instructive, and at the same time condescending. Elsa Guðrún bit her tongue. There was no way she was going to explain to him that three years ago she had been the victim of a brutal assault in her own home, and while she was making a steady recovery, there were still aspects of daily life that were challenging. She was easily startled by unexpected noises, and someone taking her by surprise could leave her a terrified wreck. In the general course of her work she was unnecessarily wary, but for the sake of her job she kept these panic attacks well hidden and tried not to let anything show.

'Ragna's here,' Máni announced, and stepped past them to open the door for an imposing middle-aged woman. She was dressed in a mustard-yellow anorak that reached down past her knees.

'I'll take those,' Máni said, taking from her hands a large bag of shopping marked with the logo of a low-cost supermarket. The woman turned and went back to a white station wagon parked half across the pavement. She opened the back and began taking out boxes of various shapes and sizes. Máni didn't bother with a coat or boots, and hurried out onto the wet pavement. Between them they carried in one box after another. Elsa Guðrún stared in astonishment at the tracks his wet socks left on the grey lino.

'They're from the police,' Máni announced as he and Ragna manhandled the last of the boxes into the wider hallway that lay beyond the entrance hall. 'They need a word with you.'

'Really?' Ragna asked, bent double as she eased off her padded snow boots. She stood up and looked them up and down. There was a questioning look on her striking face. 'Hello, and apologies for the fuss and bother. We're redecorating the living room and I went to get new shelves and tables. Máni was kind enough to paint the room for us.'

'Brightening the place up is long overdue. The cuts are just endless. Makes no difference if you do well or badly when it's run by the state,' Máni said as he pulled off his socks. Elsa Guðrún noticed there were paint stains on the soles of his feet.

'Nothing serious, I hope. We can go to my office, but please use the hand sanitiser. My people here are susceptible to infections.'

Ragna wiped a drop of perspiration from her forehead with the back of one hand, before she pumped the nozzle of a large container so energetically that sanitiser not only filled her cupped palm, but also added to the damp patches on the floor.

They exchanged glances, then did as they had been asked. Guðgeir winked at Elsa Guðrún and she felt like a small child faced with the manager's single-mindedness. Her office was a small room next to the entrance hall. She waved them to sit on a small sofa that faced the desk. Elsa Guðrún sat down, while Guðgeir chose to remain standing, which was understandable as there would barely be space there for someone of above average height, with long legs and broad shoulders. They waited silently while Ragna fussed over hanging her huge coat on a hook.

'Well, then,' she said, when her anorak had finally submitted to staying where she had hung it. 'What can I do for you? Have there been any break-ins in the area? We're constantly hearing about that kind of thing going on. That wretched dope that ruins so many lives. Dreadful! We even hear about foreign crime gangs who come to Iceland to rob innocent people. It's shocking!'

'No, it's nothing like that. Unfortunately, I could almost say,' Guðgeir replied as soon as Ragna paused. 'Do you have an Unnur Elva Jacobsdóttir living here?'

Ragna sank heavily into her office chair.

'Yes. What about her?'

'Her mother is Arnhildur Drífa Friðthjófsdóttir?' Elsa Guðrún asked, and noticing a look of deep concern spread across Ragna's face.

'Yes. Why do you ask?'

'Because she's dead. Arnhildur was found this morning, and sadly, tragic as it is, it appears that she died some time ago,' Guðgeir said calmly.

'What?' The news clearly took Ragna by surprise. She gasped and stared at them. 'I didn't even know she was missing,' she said, shaking her head as if unable to believe her own ears.

'It's not as if her death occurred a long time ago. It looks like some days,' Elsa Guðrún said. She wasn't sure how much she could safely say, and they hadn't discussed this on the way. The reality was that they had so few facts to work with that it was best to say as little as possible.

'What on earth? That's awful, absolutely horrifying,' Ragna said, as if struggling to accept what she had been told. For a moment she stared out of the window, her forehead furrowed. 'Some woman called me this morning, saying she had found Arnhildur's phone on the pavement in the western end of the city. How does that add up?'

'That was me. Arnhildur's body was found among the graves in the Hólavellir graveyard, and the phone was in her handbag,' Elsa Guðrún explained awkwardly. 'Of course, I had to avoid saying too much to keep us a step ahead ... news travels fast onto social media, and then it's not long before we get journalists calling.'

'Ah, I understand,' Ragna said. 'How did this happen?'

Guðgeir and Elsa Guðrún exchanged glances.

'At this point we can't be certain how her death occurred,' Guðgeir said in a dark, formal tone.

'You don't think she could have been...' Ragna asked, and Elsa Guðrún quickly cut her off.

'As Guðgeir said, we don't know anything yet,' her northern accent clear.

'Poor Unnur. Now she's lost her only relative,' Ragna said gloomily.

'That's true. Although it's a serious blow, she still has an aunt living, and that side of her family. So Unnur isn't completely alone,' Guðgeir sympathised, a fingertip scratching the dark stubble on his chin.

SHROUDED

There was no mistaking the astonishment on Ragna's face.

'Is that so? Well, those people have never once showed their faces here,' she said, with a new hardness in her voice. 'It's the same old story, sadly. It's all too convenient to forget the unfortunate among us. While we make every effort and do everything we can here, we can never replace family. Staff come and go, but relatives are the only fixed points our clients have in life.'

'People can live with all kinds of circumstances. No doubt some have their own reasons, and we live in a society that's changing all the time,' Guðgeir said, sounding tolerant, but also ready to move on. He wasn't here to discuss the pressures exerted by society. 'But we need to meet Unnur and give her the sad news. It won't be easy...'

'I'll speak to her,' Ragna interrupted. 'Unnur is normally placid, but the brain damage she suffered is such that she can be a danger to herself and others if she gets upset.'

'In what way?' Elsa Guðrún asked.

'Well, she can break furniture and throw things about,' Ragna replied quietly, looking serious.

'Really? She can be violent?' Guðgeir asked.

'No, I wouldn't say that. But when Unnur was a teenager she had a serious accident and among her other injuries she suffered trauma to the frontal lobe of the brain, leading to a loss of emotional control and social skills. She can become furiously angry in an instant. By that I mean completely unrestrained rage, you understand, as the damage to her brain resulted in personality disorders which mean that her behaviour is entirely in response to her environment and situation at that moment. Unnur doesn't experiences these anger spells often, and in fact these were quite rare during her first few years after I came to work here. But more recently she has lost control increasingly frequently,' Ragna said and fell silent, as if to give them an opportunity to digest her words. 'Strangers find it difficult to understand, as her appearance is quite normal.'

'In the police we get to see all sorts of results of frontal lobe brain damage,' Elsa Guðrún said.

Ragna nodded and gave them an apologetic smile.

'What I mean,' she said, 'is that I feel it would be better if I explain things to her as calmly as possible. You must understand that this is terrible news, and you are total strangers.'

'Of course,' Guðgeir agreed. 'But I trust you'll do this at the first available opportunity?'

Ragna nodded, looking grave.

'How long ago was the accident, and what happened to her?' Elsa Guðrún asked after a pause.

'She was only sixteen and had her whole life ahead of her. Unnur was staying with some people out on Snæfellsnes and was invited to go riding. She had some experience of horses, but not much, and was given a horse that was much too lively for her. The route they took wasn't suitable for a novice. Something went wrong, either the horse bolted or lost its footing, and Unnur fell off, and her head hit a rock. She was kept in a coma for some months in intensive care and then there was a long period of rehabilitation therapy. She made a reasonably good recovery in physical terms, but she has never been the same mentally, far from it. It seems that before her accident Unnur had something of a temper, but she did well at school and was a talented figure skater, according to her mother.' Ragna sighed. 'Poor woman. She was lovely and she did everything she could for her daughter. Such awful news. Poor Arnhildur and poor Unnur. I still haven't taken this on board ... I'm sorry.'

Ragna wiped away the tears that ran down her cheeks, reaching for a tissue from a box that stood on the desk. Then she blew her nose.

'You will give her the news as soon as possible, won't you?' Guðgeir reminded her.

'Yes, of course,' Ragna replied.

'All the same, we ought to see her for a moment,' Elsa Guðrún said quickly. She spoke without thinking, as she felt instinctively that she couldn't leave without having seen her. 'She doesn't need to know why we're here,' she added.

'No, of course not,' Ragna said and got to her feet. 'I expect she's in her room.'

Unnur lay on her neatly made bed, her eyes closed, wearing earphones. She was a delicate young woman, with a pleasant face, dressed in jeans and a rust-red sweater. The image of this girl's mother lying on the cold, wet ground flashed through Elsa Guðrún's mind and she felt a pang of sympathy. The room wasn't large, but it was comfortable. Elsa Guðrún couldn't help the feeling that it wasn't in step with Unnur's age. The pictures, posters and the oddments lying around were more reminiscent of a teenager than a woman in her thirties. Unnur noticed their presence, removed her headphones and sat up. Ragna explained that Guðgeir and Elsa Guðrún were visitors who were taking a look around. They appeared to attract no particular interest on Unnur's part, and the impatient look on her face made it plain that they were disturbing her.

'What are you listening to?' Guðgeir asked.

'It's a really exciting book,' Unnur replied.

'What's it about?' Elsa Guðrún asked brightly.

'A woman who had a boyfriend, and then she disappeared,' Unnur responded, unable to hide her impatience.

'How far have you got?' Guðgeir asked, so that he had something to say.

'They're searching for her, and you're interrupting,' Unnur retorted. She shook her blonde head and fiddled with her fringe.

'We're just leaving,' Elsa Guðrún said.

'Good. I'm going to listen to the rest,' Unnur said,

replaced the headphones and lay down again.

'Sorry to disturb you,' Guðgeir said as they left the room, but Unnur had retreated back into the world of the audiobook and neither saw nor heard them.

'She says exactly what she thinks,' Ragna said with a brief smile. 'It's a symptom of frontal lobe damage. No filter, if I can put it like that.'

'Good that she can enjoy audiobooks,' Guðgeir said.

'She does a lot of that,' Ragna replied. 'That's fine, mostly.'

'What do you mean?' Guðgeir asked in surprise.

'There can be occasions when she doesn't differentiate between reality and fiction,' Ragna explained. 'Sometimes she'll tell me about something that's happened to her, and then it'll turn out that it's something from a book.'

'That's very sad. How long has she been here?' Elsa Guðrún asked. She felt a weight of sympathy for Unnur, but was also aware that she had to keep difficult emotion at arm's length, otherwise she would quickly burn out.

'It must be twelve or thirteen years. She was at home with her mother after the rehabilitation therapy, but she was so emotionally damaged that she wasn't able to stay there for long. Arnhildur simply didn't have the energy to cope with such challenging circumstances, and she was already over forty when Unnur was born. That was certainly a difficult time for the two of them,' Ragna said with a frown. 'Unnur had a group of friends before the accident, and these youngsters made sure they came and visited her, but it wasn't long before they dropped away one by one. There's one who comes fairly regularly, but we don't see him all that often. He's a little older, so maybe he was more mature than the rest of them.'

'It's understandable that youngsters aren't able to deal with such a tragedy,' Elsa Guðrún said.

'Agreed,' Ragna said. 'And let's not forget that Unnur could also be very difficult to be around.'

10

They were still on the high pass of Hellisheiði, just past the Hverádalir ski slopes, when Særós called to tell them to take it easy for the next hour. She had been in touch with the priest in Hveragerði to check things out, and found that he knew Regína and Skarphéðinn well. He was already on the way to inform them of Arnhildur's death.

'We're almost there,' Guðgeir said, unable to hide his irritation. It wasn't just that Særós had interfered, but he had lost the opportunity to read their reactions to the bad news. This was not necessarily to look for a perpetrator, but it was a way of getting a handle on their personalities and relationship with the deceased. But the upside of this was that he and Elsa Guðrún would have a chance to get a bite to eat before meeting Arnhildur's sister and brother-in-law. His stomach was rumbling, it was well past midday and breakfast had been a long time ago.

'Fair enough, Særós,' he said. 'We'll take it easy for an hour or so.'

Despite Hveragerði's choice of restaurants, they went to the first hot dog stall they saw. That was the quick and easy option, Guðgeir decided, buying himself two, but leaving out the bun. Then they drove around the town for a while before coming to a halt outside a small detached house in the older part of the town. Multi-coloured Christmas lights twinkled in both windows and on the wooden fence at the edge of the plot.

'The sisters have something in common,' Elsa Guðrún said with a smirk. 'Neither of them are in a hurry to take their Christmas decorations down, even though we're well into the new year.'

'Just how many lights does a garden fence like this need?' Guðgeir mused. 'I'm sure our neighbours in Europe would get a shock if they saw how Icelanders get through electricity, considering what the situation is like in some places.'

'Ach, these bulbs use next to no energy,' Elsa Guðrún assured him, with a dreamy look on her face. 'Maybe I ought to move to Hveragerði and lose all the commuting stress. My boys could look after themselves while I'm at work. I imagine a house like this costs about as much as my little flat in the city. Always thought this was a pretty sort of place, everything close at hand and a simpler life.'

'Surely you wouldn't abandon me and Særós and join the southern region force instead?' Guðgeir asked with a grin. 'I can't believe that, and who would keep Leifur up to speed with the modern age? He'd be devastated to lose you...' His words faded away as his thoughts went back to the job in hand. 'No point hanging about,' he said, tapping at the door of the little house as there was no bell to be seen anywhere.

Voices and a cough could be heard beyond the door before it opened. A tall, balding man, but with hunched shoulders, looked them up and down with tired eyes. This had to be Skarphéðinn, the late Arnhildur's brother-in-law. From what Særós had found out, he drove coaches for a tour operator during the busy summer period, and took shifts clearing snow during the winters. Guðgeir felt that Skarphéðinn looked older than the date contained within his ID number would indicate, although having just been given bad news could account for that. He extended a hand to shake, muttering a few words that they interpreted as an invitation to step inside.

Regína sat with her elbows on the kitchen table and her head in her hands. She was clearly distressed, but made an effort to pull herself together when she saw them. The sadness on her face was unmistakeable, although it quickly gave way to a stonier countenance. Regína passed her hands over her cheeks and sniffed.

'Won't you sit down?' Skarphéðinn asked when they had introduced themselves and offered their condolences. 'The priest has just left, and it wasn't as if he could tell us much …. Just that Arnhildur had been lying there for some time, and it looks suspicious. He said you'd explain everything.'

'That's quite right,' Guðgeir said, perching on a blue-painted stool. 'There's a strong suspicion of manslaughter, and we don't know how long she had been lying there, but it could be as long as three days. That's a remarkably long time in such a busy part of the city, but it's maybe not surprising considering how bad the weather has been and how difficult it has been to get around. Normally a good few people pass through the graveyard, even in the winter. But like I said, the weather's been bad these last few days.'

Regína grimaced and it clearly hurt to have the priest's words confirmed.

'Was she left there to die?' she asked, taking a breath as she spoke, and the horror shone from her wide eyes.

'No. We consider that wasn't the case. But the investigation is at an early stage, so there's still a lot we don't know,' Guðgeir explained, his voice low but clear.

'Was this a mugging?' Skarphéðinn asked. His face hardened and his eyes narrowed angrily. 'Those junkies will do anything for their next fix.'

'Unlikely, but it goes without saying that we're open to every possibility,' Elsa Guðrún said.

'Why do you think she was … murdered?' Regína asked, a shiver passing through her at the sound of the word.

'We're not aware yet of the cause of death, although

there are visible signs of trauma. She appears to have received a blow to the head. So we feel it's likely that she was the victim of an assault, but it's unclear whether or not the assault resulted in her death. That kind of shock could trigger a heart attack,' Elsa Guðrún explained.

'So she could have lost her footing on the ice and fallen .... And hit her head,' Skarphéðinn suggested. He looked at his wife with concern, clearly doing his best to allay her concerns.

'Unfortunately, it doesn't look like that,' Guðgeir said. 'We would appreciate it if you could keep this information to yourselves, as the investigation is only just getting underway.'

The couple looked at each other in surprise, and then nodded without saying a word.

'We need to ask a few questions,' Elsa Guðrún said. 'When did you last see Arnhildur?'

They quickly glanced at each other.

'Well ... it's a good while ago,' Skarphéðinn said, while Regína said nothing, leaning forward with the tips of her fingers to her forehead, staring down at the table.

'Days or weeks? Or months? Elsa Guðrún probed.

'A long, long time,' he replied slowly.

Regína got abruptly to her feet and excused herself, saying that she needed to change, and that she had just come in from work as the priest had turned up. This was such an unexpected reaction that Elsa Guðrún asked in surprise where she worked, because as far as she could see, the woman was dressed for comfort in track suit bottoms and a thin sweater.

'She works at the clinic,' Skarphéðinn said, as his wife left the room without replying.

'What clinic?' Elsa Guðrún asked.

'It's a health clinic. The Health Spa, to give it its proper name. That's supposed to sound more posh. Regína takes shifts cleaning or in the kitchen when needed. It's hard work for her as she suffers from arthritis and things aren't easy for a woman of her age. That's the way it is. Needs must...' Skarphéðinn ran a hand awkwardly over his bald head, as if that last word was awkward to say in front of the police. 'It's easier for me, even though driving for long spells is tiring. Would you like coffee?' He stood up and fetched three cups from a cupboard without waiting for a response and placed them before them. Then he reached for a thermos and poured coffee. 'Yes, that's the way it is. We have to try and make ends meet,' he said, sipping steaming coffee as he stood by the table. 'Quite apart from the long drives in all sorts of weather, I have to watch tourists playing the fool far too close to the waves on the Black Sand Beach at Reynisfjara. It's insane what people will do to get a selfie to post online. Can I offer you anything else? There must be something in the house.' He turned and opened a drawer. Guðgeir and Elsa Guðrún exchanged glances as the man searched for something edible. His conversation had taken an unexpected turn.

'What are you doing, Skarphéðinn?'

Regína stood in the doorway, glaring at her husband. The sweater had been replaced by a long-sleeved tee-shirt, and that was the only difference, except that her eyes were even redder than before.

'Well, trying to find some biscuits for them,' Skarphéðinn replied in annoyance, continuing to root through the contents of the drawer.

'That's all right,' Guðgeir assured him. 'We've already eaten.'

'Oh, well,' Skarphéðinn said grumpily, as if they had been troubling him unnecessarily.

'We were asking when you last saw Arnhildur,' Guðgeir repeated.

'Yes,' Skarphéðinn muttered. He shut the drawer before turning to face them, and without answering right away. 'It's been quite a while. Do you remember, Regína?' He looked at his wife expectantly and leaned against the worktop with his arms folded.

'I reckon it must be eleven or twelve years since we last met,' she said heavily, and perched on the edge of a chair. 'That was far from being a happy occasion and since then neither of us have seen her, although there have been a few phone calls. But those have been few and far between.' Regína pursed her lips and ceaselessly massaged her left shoulder with her right hand. Her nails were gnawed to the quick.

'So what happened?' Elsa Guðrún asked.

'There was an accident,' Regína replied and there was an unmistakeable harshness in her voice.

'Do you mean that was when Unnur was injured?' Guðgeir asked warily. No confirmation was needed as their faces darkened. 'How did this happen?'

'The horse was one of ours,' Skarphéðinn snapped. 'We ran a farm on Snæfellsnes with a riding school. We did fairly well, right up until that accident. After that everything we had built up came crashing down. Not just our own efforts, but those of my parents and grandparents. We were forced to sell the land and move here to Hveragerði. From that moment on we've been slaves in the service of others.'

'That's it,' Regína broke in, her voice raised.

'That's the way it was. We had to leave behind everything we loved and came here to slave away for starvation wages,' Skarphéðinn snarled.

'We were given to understand that Unnur had been given a horse that hadn't been properly broken in,' Guðgeir said.

'Who told you that?' There was no mistaking the astonishment on Regína's face.

'Unnur lives in sheltered accommodation, and that was what the manager told us.'

'That's not true!' Regína said with determination. 'She's heard these lies from Arnhildur.'

'That's bullshit,' Skarphéðinn said angrily. 'What do you expect this manager would know about it? The truth of it is that Unnur demanded to ride that horse. Well, I warned her, but there was no arguing with her as she'd been used to getting her own way in everything. The girl had always been given everything she wanted.'

'That'll do!' Regína glared at her husband. 'You'll have to excuse us. We're upset and this is bringing back a very difficult time that we had tried hard to put behind us so we could get on with our lives. Arnhildur sued us and we were forced to pay her substantial damages. It was difficult to keep the business going as not only were our finances wrecked, but our reputation was ruined. The equestrian business lost customers rapidly, and at that time we had just started up the riding school that we had put everything into, and there was no way we could continue. My sister certainly didn't hold back when it came to blackening our names.'

'I see,' Guðgeir said, his eyebrows lifted. He wasn't used to getting so much information at once, and without having to dig for it. 'Tell me, Arnhildur's former husband and Unnur's father, Jacob Winter, is registered as being resident overseas. We urgently need to get hold of him. Can you help us track him down?'

'No, I don't think so. He left the country when Unnur was eight, and after that he was never in touch with them, at least, not while we were still on speaking terms,' Regína replied.

'How come?' Elsa Guðrún asked in astonishment.

'I think he had other children here in Iceland. It was amazing how long he stuck it out with Arnhildur, as he was naturally on the footloose side, or so it seemed to me. Then, one day he was just gone .... To Germany, as far as I know,' Skarphéðinn said. 'The Winter name fits perfectly, because he vanished during a cold winter, just like this one.'

'Was there any search for him?' Guðgeir asked.

'Maybe, just to go through the motions,' Skarphéðinn replied, before adding his own perspective. 'Jacob was a party animal, and quite a ladies' man. Being cooped up with Arnhildur didn't suit him, and to be truthful, she wasn't the most fun person to be around.'

'Ach,' Regína muttered. 'Rubbish!'

'These other children you mentioned. Are they in Iceland?' Guðgeir asked.

'Well, I don't doubt he was blamed for a good few, poor guy. But there's one I know of in Snæfellsnes, in Stykkishólmur, to be precise. Those of us from that part of the country keep an eye on each other. But the lad must be around forty by now, and there's no telling if he still lives there in the west.'

'Do you know his name?' Elsa Guðrún asked.

'No, I don't remember. But the mother's name is Stella Jónsdóttir,' Skarphéðinn replied with a frown. 'What do you need these names for? Like I said, these were just rumours, and I don't want to see these people pestered. It's wrong to dig into other people's lives.'

'We'll tread carefully,' Guðgeir said, getting to his feet and Elsa Guðrún followed suit. 'But to finish off, can you account for your movements since Monday?' Skarphéðinn groaned and Regína glanced from one to the other in confusion. 'I'm sorry, but I have to ask,' Guðgeir added.

'Oh, I see,' Regína said with a sigh. 'I was working at the spa every day. On Tuesday I was at a needlework class with some other ladies from the town here, and the other two evenings we were both here at home.'

'Thanks,' Guðgeir said. 'We'll check it out. And you, Skarphéðinn?'

'I've been at work. On Tuesday evening I went to help someone take down a greenhouse that had come down in the bad weather. That kept us busy well into the evening, and then I went home to get some sleep as I had to be up early to drive a tourist group on Wednesday.'

'Were you asleep when Regína came home from her class?' Guðgeir asked.

'Yes. I was snoring the moment my head hit the pillow,' Skarphéðinn said, running a hand over his bald head.

11

The working day was coming to an end as they reached the city. Guðgeir dropped Elsa Guðrún at the garage to collect her car, and then made his way down to the station to meet Særós.

He stopped at the coffee machine and punched the buttons for a double espresso, adamant that he needed the boost it would give him after a long day. He could see out of the corner of his eye through the open door of her office. Særós sat straight-backed as she faced the computer screen and was speaking on the phone. Her immaculate dark hair formed a frame around her sharp face and her long, slim neck. A fine gold chain curved over her collarbones and the pendant itself hung precisely dead centre. Guðgeir smiled as he thought of Inga, and how often he had noticed her with the clasp of a necklace at the front and the pendant hidden somewhere under her collar. His absolutely reliable legal expert could be delightfully slapdash when it came to minor details that were of no importance, and he found that side of her personality enchanting. Guðgeir paused for a moment and watched Særós without drawing attention to himself. He wanted to finish his coffee without getting a well-meaning reminder of the dangers that came with caffeine consumption. Særós was extremely competent, clever, precise and organised, and Guðgeir hoped that with a little more experience her management style would become more relaxed. He felt it was unfortunate that she seemed to have a constant need to prove herself, both professionally and personally, which could sometimes result in minor but completely unnecessary clashes with her team. Guðgeir both liked and knew her well, and he had been the one who had brought her into the department, before their roles had been reversed.

   He sipped his coffee and checked his phone. There were new messages from Inga to let him know that she would be collecting Guðgeir Jökull from nursery, as their grandson's mother was busy revising for an exam. Their daughter Ólöf had moved back home after parting company with the little boy's father, Smári, for the second time. They got on well together, although space was limited because their college student son Pétur Andri was also still living at home. Guðgeir and Inga had downsized a few years previously. Their town house in Fossvogur had been sold and they had switched to an apartment in a new block, in the expectation that before long their son would also be leaving home and the pair of them would be left at home. But things hadn't turned out that way and they would have to live with cramped conditions for a while as upscaling again wasn't on the agenda. Guðgeir knocked back the last drops of coffee, put the cup aside and made his presence known. Særós was still on the phone but gestured for him to take a seat. As always, the week's aphorism hung on the wall behind her, a printout with black letters on white in a simple Ikea frame. This week it said, **Always be the best possible version of yourself**.

   Guðgeir's eyebrows lifted and he scratched his chin. He had many times heard and seen these words that had become so commonplace a phrase, trotted out by all kinds of lifestyle gurus, that it had become a cliché. The words were certainly in the spirit of the super-organised and precise Særós, who was constantly striving to improve herself in every conceivable way, although she generally had the latest thinking at her fingertips. A new piece of advice or nugget of wisdom always made an appearance on the wall every single Friday, week in and week out. Every week there would be a sweepstake on whether or not she would forget, with the winner standing to take home a six-pack of beer. So far the beer had remained unclaimed. Guðgeir felt that Særós had no need of improvement, except that she could make an effort to relax a little. If she were to manage that, then she'd become *the best possible version of herself* – whatever that was supposed to mean. He watched his superior fondly and noticed clear signs of fatigue in her face. Her eyes were bloodshot and there were black patches beneath her eyes. Maybe it was time to stop being up at five-thirty for a training session, and to get more sleep instead. Ninety more minutes of sleep makes a difference, he reflected, although there could be something else troubling her.

'That was the Ministry of Foreign Affairs,' Særós said as she put the phone down. 'They'll do what they can to help us search for Jacob Winter. There was a rumour that he'd committed suicide by swimming out to sea, although there's always the possibility that he simply ran away from his responsibilities and left the country. At any rate, no body was ever recovered.'

'Interesting,' Guðgeir said. 'If he's living, wouldn't he have been likely to have tried to maintain some contact with his daughter?'

'Ragna at the assisted living facility isn't aware of anything of that nature, although there could have been some contact with Arnhildur that nobody else was aware of,' Særós replied. 'Some people just don't take part in the lives of their children. They just disappear, and for that they don't need to be that far away ... Just like my so-called father. He's not physically far away, but he could just as well be on the moon,' she said with a cold, humourless laugh.

Særós being unexpectedly open about her personal life took Guðgeir by surprise.

'Yes, true. All sorts of things happen,' he said. 'Maybe it's not worth putting too much effort into finding this man? Was there anything else?'

'We've spoken to people in most of the houses in the surrounding streets and nothing has come out of that so far, but there's still a chance that someone could have seen or heard something,' Særós said, and stretched in her office chair.

'And CCTV? Guðgeir asked. 'Weren't there two cameras close by?'

'Yes. One has been out of action for months, and forensics have taken the material from the other. It's always the same story with these lousy cameras,' she sighed. 'Which is crap, because it seems to me that this isn't likely to be a premeditated murder. To be honest, it seems most likely to me that some down-and-out knocked this unfortunate woman on the head.'

'That's the most obvious explanation, but somehow I'm not ready to buy it. I feel we need to be open to every possibility,' Guðgeir said.

'Of course we'll do that,' Særós said.

'That's good. Are we all right to appeal for witnesses who might have been aware of Arnhildur's movements? The next of kin have been informed and I don't think we can wait any longer,' Guðgeir said. 'Time isn't on our side.'

'Agreed. I'll pass this on to the media, without saying too much about the reasons behind it,' Særós said. 'Elsa Guðrún sent me a digest of everything you found out today. But what's your personal take on this?'

'Well...' Guðgeir ran his fingers through his dark hair and leaned back. 'There are indications that Arnhildur was struggling financially, although we haven't yet seen her bank statements.'

'I'll send Leifur a message and ask him to check,' Særós

said, tapping at the keyboard in front of her.

'Good. She wanted to increase the rent for the downstairs apartment, even though there's a rental agreement, and justified her demands by saying that a friend had moved in with the tenants. They rent the apartment as a couple, but now there are three of them living there.'

'That's a whole new angle on the property market, going by the number of people sharing,' Særós said with a smile.

'The house needs repairs. It's possible she couldn't afford it and that's why she wanted to squeeze more out of the tenants,' Guðgeir speculated. 'As well as that, there's a bedsit flat in the basement that could be rented out of it could be fixed up.'

'Could just be sloppiness,' Særós suggested, but Guðgeir shook his head.

'That doesn't ring true. Inside her apartment everything was in perfect order,' he said. 'Admittedly it's dusty, but there's no clutter there. Far from it.' Guðgeir closed his eyes for a moment so he could better bring to mind what he had seen. 'Thinking back, the place is ... how can I put it? Somehow stagnant, as if time had stood still.'

'Arnhildur could have suffered from some kind of phobia or indecisiveness. Some people have real difficulty taking decisions,' Særós said.

'Either that, or financial difficulties,' Guðgeir replied.

'We still need to check. I spoke to Ragna, the manager you met at the assisted living facility, and asked a few more questions. It turned out that three years ago Arnhildur bought a car that was intended solely for driving her daughter Unnur, going for trips, shopping, or going bowling, which she really likes. Arnhildur didn't have a driving licence herself, so the car was in the hands of the staff up there, and that all worked out well, until she announced suddenly that she was selling the car. Her reasoning was that the staff weren't looking after it properly, and that there were sweet wrappers and empty cans in the footwell. She was very angry about this, which Ragna felt was very unlike Arnhildur,' Særós said. 'Normally she'd come across as being well-balanced emotionally, not least when it came to difficulties related to her daughter.'

'Arnhildur seems to have been struggling with some serious financial difficulties, and this odd behaviour towards the tenants indicates she was getting desperate. Did you find out anything more about Regína and Skarphéðinn?' Guðgeir asked.

'I read the court files,' Særós replied. 'It was a hell of a case.'

'I had a look as well, and it must have been terrible,' Guðgeir said. 'It's clearly left a lot of bitterness behind, at least with the brother-in-law. The sister came across as being completely devastated.'

'Understandably,' Særós said. 'It's bad enough losing a sister, without there also being a matter there that will now never be resolved. Family affairs can be unbelievably difficult and complex...' Særós fell silent and stared into the middle distance, as if she had lost the thread of the conversation. Guðgeir thought of what he knew of her childhood. She had lost her mother at a young age and from then on her father drank heavily and took up with women of varying levels of unsuitability, all of them younger. Some had even been around the same age as his eldest daughter, Særós. At least two siblings had struggled with addiction and she had made efforts to support them, even though she had long since given up on their father. She was the only one of them to complete further education and to be successful at a professional level. Guðgeir wondered if Særós's ceaseless quest for perfection and the constant determination to better herself had roots in her childhood difficulties. She seemed to be obsessed with proving herself, or else gnawed by guilt over her present situation. Those who weren't aware of her background assumed she'd been born with a silver spoon in her mouth, because of the way she behaved and approached life, but Guðgeir knew better. The expensive, quality clothes, her impeccable appearance, even the beautiful apartment that would have done credit to any interior designer were her shield. These were her defences against all the old tribulations and also against those she encountered in her police work. He knew her well enough to understand that beneath the tailored exterior lay a sensitive nature, as well as a sharp intelligence and a logical way of thinking that was the basis of their profession. Guðgeir sat and watched Særós, and reflected on how fond he was of her. This woman had been through a lot in her life.

'It must weigh heavily on them,' she said at last, after a long silence.

'Certainly. There was a complete break between them following the accident. They hadn't met for years. These people have clearly been entirely estranged from each other,' Guðgeir replied.

'Shall we call it a day? I'm exhausted, for some reason,' Særós said as she abruptly got to her feet.

He watched in astonishment as she fetched the coat that hung on a hook by the door. In all the years they'd worked together, she had never once admitted being tired. Fatigue was something that other people experienced. Those were the people who didn't take proper care of themselves, didn't watch their diets or exercise, or who didn't exercise sufficient self-control. In her mind this was a sign of weakness, as although she was undoubtedly familiar with the feeling, she had repeatedly battered it into submission through sheer determination. Særós was the woman who took part in triathlons, long-distance mountain runs and who'd passed every one of the police's endurance tests with flying colours. She wasn't one to complain of fatigue or pressure.

'Are you all right? Are you ill?' The question was out of Guðgeir's mouth before he had even thought about it.

'Me? No, why would I be ill?' Særós snapped back sharply, almost angrily.

'Isn't there always a flu going round at this time of year?' Guðgeir asked, awkwardly scratching his head. 'You must surely get ill, just like everyone else.'

'Me? No. I haven't had a day's illness since I started cold water swimming ten years ago, and only occasionally before then. It's something that cures all ills, and it's best when the temperature is below freezing,' she said, buttoning her woollen overcoat.

'Yes. Sure,' Guðgeir replied, as he always did.

'Meeting in the morning. Nine sharp,' Særós said, and was gone.

That evening as he and Inga were clearing up after dinner, Guðgeir mentioned Særós's unusual behaviour.

'It wasn't just that she mentioned personal stuff, she also said she was tired,' he explained. 'She looks pale, and there are worry bags under her eyes.'

'People get worn out. That's normal,' Inga said, picking up the place mats.

'Not Særós. I've worked shifts with her that have gone beyond twenty-four hours without a break and she always said she was fine. Maybe she was telling the truth, even though I could hardly keep my eyes open,' Guðgeir said, arranging the cutlery in the dishwasher. 'She's always had unbelievable energy levels.'

'Maybe she's burned out?' Inga suggested, holding a cloth under the hot tap. 'Or maybe it's just life overload.'

'Life overload? What's that?' Guðgeir asked, looking over at his wife. 'Is this something new?'

'It's not just work, but everything …. Well, life as a whole,' Inga said and wiped the cloth over the table. She paused at the area in front of Guðgeir Jökull's high chair and fussed with some splashes of food. Ólöf had just taken the little boy into her room to put him to sleep.

'Surely not Særós? Of all people, she's the ball of fire and the health guru personified,' Guðgeir protested. He slid a tablet into the dishwasher before he set it to run.

'She's human, like the rest of us,' Inga said, twisting the cloth and wetting it again. 'And don't talk so loudly. You might wake the little one. But in all seriousness, you ought to speak to her if you get a chance.'

'You think so? Even though she's my boss?'

'Yes,' Inga said, sweeping up a book as she headed for the sofa. 'No question.'

12

Guðgeir found the meeting room empty when he arrived a few minutes before nine the following morning. He checked his phone and saw a message from Særós, postponing the meeting until eleven o'clock, so he fetched a cup of coffee and strolled to his own office. There was an alert on his computer screen from the reception desk. This told him that a woman called Thórdís Emilsdóttir wanted to speak to him. She was soon standing in his doorway. She was very thin, dressed in jeans and a heavy coat. A long, thick woollen scarf was wrapped around her neck, and she wore striking earrings, as well as a colourful scarf covering her head.

'You're Guðgeir Fransson?' she asked. Her voice was soft, but it carried.

'I am.'

'I decided I'd come and see you, as I'm going for my chemo session later and wanted to do this first,' she explained. 'My name's Thórdís and I'm here because you were asking people to come forward who might know about Arnhildur Drífa Friðriksdóttir's movements.'

'Friðthjófsdóttir,' Guðgeir corrected. 'Please, take a seat.'

'I didn't know her, and didn't even know her name until I saw the announcement in the media,' Thórdís said, perching on the edge of a chair.

'I see. So when did you see Arnhildur?' Guðgeir asked.

'That was on Tuesday evening. We were at the same meeting,' she replied. 'When I saw the picture of her on the TV, I realised right away that she was the woman who'd been sitting next to me.'

'Where was this meeting?' Guðgeir asked.

'In a place off Bergstaðastræti. I don't recall the number, but I could find it online, if you like.'

'Yes, absolutely,' Guðgeir said, turning the screen of his computer so she could see. It didn't take long to find the right building. 'Tell me, what sort of meeting was this?'

Thórdís flushed at the question.

'Well, this was a séance,' she said with a touch of awkwardness.

Guðgeir narrowly stopped himself from repeating the word. 'That's unusual,' he said, his eyebrows lifting.

'I'm going through a difficult time .... And that makes you seek for things in different places .... You see...' she said, her voice mellifluous.

'I understand,' Guðgeir said with sincerity, although this was certainly something he hadn't experienced personally. 'Could you take me through everything relating to Arnhildur that evening? Every detail?'

Thórdís gazed back at him with a serious look in her eyes.

'That's what I've been trying to recall,' she said. 'Has she gone missing, or is it more serious than that?'

It was interesting the way she worded her question, not asking if this person had vanished or disappeared. Nobody appeared to have missed Arnhildur between her murder and the discovery of her body. There hadn't been a single person so far, with the possible exception of her daughter – although he had no idea of her thoughts. Guðgeir took a deep breath and decided to tell Thórdís the truth of the matter, as the media had already put two and two together, connecting her to the discovery of a murder victim. It was just a case of how long it would be before the news was splashed across the front pages.

SHROUDED

'The reality of it is that Arnhildur was found dead, in the Hólavellir graveyard. There's a strong suspicion that her death was due to a criminal act,' he said after a moment's hesitation, instinctively slipping into official jargon.

'What?' Thórdís's voice boomed and her hands went to her mouth. 'That's terrible! She died on Tuesday night?'

'We don't know yet, which is why I would ask you to be as precise as possible. I'll record the conversation, if you have no objection?' Guðgeir said, placing his phone on the desk before taking his glasses from their case in his jacket pocket.

'Not at all,' Thórdís replied. 'I'm happy to help, but I have to be at the oncology department at ten-thirty.'

'Understood. You'll make that in good time,' Guðgeir said. He opened the case, took out his glasses and put them on. Then he tapped the button to start the recording. 'This isn't a formal statement, but it would be ideal if you could start with your name and ID number. Then give me as accurate an account as possible, as far as you remember. I'll only interrupt if I need some further explanation.'

Thórdís unzipped her coat and crossed her denim-clad legs. She was wearing a loose-necked shirt and Guðgeir couldn't help noticing a recent scar just below her left clavicle. This was an obvious chemotherapy port scar, and Thórdís had clearly been through a lot in her twenty-three years. In a low, soft voice, she recounted how Arnhildur had sat next to her at the séance, and that she would never have gone to such a gathering if the people from whom she bought stuff hadn't recommended it as being good for those coping with difficult illness.

'What sort of stuff?' Guðgeir asked.

'It's not dope, if that's what you're thinking,' Thórdís replied with a faint, momentary smile. 'It's a powder that I take with my morning boosts. It's full of vitamins and all kinds of things that are good for the immune system. It's not available in shops or from chemists, but it's sold person to person, and you can find it online.'

Guðgeir wanted to ask what evidence she might have for the effectiveness of this powder, but he held back. Her narrative flowed and he was reluctant to interrupt. No ghosts had manifested themselves at this meeting, although some of those present had received messages from the other side. She herself had been told that everything would be fine and that she would make a full recovery. A couple who had lost their son had been given the news that the boy was strong and well. There had been other messages that people understood, or not, and towards the end of the séance the medium had changed, so that spirits spoke through him. Among these was an old woman who appeared to have been Arnhildur's long-departed grandmother.

'And what did she want?' Guðgeir asked, relieved that this wasn't a formal statement.

'Ach, well. She talked mostly about some silver that had been on a dress she had owned, national dress of some kind.' Thórdís grimaced and rolled her eyes. 'I find it so odd that the dead are so obsessed with worldly stuff. So maybe people just continue the same way they were in life ... What do I know? I mean, if we believe this stuff at all. But after that, the medium's voice turned very deep and that was her long-dead grandfather coming through,' Thórdís said. 'He was angry with her, said she'd brought shame on the family.'

'What for?' Guðgeir asked, his curiosity piqued.

'Oh, something she was supposed to have done ages ago,' Thórdís replied. 'Arnhildur didn't want to speak to her grandfather and asked the medium to exclude him.'

'And he did?'

'Yes, and then the grandmother came back and was still going on about the silver,' Thórdís smiled.

'Was Arnhildur the only one to get that kind of direct connection that evening?' Guðgeir asked.

'Yes. There were others who received messages from the other side, but considering her dead ancestors came through so clearly it seems sinister that something could have happened to her, you see,' Thórdís said. 'It's as if they were checking on her.'

'What's the medium's name, and who were the others at this meeting?' Guðgeir asked.

'All I know is that his name's Valthór, but I didn't know anyone there. There were just five of us, apart from him. That's the couple who lost their son, Arnhildur, and there was an older man who sat on her other side. He left with her, I saw them go. Maybe they knew each other, I don't know.'

'And you don't have any names?' Guðgeir asked, quickly checking online for anyone called Valthór with an address on Bergstaðastræti. There was nobody of that name, although there was one Valur, and he was only fourteen. A company with a mysterious name was registered as the owner of the building where the séance had taken place.

'No, I don't know any of them, and people naturally didn't introduce themselves.'

'What sort of age is this Valthór, the medium?'

'Well...' Thórdís clicked her tongue and narrowed her eyes. 'Hard to say. Maybe forty-plus, but not more than fifty, I'd say,' she said after pausing for thought.

'This man who left with Arnhildur after the meeting, what did he look like?' Guðgeir said.

Thórdís shrugged.

''I was so uptight in there that I didn't take much notice of the others. But he had a beard and looked a bit like an old film actor. Like one of the guys who played James Bond, but gone to seed, if you know what I mean?'

'Daniel Craig?'

'Don't think so. He's much too fit.'

'Sean Connery or Pierce Brosnan?'

'You know the whole series,' she said with a smile that stretched from ear to ear.

'I've seen them all, and more than once.' Guðgeir returned the smile. 'I watch a lot of movies when I have time.'

'Ach, I couldn't be sure who he resembled. I just said that because he's that type, y'know?' Thórdís said, reaching for her phone to check the time.

'Did you get the impression they'd met before? Arnhildur and this man?'

'Don't think so. But I can't tell,' Thórdís replied. 'Look, I have to make a move. I have to be there in half an hour.'

She got to her feet.

'I understand. Thank you for coming in. You've been a great help.' Guðgeir stood up. 'I might need to speak to you again.'

'That's fine,' Thórdís said. She opened her handbag, took out a card and handed it to him. 'You can reach me any time.'

She disappeared through the door and he was left holding her card. It hadn't occurred to him that someone in their early twenties would carry a card, and that took him pleasantly by surprise. He placed it next to his computer so he could enter the information onto the system.

Thórdís Emilsdóttir
Classical singer.

That fit. That voice had immediately caught his attention.

13

Guðgeir made use of the time he had spare before the meeting to collate his notes of what had emerged from his conversation with Thórdís, and points relating to his and Elsa Guðrún's trip to Hveragerði. He sent the memo to his colleagues. By this time it was almost eleven, so he made his way to the meeting room. Særós sat at the end of the table, absorbed in her laptop, and barely looked up as he entered the room. Next to her sat Leifur with a plastic folder in front of him, clicking a biro. Elsa Guðrún made her appearance hard on Guðgeir's heels and shortly afterwards Ísgerður the pathologist – professional but always a little distant – joined them.

'Let's make a start,' Særós said.

'Isn't Helgi Már joining us?' Elsa Guðrún asked, glancing through the half-open door.

'Not now. He's busy going through samples,' Leifur replied. 'I'll bring him up to speed later on everything here.'

'So,' Særós said. 'There's nothing from CCTV and no witnesses have come forward apart from the girl who spoke to Guðgeir this morning.'

Leifur and Elsa Guðrún looked enquiringly in Guðgeir's direction.

'I sent everything to you just now,' he said.

''We'll go over that afterwards,' Særós decided, and turned to Ísgerður. 'Any results from the autopsy?'

'There's definite trauma to the base of the skull and I found metal traces in the hair. So it's likely she was hit with a tool of some description. I'm trying to work out the shape of it and that should become clear before long.'

'We can be certain she was hit, and didn't get these injuries from falling backwards?' Elsa Guðrún asked.

'Yes. That's for sure. I can be fully certain of this, as is Arnar who assisted during the autopsy, but there's also something unexpected.'

Ísgerður paused for a moment and gazed meaningfully at those present. She tucked her long brown hair behind her ears and picked an invisible speck of fluff from her patterned sweater. It was as if she relished the tension for a few dramatic seconds. Særós drummed the desk with her long, lacquered nails and glared impatiently at Ísgerður.

'Well, are we going to sit here all day long?' Leifur snorted, fiddling with his pen, and coming across as being stressed. The pen clicked at quick intervals.

'Arnhildur's coronary artery was narrowed and partially blocked, so she had heart problems, probably with a cholesterol level that was far too high,' Ísgerður announced, her expression unchanged.

'There was no medication for that kind of condition at her home,' Leifur broke in.

'Not even anything for heartburn?' Ísgerður asked.

'No. Nothing like that,' Leifur replied. 'Just Panodil painkillers and Imovane for insomnia.'

'Then she can't have been aware of this,' Ísgerður said. 'A heart problem can be quite advanced before people have the slightest idea. I can assure you that with that kind of blockage, untreated, she wouldn't have had long to live.'

'But was the cause of death the blow to the head or a heart attack?' Guðgeir asked. He leaned forward and his fists clenched. This was a vital aspect of the case.

'The head injury was the cause of her death,' Ísgerður replied. 'But it's clear that her physical condition was poor.

That wouldn't have helped.'

'So it's conceivable that whoever assaulted her could have intended to knock her out, but the attack turned into unintentional manslaughter?' Guðgeir suggested.

'Yes. But I'm confident enough to assert that she received more than one blow to the head. I speculate that she received two or even three blows, but that will become clearer once we've figured out the shape of the weapon,' Ísgerður said, fiddling with one silver earring. 'Her airway was restricted as she was choked with her scarf, but that wasn't the cause of death.'

'But what did the attacker have to gain from all this?' Elsa Guðrún asked. 'Of course it could have been a bungled mugging ... some junkie who hadn't expected things to go that far?'

'Unless Arnhildur had something on her or in her bag that we don't know about, which the attacker was determined to get,' Guðgeir said. 'People can be after other things than money.'

'Or else he wanted to simply get rid of her, for whatever reason,' Leifur pointed out.

'This woman's life doesn't appear to have been complex, and the outstanding characteristic is that everything was very regular,' Særós said, pushing her computer aside. 'I spoke to her former colleagues at the lottery. They were unanimous in saying that Arnhildur lived a simple, ordered life. Of course, that didn't extend to the difficulties that go with having a disabled child. One of them said that Arnhildur invariably ate the same thing for lunch every single day, and barely missed a day during her whole working life. She walked the same way to and from work, so she was very set in her ways, but turned up for events such as the annual office party, and that sort of thing. She was highly conscientious in her work, but the problem was that she wouldn't move with the times. She wanted to do everything exactly as she always had, and there was always some excuse for this. If there was anything that needed changing at her workplace, such as bringing in new technology, she was always completely against it. She loathed change, bringing up all kinds of objections, when the real reason for her opposition was generally that she either didn't want to or didn't trust herself to change her working routines. Finally, she was pretty much forced out and into retirement when she was 65. It was made to look as if it was her own choice, and in fact she was relieved to be free, at least to begin with, as she wanted to spend more time looking after her daughter.'

Særós paused, opened her computer and scanned the screen.

'I had an email, just now, from her former manager, who told me that something strange occurred a few weeks ago. According to him, Arnhildur, now in her seventies, turned up and asked to have her old job back. When she was told that wasn't possible, she asked if there might be any part-time work. The manager said that he was astonished and wasn't sure what to do. He talked to her over a cup of coffee and a biscuit, and even thought at first that she'd lost her mind, but that didn't appear to be the case. She turned out to be perfectly sane and was completely serious.'

'Which supports the indications that Arnhildur was in financial trouble,' Guðgeir said. 'Is there anything on that?'

'Yes,' Leifur said, leafing through his folder. 'According to official sources, Arnhildur had no bank debts. She has only one registered bank account and her pension was paid into that. It's noticeable that over the last three months she has withdrawn money as it came in, but hasn't paid it into any other accounts. Arnhildur didn't use online banking, and did everything across the counter at her branch.'

'The poor woman was firmly stuck in a bygone age,' Særós observed.

'Or maybe she just needed the personal interaction,' Leifur said. 'So much is being moved online and there are automatic checkouts where there used to be cashiers you could talk to, and it doesn't agree with everyone. It can be hard for the older generation to lose that social interaction, especially if they live alone.'

Leifur's meaningful look travelled around the room, almost as if those present were responsible for the growing tide of loneliness around the world.

Guðgeir coughed and grunted, as a reminder for Leifur to keep to the business in hand. He took the hint and continued.

'Concerning the property, there's no mortgage on it. At least, for Arnhildur's share of it. Her sister, Regína Friðthjófsdóttir, owns forty percent, and she and her husband rent a house in Hveragerði.'

'That's right. Yesterday we went to see her and her husband, Skarphéðinn, to inform them of Arnhildur's death,' Elsa Guðrún said.

'I sent some information to everyone just before this meeting with a digest of the main points concerning them, and also Thórdís, the witness who came forward this morning,' Guðgeir added quickly. 'In short, there's been no contact between the sisters since Arnhildur's daughter Unnur fell off a horse and suffered permanent brain damage. This happened at a farm on Snæfellsnes that was owned at the time by Regína and Skarphéðinn. They lost the property and their business as a consequence of the accident. There was a difficult legal process and their reputation was trashed.'

Guðgeir paused, as all those present were deep in their phones, reading through the points he'd sent them just a few minutes before the meeting – except for Særós, who had already checked over everything relating to the case.

'Family disputes are lousy,' she said as they all looked up. 'Imagine, those sisters could've long ago sold that house in the west end of the city. Regína could have bought herself an apartment, and Arnhildur could have got rid of her debts, whatever these are. All they needed to do was talk to each other in a civilised manner.'

'What about Unnur? Has she been informed?' Elsa Guðrún said suddenly.

'Yes, I've been in touch with the manager at the assisted living facility where she's a resident, and the Ministry of Foreign Affairs is working on tracking down her father,' Særós replied. 'It doesn't appear that he paid any maintenance up to the girl turning eighteen, or rather, Arnhildur didn't seek maintenance after he left. It's all so very tragic.'

14

Valthór's hands trembled and it was with trepidation that he slid the key into the lock. He hadn't been to Bergstaðastræti since Tuesday night. But today he had to pull himself together as he had a séance and then a private fortune telling session. He was nervous about this, as his strengths didn't lie in clairvoyance. After he had been forced to stop collaborating with others and to resign from the Spiritualist Society, to make ends meet there had been no choice but to take on more than he was comfortable with, as a way of making a living. Word of his talents had spread recently and he had been doing well, both in divination and communicating with the spirits. The demand was such that he had even turned people away. So he should have been satisfied with this success, but instead he felt uncomfortable.

Valthór used his phone to look up the news site. There was still a notice asking people who knew anything of Arnhildur's movements to come forward, but there was nothing new relating to the investigation. The only change was that two of the news media had downgraded the item, so it was no longer being read much. Valthór put his phone down on the sideboard in the foyer and hung up his coat. His steps were heavy as he went to the kitchenette and filled the kettle. He went back into the hall and opened windows to let in some fresh air. The memories of Tuesday evening came flooding back and it felt as if his heart shrivelled inside him. Today he would have to excel in the private session and also during the séance in the afternoon. God knows, he was in no state for anything like this, but rumours of poor performance would spread fast and he couldn't afford a downturn in business. Not again!

Deep in thought, he walked as if in a daze back to the kitchen to make some tea. He warmed his hands, clasped around the cup as he drank it, and stared into space. He had slept badly and wasn't feeling himself. He would have to get himself into the right frame of mind to be ready for three o'clock.

There was a knock on the door that startled Valthór from his thoughts. Who could it be? A few minutes later there was another knock, louder this time. Should he pretend there was nobody here? But what if this person had seen him come in? There had been a dusting of snow that morning, and there was no doubt that footsteps could be made out in the snow by the door. Or maybe it was someone looking to make an appointment? Could be. Valthór hurried out to the foyer. A mirror hung there and he was taken aback at the sight of his own bloodshot eyes and the visible stubble on his face. *Why didn't I take the time to shave this morning?* He thought to himself, running his fingers through his unkempt hair.

The door was stiff and he had to pull hard to wrench it open. The disquiet inside him grew at the sight of what he felt was an omen. There stood a tall, dark-haired man in lateish middle age and a petite woman with a broad, bright face. Her brown hair was gathered in a ponytail, giving her a girlish look. Although there was nothing out of the ordinary in the way they were dressed, he knew instantly who they were.

'Good day,' the tall man said. 'We're from the police. Are you responsible for this building?'

'Yes, well. Sort of,' he said hurriedly.

'You conduct séances here?' the female cop asked.

'Among other things. I run a spiritual centre here,' he replied in a clear voice, feeling his strength return with every word. This was going to be all right.

'Could we come in and ask a few questions?' the tall, dark man asked, placing one foot across the threshold.

Valthór nodded and invited them into the cramped kitchen. They both looked so serious that he hoped the compactness of the room would counteract their official bearing. There were two shabby chairs and he meant to invite them to sit, while he would remain standing. That would tilt the balance of power away from them. But it didn't work, as the tall man didn't even go into the kitchen.

'There must be a larger space here. We understand that séances are conducted here, so...' the woman said, glancing around.

'Of course. We can sit in the hall if you prefer. That's also quite small,' he quickly added. It would be best to get this over with as soon as possible, without generating any unnecessary emotional turmoil. He forced a courteous smile, gestured them towards the hall and switched on the lights. He fetched three chairs from the rack in the corner and lined them up by the table on which stood a heavy candelabra with many arms.

'Please take a seat,' he said as politely as he could. 'What brings you here? I have work to do, so don't have much time. How can I help you?'

'You held a séance here on Tuesday?' The dark man asked.

'Certainly did.'

Valthór cleared his throat and clasped his hands together into a ball.

'Was there a woman called Arnhildur Drífa Friðthjófsdóttir present?' the policeman continued.

'I'm afraid I couldn't tell you,' Valthór replied after a moment's silence, and with a faint smile. 'I'm bound by a confidentiality agreement with those who come to me.'

'Does it have to be that strict?' the woman asked, her voice firm and her smile polite. 'It's not exactly a Hippocratic oath.'

Valthór felt himself flush.

'No, of course not. But I make every effort to respect the trust placed in me... However, since it's the police asking, that can be waived. Arnhildur, you said? Let me think. I meet so many people.'

'I'll help jog your memory,' the woman said, her dark blue eyes gazing searchingly at him. 'There has been a public appeal in all the media for anyone with information concerning Arnhildur's movements to come forward, and now we know she attended a séance here on Tuesday evening. A young woman who was also present came forward this morning.'

'Why didn't you say so right away?' Valthór felt his heart beat faster. It was positively hammering inside his chest.

'We were hoping you'd do that,' the tall man said in a deep voice and ran his fingers through dark hair that was starting to thin on top.

'Oh, I see. Sorry. I didn't realise it was anything serious.' He took a deep breath. 'Is she missing?'

'Arnhildur was found dead yesterday morning. To be precise, in the Hólavellir graveyard,' the policeman said. Valthór felt a hand grip his heart and squeeze it tight.

'What are you saying?' he gasped. 'The poor woman...'

'It seems she was murdered on the way home from the meeting she attended here with you,' the woman continued.

Valthór swallowed, choked on his own saliva and burst into a fit of coughing. The policewoman stood up.

'Shall I fetch you some water?' she asked, but he was struggling to catch his breath and wasn't able to answer. But he managed to shake his head, in between bouts of coughing.

'I had some hot tea just before you turned up. It seems it

didn't agree with me,' he tried to explain once he was finally able to force out the words. He coughed some more. 'That's awful. Just dreadful.'

'How many people attended this meeting?' the tall policeman asked, looking around the hall.

The discomfort in his throat was such that he simply held up one hand with all the fingers extended.

'We need their names,' the man continued.

'I ask people to only give their first names, otherwise I could look them up online,' Valthór explained. 'The names they gave me are in my diary. Excuse me a moment,' he said and hurried to the other room. He was back a moment later. 'Here you are.'

The man took a picture of the page, and that seemed enough for him. Valthór was relieved that the police weren't going to take the book from him. There were no secrets to be found in it, but it contained all sorts of useful information.

'How do you get people to pay for the meeting if you only ask for first names?' the man asked. 'I don't suppose you do this for free?'

Valthór felt a stab of alarm. But now it was probably as well to tell the truth. After all these two weren't from the tax authority.

'No, of course not. I arrange it so that when people arrive they put an envelope containing a certain amount into a basket by the entrance.'

'So it's all black money?' The man asked, and Valthór nodded.

'Was there anything about Arnhildur's behaviour that attracted particular attention?' the woman asked, giving him a faint smile. There was something about her demeanour that was calming. She was down to earth, nothing underhand about her. This was an honest woman who demanded honesty in return. But now he needed to be cautious, maintain his focus, and not allow the disquiet that was becoming steadily stronger dominate his feelings.

'Arnhildur was the one who got most out of the séance. Both of her grandparents were long since called away, and both had words for her. The others said it was extremely powerful, but I remember very little of what happens when I'm in a trance,' Valthór said.

'It must have hit a nerve, or at least upset her,' the man said. 'Didn't you notice?'

'Not that I recall .... I led in a prayer of thanks as I emerged from the trance, and I had the impression there was a calmness to the group.'

Valthór heard his own voice, and realised his words were coming rapidly.

'Our witness stated that Arnhildur left here in the company of an older man. Who was he?' the policeman asked.

Valthór pointed to Markús's name in the diary.

'This person. But you have to remember that there's no guarantee at all that people give their real names.'

'Did you see where they went?'

'No. I saw the guests out of the door, and then locked up. I'm always exhausted after a session like that.'

'It would be helpful if you could describe each of the people who attended the meeting, as they appeared to you,' the policeman said, taking out his phone. 'You don't mind being recorded, do you?'

Valthór nodded uncertainly, and pointed to the names in the diary. It wasn't complicated. There had been the couple, Lovísa and Erlendur, who had lost their son, the young, sick woman, Thórdís, grey-haired Markús, and Arnhildur. He took care to describe her no more precisely than the others.

'Thanks,' the man said, took a pen from his pocket and wrote something in the diary that lay open on the table. 'My name's Guðgeir Fransson and you can reach me on that number. Please don't hesitate to call if you recall anything that could be helpful to the investigation.' He stooped again over the diary. 'I'll give you Elsa Guðrún's number as well, just in case you can't reach me.'

They stood up almost simultaneously, clearly ready to go. He felt a wave of relief and made an effort not to let it show.

'I'm just being curious, but how did you come to be a medium?' Elsa Guðrún asked, fixing him with her bright eyes. There was a strong interest in them.

'Well... I've always been receptive and open to the idea that there's more to this world than what we can feel and see with the naked eye,' he explained quickly.

'And you decided to go down this route?'

'It happened almost by itself. It runs in the family, and then I had some training from the Spiritualist Society to open the channels and focus my abilities.'

He smiled awkwardly and desperately wished for them to leave.

'Thanks for your help. That'll do for now,' Guðgeir said, opening the door.

Then they were gone. Valthór locked the door behind them and slumped into the nearest chair. He stared into empty space, and then put his face in his hands and wept.

15

Guðgeir pulled up outside a bakery and called Særós while Elsa Guðrún went to fetch them a snack. It was snowing again, although the fine powder snow that had fallen in the morning had given way to heavy snowflakes that smeared themselves across the windscreen like bird droppings. As he spoke, he watched passers-by pull up hoods and hats, or cover their heads with scarves. Having ended the conversation, he checked the weather forecast and saw that rain was expected later. These constant changes in the weather weren't going to go away any time soon.

'We'll make a fresh statement, asking those who attended the séance to come forward. Særós is putting together some text for a press release, so this should be on most media after midday,' Guðgeir said as Elsa Guðrún returned. 'Oh, and the media is all over the discovery of the body. Amazing that we were able to keep this quiet for a whole twenty-four hours! That's a job well done.'

'Co-operation makes for good results,' Elsa Guðrún said with a smile, handing him a paper cup of coffee and a filled roll in a paper bag. 'You wanted cheese and ham, didn't you?'

'Sure, whatever,' Guðgeir replied. He put the cup in the holder on the dashboard, opened the bag and bit into his roll. 'Doesn't matter, this is fine.'

'What next?' Elsa Guðrún asked, taking a cautious sip of her hot coffee.

'Let's hope those who attended the séance come forward as soon as possible. Especially the older man with the grey hair who left with Arnhildur,' Guðgeir said.

'Markús?'

'If that's his name,' Guðgeir said. 'Going by what Valthór said, people who take part in these séances don't always give their proper names.'

'Can't we turn the heater up?' Elsa Guðrún shivered.

'Yes, of course. Don't want our coffee to get cold right away,' Guðgeir smiled and turned the dial to 23 degrees. 'It's supposed to warm up later. I checked the forecast.'

'Winter seems to have been going on for ever, so surely we must get to spring eventually,' Elsa Guðrún said. 'One question – have we completely parked the theory that the murder might have been unintentional?'

'No. We shouldn't rule anything out. But it seems to me to be highly unlikely,' Guðgeir replied. 'There was some reason for this assault, but we just don't know yet what that was. The answer could have been in the handbag that Helgi found in the graveyard, or in something that whoever assaulted Arnhildur could have taken away with them.'

'Exactly,' Elsa Guðrún said. 'If that's the right theory, then it has to be something exceptionally valuable or important in the eyes of whoever attacked her.'

'I'm curious about the medium as well,' Guðgeir said. 'Did you notice how tense he was, and the boxes in the corner by the coat rack?'

'Yes. That could be the powder that Thórdís said she had been buying. This could be some pyramid sales arrangement from which he gets some income ... and he called it a spiritual centre .... presumably tax-free. Maybe that's why he was tense.'

'More than likely,' Guðgeir agreed. He ate the last of the roll, just as he remembered that he was supposed to be avoiding carbohydrates. 'Hell,' he muttered.

'What?' Elsa Guðrún asked.

'Nothing special. Just something I forgot about,' he said as he reversed out of the parking space. 'So... where are we going?'

'Now, there's a question.'

'My feeling is that it's vital to make contact with the people who attended the séance, but while we're waiting, I'd like to use what time we have to take another look at Arnhildur's flat. We know a lot more about her now, and the handbook says that a greater knowledge of the victim increases the odds of finding the perpetrator,' Guðgeir said.

'Unless there's no link between them, and encountering Arnhildur was pure coincidence,' Elsa Guðrún said, putting the empty coffee cup into the bag the roll had come in. 'But yes, let's get the keys from Leifur and take another look at the place.'

16

Embla stared out of the window as the flow of water played over the woman's hair. The image of the dead woman in the graveyard was still clear in her mind; her ankle-high boots, coat, the unearthly colour her face had taken on, and the unnatural position of the body. After she had made her statement to the police, Embla had gone straight to work, where the other women had bombarded her with questions. At first, she enjoyed the attention her experience had triggered, but now she wished they hadn't been told anything. Most of all she wished it hadn't happened. She shut off the water and reached for a bottle of conditioner. The woman whose hair she was washing closed her eyes. Embla poured the silky fluid into her palm, stroked it over the damp hair and began kneading it into the scalp as the woman murmured warmly. Embla's eyes went back to the window while her fingers did the work. Her movements became gradually firmer, until her nails bit into the woman's head. In her mind she still saw the corpse on the wet ground, a silk scarf twisted around its throat.

'Hey, stop! That hurts!' the woman protested, sitting up.

'I'm so sorry. I didn't... Didn't mean to ...'

Embla was taken aback, but noticed that Silla, the salon's owner, looked in their direction.

'You scratched me,' the woman said, her voice lower, but no less accusing.

'I do apologise. Let me finish washing your hair. I'll be really careful,' Embla said, and the woman grimaced and scowled, but lay back in the chair.

Embla rinsed her hair with all the care she could, taking care to concentrate on what she was doing. She had just finished and had wrapped the woman's head in a towel when the door opened. She saw a man come in, someone she didn't know personally, although she knew he was in the hairdressing business. This man's name was Skúli, something of a character who had a colourful career behind him. At one time he'd run a salon of his own, but sold it to open a lifestyle boutique that attracted a lot of media attention at the time, before going bankrupt a couple of years later. After that he'd turned to developing dilapidated apartments and selling them on at a profit, and Embla was sure she'd read something about that venture also having come to grief. After that, Skúli had gone back to hairdressing. From what Embla had heard, he was working part-time at a salon downtown and had a reputation as a talented hairdresser who kept on top of all the latest fashions.

'Hey, girls,' he said with a smile and shut the door behind him. 'I was passing and had to drop in and say hello. Cool layout and great accessories you have here!'

Skúli emitted a gasp that was intended to underscore his admiration as he gestured to the display shelves by the reception desk.

'Hi, Skúli,' Silla responded and the other women gave him polite smiles and murmured a greeting. 'How are you, darling?'

'Just fine. I need to grab a coffee, sweethearts,' Skúli replied. 'I don't need to be at work right away and I just know they'll grab me as soon as I walk in the door,' he said with a theatrical wink.

'Sure,' Silla said. 'Embla's our new apprentice and she'll look after you. Just go out the back, Skúli. Embla's almost finished.'

SHROUDED

Embla made haste to clear up after herself, relieved to get away from sweeping the floor and washing hair for a while. When she went to the back room, Skúli had already made himself comfortable in a chair and a spicy smell had been added to the aromas of hair products.

'Hæ,' he said. 'You're Embla?'

'That's me,' she smiled. 'How would you like your coffee?'

'A cappuccino would be great, with oat milk if you have it,' he said, examining her from head to toe. Embla felt like an exhibit being marked for style. She made the coffee and handed it to him.

'Thanks. Aren't you going to sit down? The shop looks quiet for the moment.'

'All right,' she said and took a seat, while he continued to look at her intently.

'Aren't you the one who found the body in the Hólavellir graveyard?' he asked and crossed his legs as he leaned forward with the cup of coffee in his hand. There was no mistaking the curiosity in his voice.

'Yes. How did you know?' she asked, and he gave a sharp laugh.

'In this business news travels like wildfire. Tell me about it.'

She made out that she didn't understand.

'What about it?'

'Well, the body. What it was like and what the police were asking.' Skúli sipped his coffee. 'Well, you really know how to make a great coffee,' he said admiringly.

'That's just the machine, and the sweetness is from the oat milk,' Embla stammered. 'But the body... I don't really want to go into that, if you don't mind. I'd really like to forget all about it.'

'Oh, I get you. Were you frightened?' he asked with a look of sympathy on his face, but an intensity in his voice that Embla found unnerving.

'Not exactly. But it was a really unpleasant experience. Horrible, to be honest,' she replied.

'Oh, you poor thing. Do you have to walk past that spot on the way here in the mornings?' Skúli asked, the sympathy in his voice and the sorrowful look on his face both exaggerated.

'I can go another way, but that's the shortest route,' Embla said.

'Yeah? Where do you live?'

'Right next to the bakery on Hringbraut,' she replied.

'You have a place in one of those blocks? They're so fabulously retro,' Skúli crooned.

'No, I just rent an upstairs room,' Embla said and stood up. 'I'm sorry, but I really ought to be at work. I have to dust the displays today and want to take the opportunity while it's quiet.'

'Of course. Good to see that you're keen to do well,' he said with a smirk. 'Thanks for the chat, Embla. Lovely to meet you.'

She snatched up a duster and hurried from the room. Skúli followed soon after. He placed the cup on the reception desk and muttered his thanks to Silla.

Embla felt an overwhelming discomfort as she stood at the shelves and dusted the ornaments and hair products on display. As the door closed, she nudged a vase that crashed to the rock-hard floor. Embla stood transfixed and stared down at the razor-sharp shards.

17

Arnhildur's apartment was still stuffy. The only change since Guðgeir's and Elsa Guðrún's last visit was the black powder here and there, mainly on floors, doors and switches. As soon as Ísgerður had confirmed that Arnhildur's body had been moved from the murder location to where it had been found, the forensics team had searched particularly for fingerprints and footprints in the apartment, the graveyard and the surrounding areas. Apart from that, everything was exactly as it had been. An advertisement for a genius was in a page of a newspaper, open on the table, the dirty cup was in the sink and bright rays shone from the golden star in the window.

'Ach, can't we take that down?' Elsa Guðrún said. 'Somehow it's so painfully sad to see that star there.'

'That's up to the relatives,' Guðgeir said as he went into the living room. 'But I'm sure it's all right to unplug it.'

Elsa Guðrún stooped and pulled the plug from the socket.

'Job done,' she announced as she straightened up.

Then she checked the fridge. It was empty, as the forensic team had removed the contents, so she moved on to the kitchen cupboards.

In the living room Guðgeir sat down on the sofa. In the complete tranquillity of the room, he allowed his thoughts to drift, going from one aspect of the case to the next. He tried to find a line that could be followed, knowing that to begin with it would be fragmented, although he knew that if he could find a starting point he could trace things from there on, so that the sequence of events would take on a new clarity, or there would at least be a glimmer of light somewhere in the darkness.

The estate agent's advertisement still lay on the coffee table, and Guðgeir made a mental note that this was someone he would need to speak to. He stood up and went to the doors leading out onto a small balcony. He opened them, but there was nothing there to see. The door was stiff and he had to put some effort into closing it again. While he was doing this, he noticed a change in the colour of the wall. When the door had finally given up the struggle, he took a closer look at the paint, and there was no mistake.

'Elsa Guðrún, could you come in here a moment?' he called out, drawing open the curtains as far as he could. 'Doesn't it look like there used to be a big painting hanging here, around one metre by a metre and a half wide?'

He pointed at the oblong outline.

'Yes, no doubt about it,' Elsa Guðrún replied. 'There was definitely something there for decades, judging by the colour of the wall. I'll send Helgi Már a message and ask him to find out if Arnhildur sold a painting recently.'

'Yes, please do,' Guðgeir replied and continued to look around. The dining table again attracted his interest, primarily because it was such an exceptionally well made piece of furniture. It looked as if it could be a sample piece done by a joinery apprentice, possibly the father of Arnhildur and Regína. The table had to be old, as Guðgeir had no doubt that this kind of thing was no longer made. He looked at the planed edges and the neatly finished legs, before his roving eye stopped at an irregularity at the end of the table that he hadn't noticed before. It seemed odd that a craftsman of such skill had overlooked something like that. Guðgeir ran his fingers over it, and quickly realised that there had to be a concealed compartment of some kind. As he switched on the torch in his phone to examine it more carefully, he thought to himself that this was an unusual feature for a dining table. It took him a while to open the inset drawer, but as soon as he used his pocket knife to tease it free, he was able to open it. He looked at the contents in surprise for a moment. Before him lay two memory sticks.

'Look at this,' he said to Elsa Guðrún who now stood at his side. 'A woman who owned neither a computer nor a modern phone kept memory sticks in a secret drawer.'

18

Helgi Már plugged one of the memory sticks into the computer and Elsa Guðrún could feel the tension mounting inside her. She glanced at Guðgeir and saw that he was feeling the same. Leifur appeared no less expectant, although the chagrin that his team had missed the compartment in the dining table was clear on his face.

'I'd never have noticed it if I hadn't had an eye for craftsmanship,' Guðgeir said, his hand on Leifur's shoulder.

'The main thing is that it was found, that's all that matters,' Leifur replied. His booming deep voice was unusually low.

'These are image files, and a lot of them. It'll take a minute or two for them to load,' Helgi Már said. He leaned forward in his chair and flexed his muscular arms. Elsa Guðrún's attention went from the screen to Helgi Már's back. This was a guy who was in great shape.

Guðgeir used the time to polish his glasses, and just as he finished, the images began to appear. He leaned closer to see more clearly.

'For fuck's sake! That's revolting!' Elsa Guðrún burst out, shuddering. She and Guðgeir looked at each other. They had both been taken by surprise.

'That's Arnhildur's daughter Unnur. The one who was left disabled by that accident,' Guðgeir murmured to Helgi Már and Leifur, who both shook their heads and sighed.

'This is just horrible,' he said, frowning as the pictures flashed across the screen.

Unnur was in every picture, alone, either naked or wearing scraps of provocative clothing and in sexual poses, in some of them holding sex toys. She either looked away or stared into space with a distant gaze. Most of the pictures had been taken indoors, with Unnur lying or posing on a sofa covered with a deep red spread that shone, while three had been taken outdoors, clearly in summer but the background was such that it was difficult to tell exactly where.

'Who does this kind of thing?' Elsa Guðrún raged, and answered her own questions. 'Some total arsehole! This is just revolting!'

Helgi Már took out the first memory stick and began loading the images from the second. These turned out to be much the same, but even more provocative.

'This isn't what you'd call hardcore porn, considering the way things are these days. It's more light blue stuff,' Helgi Már said. 'It's a sick world we live in.'

'Hardcore or not, Unnur is seriously disabled and this is very clearly abuse,' Guðgeir said, a serious frown on his face.

'That's obvious, and please don't get me wrong. I wasn't trying to pretend this isn't serious,' Helgi Már said.

'No. Understood,' Guðgeir replied quickly, and saw that he and Elsa Guðrún had both been affected by these unpleasant images.

'You recall that Arnhildur had printouts of information about online crime in her bedside table,' Elsa Guðrún said. 'She could have been a victim of blackmail, and that's why she was in financial difficulties.'

'Yes, and if Arnhildur was being blackmailed, it would be interesting to know who found those information sheets on the internet and printed them out for her,' Guðgeir said. 'Presumably someone who wanted to help her, but who?'

He glanced at each of them in turn, but none of them could come up with an answer to this – any more than to all of the other questions they faced.

'Shouldn't we concentrate on the perpetrator, whoever took these pictures of Unnur?' Leifur said. 'Wouldn't it be best to start with the staff at that place?'

'No question about it,' Guðgeir said. 'Elsa Guðrún and I will go up there and speak to the manager. It's best to do that before we start bringing people in for formal interviews.'

'I see,' Leifur said. 'Helgi, would you check out this material and find out if any of this has appeared on Only Fans or any other such site? The perpetrator must have tried to sell these images, considering how they're posed. But why on earth did her mother have these memory sticks?'

'It's possible that this pensioner wedded to routine wasn't being blackmailed, but had a dark side of her own?' Elsa Guðrún suggested. 'There's nothing that takes me by surprise any longer.'

'Isn't that a bit far-fetched?' Helgi Már asked. Elsa Guðrún shrugged and Guðgeir said nothing.

'How about the tenants downstairs?' Leifur speculated.

'I don't see how they could be connected to...' Elsa Guðrún said.

'You can never tell,' Leifur said. 'It's possible they had some hold over Arnhildur, and the talk of a dispute with her over the rent was a diversion.'

'Whatever the outcome, I'm pretty sure that these pictures have some connection to the murder,' Guðgeir said. 'Now we finally have something concrete that we can chase up. Then we can also hope that the people who were at the séance come forward. It's possible we'll get something out of that.'

'Where's Særós?' Helgi Már asked suddenly. 'Shouldn't she be here?'

'Hold on, I'll check,' he said, reaching for his phone. 'She's logged in as being on site,' he said. 'I'll fill her in later.'

'We'll go over the case in the morning, but give me a call if anything big crops up,' Leifur said. 'You know I have to leave early today ... because of, you know...'

'Yes, of course. And good luck,' Guðgeir replied. He put an arm around his colleague's shoulders and gave him an encouraging squeeze.

Elsa Guðrún looked expectantly at them in turn, but Leifur gave no explanation, and left.

She couldn't resist asking after Leifur's health as she and Guðgeir sat in a traffic jam on the way up to the assisted living facility in Árbær.

'So what's going on with Leifur?' she ventured after thinking it over.

'Ach, he's just disappointed because his people didn't find those memory sticks,' Guðgeir said. 'He'll get over it.'

'I can understand that ... but is he getting forgetful?' she asked cautiously, and taking care to not sound as if she were stirring up gossip about a colleague, which wasn't the case. 'He's getting on. Not far off retirement.'

'Leifur? Forgetful? Have you noticed him getting absent-minded?' Guðgeir asked, glancing quickly at her.

'Not at all, but he said earlier that he needed to go home early because of something. Is he being checked out? Or taking part in a deCODE Genetics survey? My cousin was part of one of these...'

'No, not at all,' Guðgeir replied, clearly relieved. 'He's delivering a speech ... In Honour of Women.'

The queue of traffic began to move, and he took the opportunity to change lanes.

'In Honour of Women?' Elsa Guðrún repeated. 'Is that something he knows anything about? Has he developed some psychology complex?'

She rolled her eyes and grimaced.

'Sorry, should have explained. Mind elsewhere,' Guðgeir said. 'Leifur's in the Lions Club and there's a dinner tonight. He's reading *In Honour of Women*. It's a kind of ode to the women of Iceland. Like a paean of praise.'

'Come off it!' Elsa Guðrún gasped and burst into laughter. 'You're killing me!'

'Are you telling me that the proud northerner isn't familiar with this custom?' Guðgeir grinned.

'No... Well, yes. Of course I've heard about it, but I thought that was something from the olden days. But, hey. That's something I'd love to hear. I'm sure it's a masterpiece. But aren't there only men present?'

'Yep, as far as I know,' Guðgeir said, smiling to himself.

19

It was Ragna who answered the door. They hadn't called ahead, and she seemed astonished to see them again. Before they could explain their presence, she told them that Unnur had taken the news of her mother's death badly, and that she and the other staff were seriously concerned about her mental state. Ragna glowered at them, and Elsa Guðrún had the feeling that she practically blamed her and Guðgeir for all this.

'Unnur is neither eating nor sleeping properly, so I don't feel a visit from you is likely to improve her state of mind,' Ragna said, sounding resentful. 'I'm taking her to the doctor tomorrow.'

'I'm sorry to hear that. But you're the one we're here to speak to. We need some information,' Elsa Guðrún said. 'Could we go to your office?'

'Unfortunately, it's being redecorated at the moment, but we can use the lounge. I can make sure we aren't disturbed there,' Ragna replied.

She showed them in, sanitised her hands, excused herself and left the room for a moment. They could hear a mutter of conversation from the other side of the building, and saw Ragna exchange a few words with the member of staff they had met during their previous visit.

The lounge had clearly been recently painted, as there were still strips of masking tape around the door frames and the light switches. A large sideboard filled most of one wall and on one of its shelves lay an Allen key and a set of Ikea instructions. A tool bag and some books and ornaments waiting to be put back where they belonged were piled on the floor. Guðgeir took a seat on a royal blue sofa, while Elsa Guðrún looked around the room and picked off the masking tape around a switch next to the sideboard. Her fingernails weren't up to the job, so she picked up a screwdriver and used it to scratch at the tape.

Practical as always, Guðgeir thought, but it took him by surprise when she took out her phone and used it to take a picture of the switch. Then she carefully took pictures of the lounge from every angle. He was still wondering what she had in mind when Ragna returned.

'What can I do for you?' she asked, taking a seat on a chair facing the sofa.

'It's disturbing to hear that Unnur isn't feeling well. I hope she gets all the attention she needs to cope with her bereavement.'

'All of us here are doing everything we can to support her,' Ragna said. She shifted in the chair and crossed her legs.

'I don't doubt it,' Guðgeir said in his mild voice. 'When we were here the other day you told us about the effects of the front brain damage Unnur had suffered and I recall that you mentioned her bouts of anger had become more frequent recently. Do you have any explanation for that?'

'No. Our most likely explanation is it could be due to all these audiobooks she listens to all the time. She's constantly listening, and the headphones are never off her head. We've discussed limiting her access somehow, as she tends to mix up fiction and reality, as I told you before,' Ragna explained with a patient look on her face. 'She can come out with the most bizarre narratives, which are completely confused.'

'But could the explanation lie elsewhere?' Elsa Guðrún asked. 'Could something have happened that she either can't or doesn't want to talk about? Could a real life experience have become mixed up with a fictional narrative?'

Ragna's face hardened and her defences were up.

'Such as what? We have staff on site around the clock and our clients are never unattended. What are you insinuating?'

'We have come across a number of pornographic pictures of Unnur that appear to be recent,' Guðgeir said, and left it at that so he could gauge the effect of his words. She was clearly shocked, but said nothing. So he continued. 'Considering she's under constant observation, the indication is that someone who works here must have subjected her to this abuse.'

'The pictures are taken here in this building, and some outdoors. Isn't it the case that staff had the use of a car that Arnhildur owned, for Unnur's benefit?' Elsa Guðrún asked, and although she was well aware of the facts, she wanted to hear Ragna confirm this, as she stared at them in shock, and nodded her head.

'That's correct,' she replied. 'As I told your superior, Særós I think she's called...' Guðgeir nodded. '... Arnhildur wanted to sell the car. I told her that I was very surprised at this decision because up to that point mother and daughter had both been pleased with the freedom that this allowed them, because Unnur was sometimes taken to visit her mother.'

'Have you noticed anything else unusual in Unnur's behaviour, or among the staff here?' Elsa Guðrún asked.

Ragna sat in thought. She sat with her legs crossed, the one on top swaying to and fro.

'Not among the staff, no. But thinking back, Unnur has been prone to tears,' she said after a pause. 'I wish I had paid more attention, talked more to her, asked how she's feeling, but I thought that...' Ragna said and fell silent.

'We're going to need the names and details of all the staff who have been on single-handed shifts,' Elsa Guðrún said.

'Staff are never alone with clients,' Ragna said firmly.
'Not even night shifts?' Elsa Guðrún asked.
Ragna hesitated and her eyes went to the window. She looked tired as her gaze returned to them.
'Yes, actually. It's unfortunate, but it's difficult to get staff for care work, even though I've managed pretty well to retain them. But it's always a challenge to get people for night shifts,' she said heavily, clearly distressed.
'We need all the details relating to the staff who have driven Unnur anywhere, or gone with her anywhere off the site,' Guðgeir said, making an effort to be sympathetic.
'You've no idea how difficult it is to find staff, and to hold on to them,' Ragna said, her voice almost robotic.
'We fully appreciate that, but we need to have this information,' Elsa Guðrún said, leaning forward, looking intently at Ragna.
'The staff here are excellent, and I'm certain that none of them...' Ragna said, her voice tailing off. She failed to finish her sentence, apparently aware that such a statement wasn't acceptable.
'Let's not forget that many wolves turn out to be wearing sheep's clothing,' Guðgeir said.
'I'm sure I remember everything,' Ragna said as she got to her feet. 'But to be sure I'll check the rota on the computer.'
'We'll go with you, and you can send me everything as soon as possible, along with the details of the staff,' Guðgeir said, and stood up.

The visit to the assisted living facility had left them both deep in thought and they drove for some time in silence. The clouds were low and it had begun to rain. Elsa Guðrún watched absently as pedestrians splashed through the slush and the windscreen wipers gave out a rhythmic squeal. The abuse Unnur had suffered hit her hard emotionally, and it didn't help that the perpetrator had to have been someone Unnur should have been able to trust. During her career Elsa Guðrún had seen much that had been worse than this, and had also experienced her own sheer horror – but it never failed to hurt when she witnessed such a vile exhibition of power wielded against someone unable to protect themselves. A bus overtook them, sending a sheet of water over people waiting at a crossing. Hell, this endless winter has to end at some point, she thought, and the spring sun will shine again as the colourful crocuses push their way up from the ground.

'Was it the same guy who was preparing Ragna's office for painting, the one we met the other day? The one who carried the boxes in for her, remember?' Elsa Guðrún asked.

'Yes. His name's Máni, I think,' Guðgeir replied.

'That time he was painting the lounge,' Elsa Guðrún said. 'I noticed there were paint stains on the soles of his feet when we were there to inform them of Arnhildur's death. You remember he ran outside in his socks to help Ragna and his feet got wet.'

'Go on,' Guðgeir prompted.

'I pulled up the masking tape and could see what the old colour was. The lounge used to be green.'

'Interesting,' Guðgeir said, glancing at her with interest.

'It looks to me like the same shade of green in the room where the indoor pictures of Unnur were taken. Máni could have offered to paint it, as a way of covering his tracks.'

'I see where you're going with this,' Guðgeir said thoughtfully. 'So it could be that we know already who we're dealing with?'

20

The night had been a hard one. Valthór slept in snatches, and his dreams were bad ones. In between dozing off, he lay awake, anxious and with a terrible gnawing feeling in his chest. Arnhildur was close by. He could feel her presence. She had an errand with him that he wasn't sure he wanted to acknowledge. It was before six in the morning that he gave up trying to sleep and got up. He dressed and gulped a cup of coffee before pulling on a warm coat and a hat. Ready for the cold outside, he pushed through the snow of the icy winter morning. There wasn't a soul to be seen in the sleeping street. He marched with determination down through the Thingholt district and with ever greater certainty along Skothúsvegur and over the bridge crossing the lake. His pace slowed as the concrete wall of the graveyard appeared in the darkness. His heart beat irregularly and he could feel an emotional weight as he knew he was walking in Arnhildur's tracks. His awareness became even stronger as he turned onto Suðurgata, along the perimeter of the graveyard.

He glanced at intervals over the concrete wall at the gravestones, large and small, but looked mostly down at his own feet. He could feel Arnhildur accompanying him. There was no doubt in his mind and he could feel her presence with every fibre of his being. He could sense her at his side, occupying the same space as him. Here was the place where the streetlight was broken and there was no house on the opposite side. His breathing became strained and he felt the hands around his heart squeeze tighter. He walked faster, hoping to take himself as fast as possible past this terrible place. In his hurry, he caught his toe against a crack in the pavement and he almost tumbled forwards. It wasn't until he had made his way onto Hofsvallagata that he could relax a little, but he continued down into the old western part of the city. Every step he took became more of an effort and as he stood in front of the red house he felt a surge of sorrow and horror sweep through his body and soul. He trembled as he stared at the darkened window with its gilded Christmas star. Its light had been switched off.

21

Ólöf was deep in revision for a criminal law exam. Guðgeir had gone to the toilet during the night and had seen her hunched over her books at the dining table. He woke again at seven, and the day began with him overhearing his three-year-old namesake chattering, keen to tell his half-asleep mother all about flying yellow cats that wore Batman cloaks.

'Come on, little man. Let's get dressed here and go and get ourselves some breakfast. Then I'll take you to nursery,' Guðgeir said as he led the little boy away. 'Your Mum needs her sleep.'

An hour later he was alone in the car and heading for work. He felt a flutter of anticipation for the day ahead. Three of the assisted living facility's staff had been asked to come to the station to be interviewed, and the first was scheduled for nine o'clock. This was going to be Máni. He had most frequently been single-handed on night shifts, and had taken Unnur out in the car seven times. Guðgeir was fairly positive that Máni was the man they were looking for. Sigurður was due at eleven. He was an elementary school teacher who earned a little extra by taking a few shifts each month, as well as the occasional night shift. The last one to come in would be Fríða, a twenty-five-year-old university student who had occasionally driven Unnur, and had once taken a night shift alone. The reason for that had been that the other person had been taken ill suddenly. Fríða was the least likely of the three.

As well as the interviews, Guðgeir expected some, or even all, of those who had attended the séance to come forward. It would be interesting to have some information on what had taken place at the gathering, and whether or not Arnhildur's behaviour had attracted any attention. Most of all, he hoped the grey-haired man would show his face. Guðgeir drummed his fingers on the wheel and turned into the police station's yard. He was expecting an eventful day.

He saw Helgi Már parking his car nearby. He had a positive feeling about their new colleague. He was a solidly built man, self-confident and with a straightforward approach – exactly the qualities Guðgeir appreciated in a colleague.

He whistled the melody of a ballad that had been playing in the car on the way to work, and waved to Helgi Már. Inside the station, he fetched himself a cup of coffee and strolled over to Særós's office. As usual, her sports bag was on the floor beside her desk and she was in front of her computer. The only thing that stood out as unusual was that instead of her hair being blow-dried and glossy, it was damp and unkempt. For Særós, such an oversight was very much out of character, and Guðgeir was almost relieved to notice that her make-up had been applied and was as immaculate as ever. She could have been running late, something that could happen to anyone – even to Særós. He tapped at the half-open door to attract her attention. She looked up.

'Good morning,' she said with a smile. 'I see there's progress. Good work!'

'Yes, it'll be interesting to see how things develop today,' Guðgeir replied. 'Elsa Guðrún and I are going to be busy with interviews all morning.'

'And I'll be keeping a close eye on everything,' Særós

said, clicking the mouse with her eyes on the screen.

'Is there anything new on the people who were at the séance? Anyone come forward?' Guðgeir asked.

Særós looked up at him, her eyes wide.

'Ach, that's what I forgot,' she said, and the look of vexation on her face showed clearly how annoyed she was with herself. 'It completely slipped my mind.'

At first, Guðgeir was astonished, before his temper got the better of him.

'What do you mean? You forgot the press release?'

Særós was obviously upset.

'I'll do it right away. I don't understand... It's not like me to screw up like that, especially with a case that's so serious. I'm so sorry.'

'Well, that's true,' he said in a harsher tone that he meant, but he was angry. 'Look, we've always been able to talk, Særós. So if there's something bothering you, you can always come to me.'

She fixed him with a serious gaze, clearly undecided whether or not to continue the conversation, when he realised that it was eight-thirty. Time was pressing and he needed to prepare himself for the interview.

'Let's talk later today, or tomorrow,' he said, squeezing out a smile. 'But could you make sure the press release goes out as soon as possible?'

Lips pursed and scowling, she nodded.

Guðgeir had barely left Særós's office before he slammed his right fist into his left palm, again and again. He had no tolerance for any kind of incompetence, but felt a rising concern for his superior. Forgetfulness and fatigue were well-known burnout symptoms, so maybe Inga had been right when she suggested this could be behind the change in Særós's behaviour.

Twenty minutes later, Elsa Guðrún and Guðgeir went to interview room number three. The message had come through minutes before from Helgi Már that none of the images from the memory sticks had been found online.

'We'll keep going and dig deeper,' he told them.

This morning hadn't got off to a good enough start.

'It's only just nine o'clock, and we have two setbacks to the investigation already,' he grumbled to Elsa Guðrún as they made themselves comfortable in the interview room. A few minutes later, Máni was escorted in. The first time they had met, Guðgeir hadn't paid him much attention, but this time he examined the man closely. A man of average height, Máni was slim, but nonetheless with something of a belly, dressed in jeans and a blue shirt over a white singlet. His light brown hair was cut very short. His face had a very ordinary look to it, and his large spectacles were its most noticeable feature. In general, Máni had the look of a thoroughly unremarkable person. His handshake was limp, and a damp patch appeared under his arm as he extended a hand.

Elsa Guðrún started the recording and Guðgeir went quickly through the formal questions, with Máni answering quickly and easily. Then Guðgeir reached to pick up a numbered evidence bag.

'Do these look familiar?' he asked, placing the memory sticks on the desk. Máni's surprise was obvious.

'I don't know .... Don't most people have a few of these?' he asked, staring back at them.

'We found on these memory sticks sexual images of Unnur Elva Jacobsdóttir, who is in your care at the assisted living facility,' Guðgeir continued, watching beads of sweat appear on Máni's forehead. This guy wasn't going to be hard to handle. He decided to give him time to sweat as he reached for the spectacle case in his jacket pocket. He opened it and took his time polishing the lenses of his glasses, before putting them on and continuing. 'The pictures are taken somewhere out of doors, and in the lounge at the facility. The colour of the walls gives away the location. By that I mean the original colour before you gave the walls a fresh coat of paint. On closer inspection, everything else about the location fits perfectly. Elsa Guðrún, could you show him the pictures in the folder?'

She arranged them on the table while Guðgeir carefully watched Máni's reactions. Next to each photograph of Unnur was another taken from the same point of view in the freshly-painted lounge. Máni's eyes widened and a flush of red patches appeared around his throat. Elsa Guðrún placed a small can of paint on the desk.

'Here we have remnants of the original colour, and according to the expert at the paint dealership, there's an overwhelming likelihood that this is the same colour as we can see on the walls in the picture of Unnur,' she said. 'Practically 100% certain. Take a look at the picture there that's closest to you. The throw has been pulled aside and you can see the royal blue of the sofa. Doesn't that look familiar?'

'I don't know what you're talking about,' Máni whispered hoarsely, as his eyes flickered between the printouts on the desk in front of him. Arrows indicating the similarities had been drawn on them.

'Did you take these pictures of Unnur?' Guðgeir asked. He leaned forward over the desk and looked into Máni's eyes. 'Tell us the truth.'

'Me? No, I didn't,' Máni said stubbornly. By now the red patches had reached his face.

'You had plenty of opportunity. None of the staff have taken as many night shifts as you have. We also have it on good authority that you've always been prepared to jump in when it's been difficult to find staff for a shift.' Guðgeir glared at the man who was slumped in the chair opposite. 'Two sets of fingerprints were found on the memory sticks. One is those of Arnhildur, Unnur's mother, who as you presumably are aware, was found dead a few days ago in the Hólavellir graveyard.' Guðgeir paused to allow Máni a moment to take in that he was being implicated in a murder, before continuing. 'The other set of prints hasn't been identified, but as you deny any involvement, then you'll presumably have no objection to coming with us over to forensics. It won't take long, and as this case is top priority, we won't have to wait long for the results. How about it?'

By now the dark patches under Máni's arms extended down to his midriff. He sat hunched over, twisting his hands without responding to the question. Guðgeir and Elsa Guðrún quickly exchanged glances. Was this going to be enough, or would more pressure be needed?

'Is this turning into an interrogation?' Máni asked finally, in a strangled voice. 'Don't I have a right to a lawyer?'

'No, you're simply here to give a statement. All I'm doing is offering you the opportunity to make it absolutely clear that you haven't ever handled these memory sticks by having your fingerprints checked,' Guðgeir said calmly, while observing the man's inner battle going on.

'There's no need for that. Arnhildur got those from me, and I took the pictures,' Máni admitted through gritted teeth.

'Why did she keep these memory sticks?' Guðgeir asked.

'I sold them to her,' Máni muttered, without looking up at them.

'And why did she want to buy them?' Elsa Guðrún asked. This had all become so weird that she couldn't help herself, even though they had agreed beforehand that Guðgeir would lead with the questions.

'Arnhildur found out that I had been taking these pictures of Unnur and she wanted to deal with the whole thing discreetly, so I sold them to her, one at a time,' the downcast Máni replied.

'One picture at a time?' Guðgeir asked.

Máni shook his head.

'I would ask you to speak clearly, so we don't have to

drag words out of you. You've already confessed to a crime,' Guðgeir said.

'No, I sold her one memory stick at a time. I had my laptop with me and let her watch as I copied the picture files across. She was under the impression that by doing that, the images were no longer on my computer. She paid a certain amount into my bank account, and that was a pain as she didn't use anything online and I had to drive her to the bank myself. When she'd made each payment, I handed over the memory stick. She'd had two, and there were two more to come, or so I told her,' Máni said, and wiped away the sweat from his face with his sleeve.

'Yes, but...' Elsa Guðrún said, baffled. 'But you still had the pictures ... I don't see why she would...'

'Arnhildur was the most technologically ignorant person I have ever encountered. I hardly knew that such people existed...' Máni hesitated. 'Well, yeah. My granddad's almost as innocent of this kind of thing. He can hardly even manage the TV remote,' he explained in a mumble, and fell silent.

'Go on,' Guðgeir said. 'It could be in your favour if you tell us everything clearly and correctly.'

Máni held his head in his hands and rocked back and forth in the chair that wasn't made for this kind of use. He seemed to be working out whether to retract everything, or to continue. He finally took the decision to keep going.

'When I realised it, then it was too much of a temptation and Arnhildur genuinely believed that I'd handed the pictures over to her. As far as she was concerned, those memory sticks were the same as the photographic film people used in the old days. She either didn't understand, or didn't know how electronic images work,' Máni said and wiped his shirt sleeve yet again over his face to wipe away the beads of sweat. Elsa Guðrún handed him a tissue.

'Wouldn't you rather use this?' she asked, her voice expressionless.

'Yeah. Thanks,' Máni replied and wiped his forehead with trembling fingers.

'You still have the pictures in your computer?' Guðgeir asked, aware of just how cold his voice was. This man appeared to be unable to understand that he had abused the mother's lack of understanding and her daughter's disability in a particularly venal manner – or maybe he didn't want to see that for himself.

'Just a few. I deleted most of them. So you can see I was at least partly telling her the truth. To start with I just took pictures for myself and then I thought I might sell them, but there was no need for that once Arnhildur was involved. She had more money than she needed. I mean, she could just as well give some of it to me, doing a tough job for shit money, instead of wasting it. Y'know, a type like that, a loner, could have ended up leaving a third of her estate to a cats' home and the rest would have gone to Unnur, who's no use for money,' Máni replied.

Guðgeir drew a deep breath and closed his eyes for a moment. He was becoming increasingly irritated at Máni's facile protestations and assertions about things of which he knew nothing, but he took care to show no emotion. But he allowed himself another question.

'You said that your grandfather has no understanding of modern technology. Do you feel it would have been fair for someone to abuse his ignorance to extort money from him?'

The question took Máni off guard. It was as if this angle had never occurred to him. He tried to bluff it out with false confidence, but mumbled his reply.

'That's different. Grandad doesn't have any money.'

'What gave you the impression that Arnhildur was wealthy?' Guðgeir asked.

'Speaks for itself, doesn't it? She'd worked all her life, spent nothing on herself, she had a house and could afford a car for Unnur. It wasn't a new one, but all the same ... She was rolling in it and could well afford to pay for the memory sticks.'

'How did she find out that you had taken these pictures?' Elsa Guðrún asked.

'It was Unnur who spilled the beans and her mother listened, unlike the others,' Máni grunted, and stretched. He had regained his confidence and his tone of voice had hardened. 'Look, let's be clear about one thing. Unnur was totally up for this. She enjoyed having the pictures taken, liked the attention, and it didn't do her any harm. I mean, I hardly touched her, just told her what to do and piled on the praise. It's not as if I raped her or anything!'

'What indicated to you that Unnur got pleasure from having these pictures taken?' Elsa Guðrún asked, ice-cold.

'She was just relaxed. Didn't complain or...' Máni appeared to have realised it was best for him to say no more, and his mouth clamped shut.

'Did you give her any drugs?' Guðgeir asked.

'She'd taken a sedative, the pills that calm her down that she takes in the evenings ... But, yeah. I admit to all the stuff with Unnur. I shouldn't have done it, but I have no idea about how Arnhildur died. Don't even imagine that I went anywhere near her! I mean, I was still up for getting a bunch of money out of her, so why would I do her any harm? I'm not stupid, and I'm not saying another word without a lawyer!'

22

Once Máni's statement session was over, Guðgeir made sure he spoke to the reception administrators.

'Fríða isn't here yet, but Sigurður is waiting,' said Bogga, who was there to answer his queries. 'Shall I send him home?'

'Yes, and please thank him for the taking the time to come in,' Guðgeir said.

'I'll do that, and while I remember, there was a man who called this morning and wanted to give you a message,' Bogga said. 'I've a feeling he's one of those nutcases with too much time on his hands.'

'Really?'

'He said he's a medium,' Bogga laughed.

'What did he have to say?' Guðgeir asked, his interest immediately sparked. 'This could be connected to a case we're working on. Do you have the number he called from?'

'It's unregistered. But we can deal with that.'

'Let's wait before we do that. What was his message?'

'He said you ought to search for memory sticks, and take a closer look at a man who works at an assisted living facility,' Bogga replied. 'It seemed to me a very odd conversation.'

'Interesting! Did he say anything about where we should look for these memory sticks, or mention any names?' Guðgeir asked, aware of a growing inner tension.

'No, but he whispered "the red house" in a pretty creepy sort of way before he hung up,' Bogga said. 'Does any of this make sense?'

'It certainly does, but it's on the late side. These are things that we already have confirmed. When did this man call?'

'It was just before eight. I had just got here,' she replied. 'Are you telling me that he really is a medium? Do you know who he is?'

Guðgeir could hear from Bogga's tone of voice that she was genuinely intrigued and wanted to know more about this mysterious man.

'I've a feeling I know. If it's the man I think it is, then he has my number. He could contact me directly, or he could simply call the line for anonymous tip-offs to leave a message,' Guðgeir said, thinking aloud. 'So it's remarkable that he should choose this option.'

'I see. This must be connected to the séance and the people you're asking to come forward? Særós was here just now and the press release has been sent out. But tell me, a red house... Is that the Red House restaurant in Eyrarbakki? You know the one?' Bogga asked, clearly excited by all this.

'No, far from it. But I can't spend all day chatting. I need to get back to work,' Guðgeir said.

'Hold on. We had an anonymous tip-off from some woman who said that a man followed her late last night,' Bogga said.

'Is this something for me?' Guðgeir asked.

'I thought you should know because the woman was walking along Suðurgata, by the old graveyard.'

'Did he molest her at all?'

'Didn't say. But she did say that she was very frightened,' Bogga replied.

'Thanks for letting me know,' Guðgeir said, and ended the call. He shook his head at Bogga's excitement. He clasped his hands behind his head and leaned back in his chair. How could Valthór, who claimed to be a medium, have known about both the memory sticks and Máni? The creepy guy would undoubtedly receive a dismissal notice right away, as Elsa Guðrún had wasted no time in going up to Árbær to inform Ragna of what had taken place. As well as losing his job, he could also expect to be prosecuted, but Guðgeir's mind was no longer on that, but on Valthór's message. He had to be either connected to the case, possibly even an accessory along with Máni, or Arnhildur must have confided in him. He knew that those who dabbled in séances, fortune-telling and other such sorcery could often become the confidantes of those who sought them out. To Guðgeir's mind, it was understandable that people would open themselves under such circumstances. That is, unless Valthór genuinely had a talent as a medium. That thought had occurred to Guðgeir, but he had kept it to himself when Bogga had given him the message. Growing up in the west of Iceland, he had been aware that most older people had some belief in an afterlife, and that there were a few people with the ability to converse with the dead. Many of them also believed in premonitions, dreams and prophecies. The people with whom Guðgeir had grown up had fought for their existence, in close touch with the brutal forces of nature that regularly demanded people's lives. These people had been more down-to-earth than any Guðgeir knew today, and he was still convinced that there was much about the world that could be neither felt nor seen.

Guðgeir understood this clearly, despite treating such beliefs with caution and these days his faith in anything supernatural had receded. He was also keenly aware that such beliefs were seen as juvenile in the modern world of science and knowledge, and decided that he would have to tread carefully in dealing with this medium. The last thing he wanted was to fall into the trap of giving people the opportunity of thinking that he believed in any of this paranormal stuff. Guðgeir took off his glasses and rubbed his eyes. Since the discovery of the body on Hólavallagata he had found time for neither the gym nor the swimming pool, and the effects were starting to make themselves felt. He'd have to find time for a swim today or tomorrow to regain his energy.

Guðgeir put his glasses on and opened the folder containing the case notes. He went through each document calmly, lining them up in order of priority. He would certainly make time to meet the medium, but that would have to wait. What was a priority now was to establish whether or not there was a link between Máni and the murder. If he had caused Arnhildur's death, what could have been the motive? Could she have threatened to go to the police and report Máni for abuse and extortion? The printouts about online crime that had been in the drawer of Arnhildur's bedside table indicated that she'd been thinking along those lines. Could he have murdered her to prevent her reporting him? Guðgeir didn't feel this was likely, as they hadn't had to apply much pressure for Máni to confess during the statement interview that morning. Or could his confession have been to cover up for something worse? He moved on to the next document. This was a photo he had taken at Arnhildur's house of the estate agent's advertisement. Guðgeir reached for the phone and called the number. A short conversation informed him that for years Arnhildur's sister Regína and her husband Skarphéðinn had wanted to sell the house, but Arnhildur had been the majority owner of the property and had steadfastly refused to sell up.

'It was incredibly frustrating for them,' the estate agent said. 'They rent a place in Hveragerði. It seems they went bankrupt a few years ago and desperately need the cash, but Arnhildur wouldn't have it. She flatly refused to sell. I've heard I'm not the only one they got to try and change her mind, but no way. The old lady's as stubborn as a mule and completely set in her ways. I went to see her and did my best, but there was no changing her mind.'

The estate agent spoke about Arnhildur in the present tense, and Guðgeir didn't trouble to correct him, as he had explained just that the police were looking for information relating to a certain case, without going into any further detail.

The conversation left Guðgeir thoughtful. The couple in Hveragerði were short of money, and Arnhildur had needed a lot of cash. Millions of krónur had gone into paying for Máni's memory sticks, so why on earth was she so opposed to selling the red house, and where had she found the money?

He pulled on his jacket and dropped his phone into his pocket. Then he let the others know that he wouldn't be around for the next two or three hours. He was going to take a drive out to Hveragerði to talk to them again. He wanted to meet them, see their reactions for himself, get to the truth of the matter.

23

The afternoon traffic was light and Guðgeir enjoyed the feeling of putting the city behind him. Even though it was still February, there was more light with every passing day and it made a difference. His spirits felt lighter and with that came a need to spend more time outside. Passing the turnoff for the Blue Hills, he gazed longingly in the direction of the ski slopes that were just out of sight. There was probably still enough snow, maybe even a queue for the ski lifts. All the same, his thoughts quickly left behind the temptations of the slopes as he wondered if making this journey out east was a good use of his time, or if this had been down to his need to get out of the office for a while. He heard the beginning of the news bulletin and turned the radio up.

The police request that anyone who attended a séance in a building on Bergstaðastræti on Tuesday 7th of February come forward as a matter of urgency...

The text was the same as had been read out before, even though most of those who had been at the séance had already been in touch. Everyone but the grey-haired man had come forward, and this person was increasingly on Guðgeir's mind. It could well be that this Markús, if that was his real name, had nothing to hide. There was a chance he'd neither heard the announcement on the radio nor seen it in any other media. It was becoming increasingly common for people to pay little or even no attention at all to news or social media, preferring to live their lives without the stress that came with disaster headlines and constant aggravation. Maybe the grey-haired man was one of these people?

There was a beautiful view of the steam rising from here and there in Hveragerði as he drove down the hairpin bends. In the town, he went straight to the little detached house that Regína and Skarphéðinn rented. He had mulled over whether or not to call ahead, but preferred not to do so as he felt he got more out of such visits if people hadn't prepared their answers in advance. The downside of that was that it seemed nobody was home. He strolled back to the car and waited a while, in case one or other of the couple should turn up, and then drove towards the Health Spa. A very welcoming man at reception invited Guðgeir to take a seat and said he'd go himself to find Regína. He sat for some time, and watched people come and go along the long corridors. Some were dressed in track suits and indoor shoes, while others were wrapped up against the cold for a walk in the winter frost. The man returned, and asked Guðgeir to take a seat in the canteen, where Regína would meet him in half an hour when her shift ended. He followed the man through an endless succession of twists and turns to a wide, bright room where some of the spa's guests sat and chatted at a table.

'Make yourself comfortable, and help yourself to herbal tea while you're waiting,' the man said with a smile as he left the room. 'It's great for you and it tastes good.'

Guðgeir took the man at his word and was finishing his third cup when Regína appeared. She was taller than he remembered, but that could have been because her husband wasn't at her side this time. Her pale grey hair was cut short just below her ears and a thin fringe covered her forehead. She waved, acknowledging his presence, and went to fetch herself a glass of water.

'Let's sit in the corner,' she said, gesturing. 'We can

expect a crowd in here in the next few minutes.'

'You're sure you wouldn't prefer to be somewhere more private?' Guðgeir asked. 'I don't have good news.'

'I've probably heard the worst already,' Regína said, taking a seat facing Guðgeir but with her back to the rest of the room.

He told her about the pictures of Unnur, the memory sticks and Máni's extortion of money from Arnhildur, but made no mention of the murder itself. Regína's face was pale by the time he finished his account.

'I don't know what to say,' she said, shaking her head with a look of sorrow on her face.

'You and your husband own a minority share of the house where your sister lived,' Guðgeir said.

'Yes. That's correct,' Regína replied, and sipped her water. Her hand trembled and he noticed her swollen knuckles and twisted fingers. She was clearly suffering from arthritis.

'I saw an estate agent's advertisement in her flat, and I spoke to the man. He told me that you and your husband had been keen to see the property sold, and that your sister had been implacably against it. Those of us who are working on this case find this stance of hers strange, considering she was the victim of extortion and certainly needed money. Do you have any explanation for this?' Guðgeir asked and waited for an answer that didn't come right away. Regína leaned forward, elbows on the table and her forehead resting against her outstretched fingers. Her lips quivered and she swallowed repeatedly. 'Take your time. I'm in no hurry,' Guðgeir assured her.

'I'm sorry. It's come as a shock to hear that Unnur has been abused by this vile man. The poor girl,' Regína said when she finally broke her silence. 'This is another shock on top of... You in the police are used to this kind of thing, no doubt see it all the time, but for ordinary people like me this is simply too much.'

Regína got to her feet and fetched a tissue from a neighbouring table. She dabbed her eyes and blew her nose before sitting down again.

'Where's the toilet here?' Guðgeir asked. The effects of the tea were making themselves felt, and even though the conversation was at a delicate stage, he couldn't wait any longer.

'Just the other side of the door,' Regína said, pointing.

Guðgeir was as quick as he could be, and when he returned, she was calmer.

'Yes, that's the way it's been,' she said. 'For years Skarphéðinn and I have been trying to get her to sell up, but without success. We get precious little out of this property, even though our share of it is equivalent to the rented apartment. Every quarter, Arnhildur has paid peanuts into my account and held on to the rest of the rent, saying it covers property taxes and maintenance. It's been driving us crazy, especially Skarphéðinn, not least because it's obvious that the house is in a poor state of repair. But I haven't wanted to push it too far, because of Unnur and the accident. I simply can't bring myself to re-live all that again, and the toll it took on my nerves.'

'I can understand. I read the court documents,' Guðgeir said. 'It must have been a difficult time for you.'

'You wouldn't believe it, and there's only the two of us sisters...' Regína said. 'Or, were,' she added dully.

'Was this some sort of revenge?' Guðgeir asked. 'Refusing to sell up, and being tight with money?'

'It's possible. But take Arnhildur's personality into account as well. She was always deeply set in her ways and struggled with change. Then she suffered this terrible tragedy that turned her life on its head,' Regína said. 'It wasn't just the accident that befell Unnur, but also Jacob leaving her. Arnhildur loved him so much. She adored him and was so incredibly proud of them being a couple. The four of us were close at that time and Arnhildur just lost the power of speech when he left her … I mean it, literally … she wasn't able to speak, and it lasted for weeks, even months. I wanted to take little Unnur and look after her, as I felt her mother wasn't capable of looking after her, but Arnhildur wouldn't allow her out of her sight so all I could do was bring them food and clean for them. I felt at the time that it wasn't fair on the child. Fortunately, Arnhildur made a recovery, gradually.'

'Did Jacob threaten to take Unnur from her?' Guðgeir asked.

'I don't know what went on between them, but it was all a colossal shock,' Regína replied. 'It was the same when the accident happened. She couldn't say a word for days on end.'

'So it seems that Arnhildur suffered serious emotional trauma on two occasions in her life,' Guðgeir said and he could feel his sympathy for the dead woman growing by the minute.

'Yes, that's the way things were and of course it's best to not beat about the bush. It's best to be open about these things,' Regína said. 'Skarphéðinn and I can see for ourselves now that she should have been in hospital, but Arnhildur wouldn't even consider seeking medical or psychological help. She changed after the shock of it, and struggled to cope with the sorrow, and no doubt suffered the shock of rejection, or even shame of Jacob leaving her. She'd always been so proud of him. We did our best to support her, but it was never discussed fully, just superficial stuff. We sisters have never been able to talk about feelings, and neither has Skarphéðinn. The way we were brought up was to bottle up all the bad stuff and get on with life. Jacob and Arnhildur were renovating the little studio apartment so it could be rented out, when he disappeared. Skarphéðinn had twice been there all the way from Snæfellsnes with a jackhammer to help them, and he'd promised to help Jacob tile the kitchen and bathroom.

But then Jacob walked out on his wife and child. It didn't come as a huge surprise: everyone could see that he was only staying in the relationship for the sake of his daughter. Arnhildur's affection was undoubtedly stifling, as Jacob confided in Skarphéðinn that she'd threatened to take her own life if he were ever to leave her. It's not just that they were married to sisters, but they were also close friends and Skarphéðinn was deeply hurt when Jacob made himself scarce, but there was no understanding that my sister wasn't the only one mourning a loss. So he left, and Arnhildur wallowed in her own martyrdom. Nothing more was done to the flat and of course it was never let. So that was income lost. That's the way things turned out, and we were tired of her behaviour, and at the same time felt sorry for her. We spent a lot of time with Arnhildur and Unnur, tried to find fun things for the girl to do, right up to the accident for which Arnhildur completely blamed Skarphéðinn. We didn't get to see her after that, and it was incredibly tough. It was as if all Arnhildur's bitterness for the way life had treated her was focused on us.'

Regína sighed and massaged her upper left arm with the palm of her right hand.

'So that's it.'

'Your sister was on the way home from a séance when she was assaulted. The medium's name is Valthór and he lives on Bergstaðastræti. Do you know anything about this?' Guðgeir asked.

'I heard earlier that you're trying to get in touch with people who were there, but I don't know anything. As I told you, I haven't been in touch with Arnhildur for many years but I know my sister to be a very rational person. Boringly rational, if you know what I mean,' Regína said. 'That's why to my mind it doesn't add up that she was a victim of extortion, needed the money, but still refused to sell the house.'

'She could've changed her mind, considering the estate

agent's advertisement was there on the living room table. She'd even underlined his name and phone number,' Guðgeir said in an upbeat tone, even though he knew better.

'Well, it wouldn't have been a bad thing, unless her natural stubbornness had won, and she'd been seeking help from beyond the grave,' Regína said, and for the first time Guðgeir saw a shadow of a smile appear on her face.

24

'Go away! Leave me in peace!' Valthór yelled, thrashing in his bed. 'Get away from me!'

The nightmare crept up on him every time he fell asleep and he fought his way into wakefulness. He was finally able to open his eyes and before becoming fully conscious, he managed to sit up in bed. He buried his face, damp with sweat, in his hands as he tried to get his bearings. His heart hammered so hard that he was afraid that the veins of his neck could burst at any moment. As he struggled to regain control of himself, he felt a cold draught from one corner of the room. Valthór opened his eyes and stared transfixed into the darkness. In the corner by the wardrobe was a faint vision of a dark shadow. It had to be her, there was no doubt about it.

'Go. Leave me alone,' he hissed, but she didn't move. 'Allow your soul peace and eternal rest,' he whispered in a gentler tone as he fumbled for the switch of the bedside lamp and pressed it. He was sure he saw a wisp of thin, black smoke dissipate in its dim light. He made himself get out of bed and switched on the main light. He searched every nook and cranny. There was nothing. He was alone in the room. Drained, he rubbed his eyes. He hadn't slept properly for many nights. Couldn't she leave him in peace?

Valthór sat on the edge of the bed and concentrated on calming his heartbeat. Breathe in, breathe out, slowly in, slowly out. His pulse rate gradually slowed. There was nobody there. He was alone. He went to the bathroom, switching on every light on the way. Red eyes in an exhausted face gazed back at him in the mirror and he was shocked at the change he saw in himself in the space of just a few days. He peed, and then pulled off his sweat-soaked tee-shirt. He washed. Then he went back to the bedroom, leaving all the lights burning. He tried to get back to sleep, but couldn't in the brightly lit room, so he switched off the main light, but left the lamp on the bedside table. He tossed and turned. It was no use. He opened the drawer of the bedside table and took out his phone. He searched for the audiobook he had begun listening to a day or two ago, which he'd found dull. He set it to the right place and tried to give it his attention. He managed to keep his mind on it well enough to stifle the worst of his fear. The soft-voiced male reader intoned the text clearly, but in a monotone that was ideal for Valthór as he tried to fall asleep. The story recounted in precise detail the author's activities in local politics in a rural community in the east of Iceland and his travels around the district. Valthór felt his mind relax as he tried to keep track of the narrative. He dozed off and heard the sound of his own snoring as the narrator described the roads of a remote eastern fjord deep in snow. The road climbed a steep mountain slope and boulders had rolled onto it. The narrator's fear of something terrible happening became increasingly urgent. This anxiety permeated the reading and the monotone delivery began to change. It became thinner and higher in pitch, and more insistent. Valthór tried to hold onto sleep, but the voice became more demanding. Now he knew this voice. This was Arnhildur and she was speaking to him. She was ordering him to go out. Right now!

Like a sleepwalker, he rose from the bed and dressed in the clothes he had taken off a few hours previously. She spoke constantly, her voice gaining in volume. He tried to tell her to be quiet, but that just angered her. Then he begged for peace, but she was as immovable as a rock. Cowed, he got to his feet and made for the hall. He put on a coat, hat, gloves and a scarf, and pulled on a pair of snow boots. He shut the door behind him and set off, not for the first time, on this ineluctable night walk.

25

By now Embla really wanted to be in her own bed at home. She was tired, had already had enough when the girls decided to celebrate Día's birthday. As she was her best friend, there was no getting away from going to a bar with them. Día was always a laugh to be around and was even more fun when she'd had a drink – and tonight she'd surpassed herself. They found themselves honking with laughter at one story after another, each crazier than the last. Embla leaned forward over the table and tried to keep up with what the girls were talking about. As far as she could make out, this was a morsel of extra-juicy gossip, as there were frequent gasps of shock or amazement. Then the waiter appeared with another round of cocktails. Embla couldn't remember having ordered another drink. This was an expensive place to drink and happy hour had come to an end long ago. She gave the waiter a questioning look.

'This one's paid for,' he said with a smile, placing it in front of her.

'Oh, really?'

She could hear herself slurring her words. It had to have been Día, whose parents were wealthy enough to fund their daughter's demanding lifestyle. The other girls giggled and clinked glasses. Embla didn't really want any more to drink, but this tasted heavenly and it was an expensive cocktail she didn't dare waste. She'd finish this one and then get home to bed. She took the odd sip as she tried to keep track of what the others were discussing. The noise level in this place had increased as the evening wore on, and as she sat at the end of the table she couldn't hear properly and wasn't able to keep up. She finished her drink, stood up and picked up her coat from the back of the chair, which she had to support herself against as she felt unsteady on her feet.

'You're not going already?' Día yelped to her. Her words barely carried through the din of music and the squawking of the drunk girls.

'Girls, you're fab, the best there is, but I need to get home,' she slurred back. 'Love you all the way to the moon, love you all to bits, but I have to get some sleep.'

Embla blew kisses to them and then plunged into the crowd, aiming for the door. Unfamiliar bodies pressed against her as she pushed her way between them. A sense of claustrophobia was added to the overwhelming effects of the cocktails, and she felt she was about to suffocate. Finally, she emerged in the cold night air and felt a little better. She set off homewards, but realised that she was drunker than she had thought, staggering along the pavement.

'Hey, are you all right?' a woman's voice asked.

'Just fine,' Embla mumbled. 'I live just along here.'

She somehow meandered on her way and before she knew it, was walking along Suðurgata. This had always been her route to and from the city centre, right up until she had stumbled across that body. Embla came to a halt. She felt herself swaying.

'Wasn't going to go anywhere near this graveyard again,' she muttered to herself. 'Go back and along Tjarnargata instead. That's a better way.'

She spun around, so quickly that she lost her balance and fell flat on the frozen pavement.

'Hey, well if it isn't little Embla, had a drink or two? What sort of a state are you in, you silly girl?' She heard a low laugh and heavy breaths at her ear. 'Here, I'll help you.'

She saw a face through the haze, sensing the spicy smell and hearing a familiar voice. It was Skúli, the hairdresser she had made a coffee for earlier in the week.

'I can make my own way,' she tried to say.

'Doesn't look that way to me. You were flat on the floor when I found you,' he said with decision, and struggled to pull her to her feet.

'I can do it,' Embla said, taking care with every word. It was a battle, she could feel her stomach churning, but Skúli took no notice, simply held her close and set off. She felt ill and laid her head against his shoulder. Together they took the route she hadn't intended to take.

'Wasn't it past this gate in the middle of the graveyard that you found Arnhildur's body?' she heard Skúli ask. In the darkness she could discern the outline of the black iron bars and muttered her agreement.

'Shall we go inside and take a look at the place?'

'No!' she snapped, pulling herself free. 'I don't want to!'

'It's all right, I was joking,' he said and took hold of her again.

'I can make my own way home,' Embla told him, unconvincingly.

'It doesn't look like it to me,' Skúli replied with a light-hearted laugh. 'It's not out of my way to take you home, I live close by.'

He stroked her hair and pulled her along. She again laid her head against his shoulder and began to doze. When she next opened her eyes, she saw they were on Hringbraut. The lights of cars glittered and somehow the sight of them made her feel better. Skúli held her even tighter and she could feel something around her throat. Was he twisting her hair around her neck? She fought to free herself, but he gripped her even tighter.

'There's no way you can stand on your own feet, little Embla,' he said firmly.

SHROUDED

She was feeling nauseous, although this passed for a moment when she caught sight of the florist and the bakery, right next to the block where she lived, so there wasn't far to go. Her bed was just out of reach and she had to get there on her own. But it was hard to keep her eyes open and in a daze she held onto the man who was pulling her along. Suddenly, the nausea welled up.

'Gonna honk,' she gasped. Skúli smartly let go.

She bent forward, shivering and trembling as she brought up the contents of her stomach. When she was able to straighten up, she looked around. Her surroundings were still undulating, but Skúli was nowhere to be seen.

26

The weekend was uneventful, but Monday afternoon brought the third team meeting for what had become known as the graveyard case or the séance case. The whole team was present, except for Leifur, who had picked up a virulent case of flu at the Lions Club gathering. Guðgeir took a seat next to Særós and helped himself to a slice of apple from the tray of chopped fruit on the table. He was keen to hear Ísgerður's report now that the autopsy results had been collated.

'Any news of Leifur?' Særós asked, directing her question to Helgi Már.

'He called just now, so hoarse he could hardly speak and still under the weather, so he'll be staying home today,' Helgi Már replied.

'That's right. That's exactly where Leifur should be until his health's back to normal,' Ísgerður said, giving her professional opinion as a doctor. 'Since the pandemic people come to work less frequently when they're sick, and that's a big improvement.'

'True, as long as it's not taken to extremes,' said Særós, who had never missed a single day's work. 'We can't have people being too soft on themselves and sometimes it's as well to push yourself through it to get better.'

Ísgerður raised an eyebrow, clearly not inclined to agree, but it didn't escape Guðgeir that there was more habit than conviction in Særós's words.

'That doesn't apply to Leifur, surely?' Elsa Guðrún asked in surprise. 'He pushed himself to the limits when he should be taking care of his health.'

Guðgeir allowed himself a smile. His northern colleague's reaction was only to be expected, leaping to Leifur's defence when she felt he was being maligned, even though she had her own axe to grind with him on occasions.

'Of course not, no. He's totally reliable,' Særós replied with an apologetic smile. 'Well, let's start with the medical side of things. All yours, Ísgerður.'

The autopsy findings were that Arnhildur had lost her life sometime between eleven on Tuesday evening and three or four o'clock on Wednesday morning. The cause of death had been two or more heavy blows to the back of the head. In addition to this, her airway had been restricted using the silk scarf she wore around her neck. There were indications that the murder weapon was a metal implement, cylindrical in shape, so possibly a length of pipe, hammer or some other tool. Ísgerður paused as Særós gestured for her to slow down as she tapped at her keyboard, making notes that could be passed on. An organised search for an item matching this description would start shortly.

'There were bruises, grazes and scratches on her body that suggest she was dragged from one location to another,' Ísgerður continued. 'There were no other signs of trauma on her body.'

'Was she dragged far?' Elsa Guðrún asked.

'Some metres, possibly, over uneven terrain, I'd guess without being certain. But it's possible that the perpetrator wanted to find a more secluded place to finish what he had begun,' Ísgerður said. 'I'd also like to make it plain that Arnhildur's heart was in poor shape. Her coronary arteries were heavily blocked, around 50 to 80 percent, and other arteries show evidence of high blood pressure.'

'Is there anything you can tell us about the perpetrator?' Guðgeir asked.

'He would have had to exert considerable force, unless he was higher than the victim. I mean, standing on one of the graves, for instance. Some of them are raised quite high there in the Hólavellir graveyard,' Ísgerður said.

'Unless the killer had been hiding behind the graveyard wall and Arnhildur had been walking along Suðurgata,' Elsa Guðrún said. 'In some places the graveyard is a good bit higher than the street.'

'That's interesting,' Guðgeir said thoughtfully. 'It would've required considerable strength to haul her towards the centre of the graveyard.'

'There are several gates in the graveyard wall, so if the assault took place close to one of those, then it's certainly a possibility,' Elsa Guðrún said, sounding convinced.

'Forensics will examine the location in more detail,' Helgi Már said. 'No question.'

'There's every reason to check it very closely,' Særós said. 'Anything else?'

'The sister, Regína, and Skarphéðinn the brother-in-law both have confirmed alibis,' Guðgeir said.

'And what about Máni?' Ísgerður asked.

'He admitted to abusing the girl and extortion, and that's all in the system now, but we don't have anything else to pin on him. While we don't have any further evidence, the best we can do is keep an eye on him,' Særós said. 'Guðgeir, would you take over?'

He nodded.

'As you all presumably know, all of those who attended the séance have come forward, with the exception of the grey-haired man who accompanied Arnhildur from the place on Bergstaðastræti. This morning a young man who lives on Tjarnargata got in touch after reading about the investigation. He reported seeing a woman who fits Arnhildur's description walking past at that time. This man is certain that she was alone as she crossed Tjarnargata on her way up Skothúsvegur. So it's clear that this grey-haired Markús, if that's his name, wasn't with her at that point.'

Guðgeir fell silent and scratched the dark stubble on his face, and Elsa Guðrún broke in.

'But the grey-haired guy could have gone another way and waited behind the graveyard wall for her.'

'Exactly,' Guðgeir agreed. 'I suggest we put out a specific request for this man to come forward.'

'Agreed,' Særós said. 'Anything else?'

'Yes. We have confirmation of withdrawals from Arnhildur's account and deposits to Máni's bank account. He doesn't have a lot left.' Guðgeir scowled and clicked his tongue. 'Don't they say that ill-gotten gains don't last long? Máni appears to have spent the money more or less as soon as he got it. He says he's spent his weekends on the town and he's up to his ears in debt.'

'After having looked into his affairs, it seems to me that he's been snorting it up his nose,' Helgi Már said, rolling his eyes like a teenager.

'That'll do for now,' Særós said, getting to her feet. 'Let's keep going.'

Helgi Már, Elsa Guðrún and Ísgerður all stood up, leaving Guðgeir alone still seated.

'Could I have word in private, Særós?' he said, hesitatingly.

'Yes, of course,' she said and glanced at the clock. 'What's bothering you?'

She went to the door and closed it.

He waited until she had taken a seat. Then he cleared his throat and screwed up his courage.

'We've always been able to talk, Særós ... Always been honest with each other. Haven't we?'

She shifted in her seat and the boss expression he had come to know so well appeared on her face.

'Of course. You can always talk to me,' she said in an understanding tone of voice. 'What's troubling you?'

'There's nothing troubling me, fortunately. But I can't help noticing that you're not at your best,' he said cautiously, but firmly.

She was instantly on the defensive.

'Don't talk rubbish! I'm just fine.'

Her laughter was forced.

'I know you, Særós. You never oversleep. You don't forget important aspects of procedure. It's not like you to turn up for work with wet hair and you...' he said, until she lifted a hand to stop him.

'Listen, my dear Guðgeir. Isn't this going too far? If you've a problem with the way I do my job, then take it higher,' she said with a contrived laugh and slapped the arms of her chair with both hands.

Guðgeir stared at her in astonishment. It hadn't occurred to him that she would respond like this to questions he was asking in all sincerity.

'You know me better than that, Særós. I've no criticism to make,' he said, hoping she wouldn't hear in his voice that he was hurt. 'I want only the best for you and I've a strong suspicion that there's something bothering you, and I'm asking if you could trust me as your friend? I don't know if I can help you, but it might do you some good to talk about whatever is bothering you. Because there's something on your mind, and maybe has been for a long time.'

He fell silent and waited for an answer that didn't come. Særós didn't look at him, but stared at the screen of her laptop, her lips pursed.

'You've always worked hard and don't spare yourself ... always at full throttle ... that can lead to burnout...'

He was silent again and this time her eyes were on him.

'That's enough,' she said firmly, getting to her feet. 'I'm starting to feel as if I'm speaking to a psychiatrist.'

'Are you not getting enough sleep, or on some diet that's leaving you with a vitamin deficiency? Are you suffering from orthorexia?' Guðgeir asked as he felt forced to get to his feet, even though he wasn't ready to give up trying to help.

'What's that?' Særós asked, and he saw a faint smile start to form.

'Ah, well. I don't remember exactly, but I read something about it. As I understand it, there are people who develop an obsession with eating the right stuff, and that triggers some high stress levels,' Guðgeir explained. He felt that this could well apply to Særós, but she laughed in response. 'I'm not quite sure what it's all about, and I understand completely about the carbohydrates,' he said with a smile. 'But you know you can trust me if you want to talk about anything that's troubling you.'

'You're quite right that there's a certain matter that's been preying on my mind and has done so for a long time. But I'm not ready to discuss it right away,' Særós said, her smile vanishing like the sun behind a cloud.

'Look at your latest nugget of wisdom on the wall,' Guðgeir said. He pointed and read out loud, '**Be the best version of yourself you can be**'. It helps to open up and trust your friends, doesn't it?'

'Ach, that's such a stupid cliché! I don't know why I bother pinning this rubbish up every week. I long ago got tired of this,' Særós said, a look of fatigue appearing on her face.

Now it was Guðgeir's turn to be surprised.

'Listen to me. There's nothing that says you have to post a weekly piece of wisdom on the wall, any more than there's a law that requires you to keep precise records of training sessions, blood sugar levels, deep sleep or whatever, all the stuff that you conscientiously register in some system. You don't have to do any of this stuff if you don't want to. But if you just left out the stuff I've just mentioned, then that would undoubtedly help you relax,' he said, feeling at a loss.

Særós stepped towards Guðgeir, placed her hands on his cheeks and kissed him.

'You're a star and if I tell anyone, it'll be you. Promise.'

'Thank you, Særós. I just want to help you,' Guðgeir said, his arms loosely around her. 'You know you can always trust me.'

At that moment Helgi Már came into the room. No doubt he had knocked, without them having heard.

'Wh... Oh, sorry! I ... I didn't mean to burst in,' he said, visibly embarrassed, and about to rush from the room.

'Don't go, Helgi, and for heaven's sake don't jump to the wrong conclusion. We were just talking,' Særós said firmly, and stepped away from Guðgeir. 'What is it?'

Helgi Már stepped hesitantly closer, his cheeks noticeably pink.

'I was just going to let you know that Freyja, one of the tenants on the ground floor of Arnhildur's place, was in touch just now. She says she woke up during the night and saw a man dressed in dark-coloured clothing standing perfectly still outside the house. He stood there for a long time and stared in through the windows. The spooky part of it is that this isn't the first time this has happened.'

27

'I'm looking at this area here, a five- to ten-metre radius,' Elsa Guðrún said, and pointed at the black iron gate that opened onto the graveyard. They stopped and glanced around at their surroundings.

'This was Arnhildur's quickest route home. It strikes me as unlikely that she'd have taken the Hringbraut side of the graveyard. There's always traffic, so someone would have seen her,' she continued. 'You can see that this stretch of Suðurgata must have been the place. There's no house on the other side of the street and that streetlight isn't working.'

'Yes, if we work on the assumption that Arnhildur wasn't inside the graveyard when the assault took place,' Guðgeir said. He took pictures and sent them to Helgi Már, with an explanation of the location. Presumably there would be nothing to be found on the graveyard wall or the pavement, but it would do no harm to check if there were even the slightest residues of contact on the coarse concrete.

'It's both rained and snowed over the last few days,' Elsa Guðrún said. 'All the same, I hope forensics will check this out as a possibility.'

'I think their investigation focused on the area where Arnhildur's body was found. The wall wasn't checked particularly, so it seems to me there's every reason...' Guðgeir fell silent, put on his glasses and peered at his phone, which had pinged an alert. 'Helgi Már just replied. He promises to make a start on it first thing tomorrow. The forecast is for it to stay dry, so that should work out.'

'Why not right away?' Elsa Guðrún asked, failing to hide her frustration.

'It's late in the day,' Guðgeir muttered. 'I'll let Leifur know as well. He must be feeling better and ready to get back to work.'

'But can't you push them on this? Arnhildur was bruised and she had scratches that Ísgerður said were consistent with having been dragged some distance. I'm not saying this could have happened precisely here, but we know she went along Suðurgata, and somehow it seems unlikely that she'd have taken a shortcut through the graveyard – alone, late in the evening and coming from a séance. Wouldn't that have been pretty crazy?'

Elsa Guðrún's wide eyes were fixed on Guðgeir, who could only agree with her theory.

'Unless she had absolutely no fear of the dark, a rational thinker,' Elsa Guðrún said suddenly. 'Or she might have had a taste for the uncanny?'

'Neither. The woman had been at a séance, and as for the uncanny stuff, I hardly think so,' Guðgeir said. 'Come on, let's make a move and find out what Freyja has to say. She's the only one of the tenants there we haven't met so far.'

*

'He was standing right here, like he was rooted to the spot, staring at the house. It must have been twenty minutes or more. The first time, I didn't really worry about it, but then I saw he was back and doing exactly the same thing as before. Well, then I was properly scared.'

Freyja shuddered and pulled her shawl tighter around her over a thin, shabby coat. The frost had electrified her thick, frizzy hair into a restless halo.

SHROUDED

'That's two nights in a row after Arnhildur was murdered, at exactly the same time. Maybe he's been there more times than that.' She put her hand dramatically to her mouth and shuddered. 'Creepy, totally creepy.'

'Are you finding it difficult to sleep?' Guðgeir asked, catching himself looking longer than necessary at the dark patches under Freyja's eyes.

'I get up sometimes to go to the toilet…'

'All right … I see,' Guðgeir interrupted. 'Could you describe this man?'

'He wore a thick coat, with a hat, dark trousers,' Freyja intoned, eyes gazing up at the sky as she spoke, before falling silent and looking back at them.

'We're going to need a better description than that,' Elsa Guðrún said. 'Age, complexion, height, size – everything. And be as precise as you can.'

'He's sort of average height, quite thin, but maybe because the coat looks so big on him. His complexion is pale, almost ghostly.' Freyja shivered again and scowled. 'I don't really know what his hair colour is because he was wearing a hat, but what I could see might have been quite pale.'

'Fair hair or grey?' Guðgeir asked quickly.

'Don't know,' Freyja replied, again looking skywards. 'Like I said, he was wearing a hat so I could hardly see.'

'Any idea of his age?' Guðgeir said.

'Ach, it's always so difficult to guess someone's age. Somewhere between thirty and fifty, or maybe older…' Freyja shook her head, a hopeless look on her face.

'That's a pretty broad range,' Elsa Guðrún said.

'I know, but it's so hard to tell at that distance, and he was so well wrapped up,' Freyja replied. 'It's horrible to think that this could be Arnhildur's murderer.'

'Did you take a picture of him?' Guðgeir asked.

'Oh!' Freyja gasped. 'Of course, I should have. Don't know what I was thinking.'

'No problem. Hindsight is a wonderful thing,' Guðgeir said and glanced at Elsa Guðrún, who was looking around the garden. 'If you see him again, then take a picture and send it to us.'

'Couldn't you have a police car outside during the night? It's really making me nervous,' Freyja sighed, puffing her cheeks.

'We'll see about that,' Guðgeir replied, ready to leave. 'But I'll make sure that there's a patrol car checking this street regularly over the next few nights.'

'Where was he standing, exactly?' Elsa Guðrún called from some distance away.

'More or less where you are now. Next to that birch hedge. He was staring at the wall as if he wanted to kill someone inside the house. Creepy as fuck!' Freyja dug her hands into her pockets and rolled her shoulders high. 'Poor, poor Arnhildur,' she said in a tone that was almost petulant.

'You weren't home the day we found her, so I'm not aware of how well you knew Arnhildur,' Guðgeir said. 'But I spoke to your fellow tenants.'

'I'm sort of the extra person in the apartment. Arnhildur wasn't happy about it, but the day before she died I sat upstairs with her and we talked for ages,' Freyja said.

'Really?'

Guðgeir's interest was instantly sparked.

'Yes, I knocked on her door and offered to fix up the spare space in the basement. It occurred to me that it could make a neat little apartment. I'm training as a joiner. She didn't turn out to be all that keen, but at least I put the idea in her head. We had a long talk.'

'About what?' Guðgeir asked, his attention now focused on Freyja.

'Mostly the internet. She asked me to explain all sorts of things for her because there was stuff she was curious about, cybercrime and so on. It had to be something she'd read about somewhere, but I thought it was cool she was so interested. I was going up to college and offered to print out some information for her. I found an info sheet of yours, the police, I mean, for her to read. Nice lady, I thought.' Freyja put a hand to her cheek and sniffed. 'Can I go back inside now? It's freezing and I'll end up with a cold if I stay out here much longer. But will you please check on the creepy guy?'

'We'll do that,' Guðgeir assured her and strolled with her towards the door. 'Was there anything else that Arnhildur discussed with you? It could be important for the investigation.'

'Really?' Freyja asked, apparently excited at the thought. 'She asked about USB, you know, memory sticks. I told her you could store information on them. And I told her all about saving to flash sticks, hard drives and even the cloud. Arnhildur was amazingly interested in all this.'

28

Guðgeir looked up at the huge clock on the swimming pool wall and saw that he had half an hour before he needed to be home to change and fetch Inga. They'd arranged to go out that evening with friends, a meal in a restaurant and then the theatre. Steam rose from the hottest of the hot tubs where Guðgeir sat, watching people coming and going. Everyone's movements in the forty-degree water were slow and cautious. One of the advantages of the hottest tub was that the sheer heat wasn't conducive to long conversations, which suited Guðgeir perfectly as after a long working day what he desired, more than anything, was an opportunity to clear his mind of anything superficial. He nodded to a man he recognised, moved closer to the steps and climbed out. From there he strolled through the thin covering of snow to the cold tub. The glacier-cold water lapped at his chin and he allowed two minutes to pass before going to his cubicle. He spent a long time under the hot shower and let the powerful jets pummel his sore shoulder muscles as he thought over the events of the day.

Now they knew that Arnhildur had understood Máni's duplicity, and the day after she had become aware of how he had exploited her innocence, she had been murdered. There was every reason to suspect Máni, and Guðgeir hoped that this new piece of information would suffice to request a long period of detention. They hadn't needed to apply much pressure to Máni before he'd admitted taking the photographs of Unnur and extorting money from her mother. Could he have done that to deflect attention from a much more serious crime? If that were the case, then there had to be something behind it. Guðgeir turned off the water, dried himself off and dressed under the crisply invigorating winter air. At ease both physically and mentally, he was certain that the next day would see them make real progress.

Inga was almost ready when he came home. She wore a patterned silk blouse in bright colours, loose black trousers and high-heeled shoes.

'We're going to be late,' she called out to him, as she applied lipstick. Guðgeir felt a longing to throw himself on the couch and think, to prepare himself mentally for the following day, try to identify more connections and plan the case's next steps from different angles.

'Why are you looking at me like that?' Inga asked, her eyebrows lifting questioningly.

'You're so beautiful,' he replied, and meant it sincerely, even though his thoughts were elsewhere.

'Thank you, sweetheart. You're lovely as well, but won't you get ready?' Inga said, taking her coat from its hook.

He hurried to the bedroom to change, found a jacket, a freshly-ironed shirt and dark trousers. He checked himself out in the mirror and a moment later was ready in the hall with the car keys in his hand.

'You're taking the car?' she asked, a little disappointed. 'Let's take a taxi so you can have a glass or two of wine with dinner. It's so rare that we go out these days, and we don't need to hurry home...'

'Sorry. There's so much going on at work that I daren't,' he replied and opened the door for Inga with a flourish. 'After you, pretty lady!'

At the restaurant he made an effort to be animated and to take part in the conversation, even though for much of the time his thoughts were somewhere far away. He consoled himself with the thought that in the theatre he would have the mental space to concentrate on the next stages of the graveyard case. But that didn't work out, as he enjoyed the performance, found it engrossing and for a while even forgot work. During the interval they sat at a small table with the drinks they had ordered in advance. Guðgeir got to his feet, saying that he was going to fetch some water, but instead took himself off to one side to call the station. Everything was quiet, except that there had been two reports of suspicious activity around the old graveyard and a patrol car had been dispatched to investigate.

'Any description?' Guðgeir asked, his eyes on a painting of a long dead star of the National Theatre as he spoke.

'Both times a man in a coat and hat.'

'Did he do anything?' Guðgeir asked.

'No, not exactly. Just approaching uncomfortably close.'

'Who called this in?'

'One was the mother of a teenage girl and the other was an older woman.'

The piercing peal of a bell told him that the second act was about to begin now that the interval was over, so he ended the call and hurried back to the others, who were making their way into the auditorium.

It took Guðgeir a few minutes to pick up the thread of the performance and concentrate again, but he managed it. But the play didn't appear to have gripped Inga and the other couple as it had him, and they had little to say as they parted sleepily on the theatre steps. Inga asked on the way home if he had been able to speak to Særós.

'Yes, we had a talk,' Guðgeir said truthfully.

'And?' Inga was curious.

'There's something bothering her and she's not ready to confide in me. At least, not yet,' Guðgeir said. 'I mentioned to her that it might be worth cutting down on stuff that's unnecessarily stressful and to lower her own expectations for herself.'

'And how did she react to that idea?' Inga asked.

'Fairly well, I think.'

'That's good,' Inga said, yawning.

29

An older gentleman with grey hair and wearing an overcoat was waiting when Guðgeir arrived at the station the following morning. He introduced himself as Markús Sigurbergsson.

'It's because of this séance,' he said, his words accompanied by a firm handshake. 'I was there.'

'Thanks for coming forward. We'd been hoping to see you as we've spoken to others who attended,' Guðgeir said, and gestured for Markús to be seated.

He was a smartish man in an unbuttoned dark overcoat, under which was a blue cardigan with eye-catching buttons of pressed black leather. Guðgeir noticed that one hung by a thread and another was missing.

'Well, what a terrible thing to happen. The poor woman! I'm afraid the whole thing passed me by, and it was only when my friends at the Rotary Club were joking about your request that I asked a few questions and they told me what it was all about.' He hesitated and smiled apologetically. 'Anyway, I'm here, and what can I do to assist the police?'

Markús wrinkled his nose slightly and fiddled with his moustache.

'You could tell me precisely what happened that evening, and especially about your interaction with Arnhildur,' Guðgeir said, getting directly to the point and watching the man with interest. There was something out of the ordinary about him, but it was difficult to pin down exactly what.

'Well, I don't make a habit of going to this kind of thing. It was all rather silly, in my opinion,' Markús said. 'These so-called mediums don't have any supernatural talents, and all they need is to be able to read people and to think quickly. Yes, and I suppose it doesn't do any harm to have some skill in hypnosis.' Markús barked with sudden laughter that just as quickly died away. 'So I went to this séance and sat next to the unfortunate woman. We walked together a little distance before our ways parted. I can hardly say that we exchanged many words. I tried to chat a little to her, but she barely responded.'

'I see,' Guðgeir said, sneaking a glance at the clock. It was particularly awkward that Markús had made his appearance just as Máni was being brought in for further questioning. After a moment's thought he decided to let Markús take precedence. Elsa Guðrún was fully capable of leading the questioning. He stood up and asked Markús to excuse him for a moment, intending to ask Særós to take his place at Elsa Guðrún's side. He was out of the room for no more than a few minutes, but when he returned Markús was on his feet and appeared ready to be on his way.

'Don't go yet, I could use some more information,' Guðgeir said politely, wondering why the man seemed ready to rush off, considering he'd just arrived.

'There's no more to say,' Markús said.

'Tell me about the séance.'

'Ach, that was all pretty foolish.' Markús sat down, but perched on the edge of the chair, gloves in his hands, as if anxious to leave. 'I don't believe in that kind of nonsense.'

'So you said already. So why were you there?' Guðgeir asked.

'I lost my wife four years ago and time hangs heavy through the winter days. I can't be having with gawping at the TV or getting into arguments on social media, as many people of my age do. Instead I do this and that, and it doesn't do any harm if it costs not much or maybe nothing at all. I've joined knitting circles in libraries and been on all kinds of courses and seminars, and when I saw this Valthór's advert it looked like it could be interesting,' Markús said as he wrinkled his nose again and stroked his moustache with two fingers. 'In fact, the séance wasn't cheap, but I found the whole premise fascinating.'

'Where did you see this advertised?' Guðgeir asked.

'I don't remember. Probably at some seminar, but I made a note of it.' Markús took a small notebook from his pocket and flipped through the pages. 'Here's the address and the date,' he said, holding it out so that Guðgeir could read what he had written. 'But I don't recall when I wrote this down.'

'Fair enough. Tell me about the séance,' Guðgeir said, his hands tensed as he listened.

'In many ways it was interesting. The medium is an accomplished reader of people and knows how to fish information out of people without their realising,' Markús said. 'He no doubt made use of all his skills, but he got nowhere with me.'

'And Arnhildur?' Guðgeir asked.

'She was the number one target. There were all sorts of dead people with all kinds of messages for her,' Markús snorted. 'It was all so theatrical that it was almost laughable.'

'And it wasn't long before she was among them,' Guðgeir pointed out quietly.

'Apologies for the sarcasm, it wasn't meant like that,' Markús said. He looked awkward and shifted in his chair. 'Well, that's all. I have no more to tell you.'

'What did they have to say, these dead people, if we can call them that, to Arnhildur?' Guðgeir said, and it occurred to him that the medium would have found no personal information about her online.

'Ach, I don't recall. It was all so unremarkable. Some crap about the silver decoration from a set of national dress, and then there was her long-dead grandfather. The grandmother made a repeat appearance as well,' Markús said with a shake of his head.

'The two of you left together. Where did you go your separate ways?' Guðgeir probed.

'Now ... let me think...' Markús drew out his words as he twisted his leather gloves in his hands. 'I recollect walking up Baldursgata and she continued straight on. Where she went, I have no idea...'

'The body was found in the Hólavellir graveyard, the old cemetery on Suðurgata. Presumably you were aware of that,' Guðgeir said in an expressionless tone, although his eyes didn't leave the man's face.

'Of course! What am I talking about?' Markús said apologetically. He smiled and shook his head at his own forgetfulness.

'Where did you go after the séance?'

'Home to Norðurmýri. It was late and I went straight to bed.' Markús's response came quickly. 'I live on Hrefnugata.'

'Are there any witnesses who could confirm you came home at that time of the evening? Or did you meet anyone on the way? A neighbour?'

Guðgeir's questioning gaze remained on Markús, whose expression had hardened, while his smile had become strained.

'No, not that I recall. Since my wife died, I live alone. Well, I've done my bit by coming here to talk to you.'

Markús rose smartly to his feet, ready to leave.

'As I said earlier, you were the last one to have any contact with Arnhildur while she was alive,' Guðgeir said slow deliberation, looking directly into Markús's intelligent green-blue eyes. 'With the exception of the murderer, of course.'

The smile was wiped from the grey-haired man's face, replaced by a scowl.

'It's remarkable how you in the police have a knack for making innocent people feel like criminals,' he said in an ice-cold voice. 'I've done my duty to society, and now I've had enough of this conversation.'

The words had barely left Markús's lips before he disappeared through the door.

30

Máni had been as slippery as an eel, Elsa Guðrún said, much more sure of himself than on the previous occasion. All the same, her repeated questions about where he had been the on the evening and night of Arnhildur's death had made him sweat. According to him, he had been at home, watching a popular programme on TV that went on past midnight, after which he'd gone to bed. It went without saying that he slept alone, and he seemed to think that a text message sent to a friend at 23:09 saying that 'the star of H is rubbish' would be effective confirmation. His friend had responded at 23:15 with a vomiting emoji, and that had been the end of the exchange. This proved nothing, and now they were waiting for a judge to confirm the police request to detain him.

'Máni was very quick to admit his abusive behaviour and extortion. So don't you think it's possible that he's hiding something more and worse?' Guðgeir asked.

'It could well be that he's not the sharpest knife in the drawer, and he simply figured out that he didn't have much of a choice,' Elsa Guðrún replied. 'Better to admit it right away and hope for a lenient sentence.'

'Could be,' Guðgeir said thoughtfully.

'I'll get to work on the statement,' Elsa Guðrún said, and left the room, and a moment later Bogga's head appeared around the door.

'You don't pick up messages,' she said with a note of

reproof in her voice.

'Really? What now?' Guðgeir said, massaging the back of his neck with his fingertips. Inflamed muscles were again plaguing him.

'A woman called Freyja is driving me crazy. She keeps calling, about some man who hangs around outside her house at night,' Bogga explained.

Guðgeir raised an eyebrow.

'I'm aware of the case, but is there something that's bothering her?' he asked, taking off his glasses.

'She's clearly frightened of him,' Bogga replied. 'It's not as if the guy is standing on the street. He's in their garden, right up by the house itself.'

'Any threatening behaviour?' Guðgeir asked as he leaned back in his office chair.

'Freyja seems to think so, but I don't get the impression he's done anything of that nature. Won't you have a word with her?' Bogga said, her tone making it clear that she expected him to.

'Of course I will.' He put his glasses in their case and dropped it into the inside pocket of his jacket. 'Do you recall the man who called, saying he was a medium? I recollect that he called the same day we brought Máni in for questioning. Didn't he say something about a red house?'

'Yes! I couldn't forget that. He almost whispered in a breathless voice. Kinda creepy.' Bogga shivered at the recollection. 'You think it's him?'

'I don't know, but I'm going to check it out,' Guðgeir said. He took his coat from its hook. 'I'm off. Could you call Freyja and let her know I'm on my way?'

This time Freyja and Hafdís had been watching a movie together late the previous evening. Hafdís had fallen asleep on the sofa and Freyja had been sleepy, so she decided to go to bed. She noticed the man in the garden as she went past the living room window, standing in exactly the same spot as before, staring at the house. Her phone was on charge in the kitchen, so she reached for Hafdís's phone to take a picture, but it turned out to be locked. When she looked again out of the window, the man was gone.

'I know it sounds mad, but it seemed to me like he wasn't alive,' Freyja said, her untamed hair fluttering around her head.

'You think this was a ghost?' Guðgeir asked seriously as he looked around the garden.

'No, of course not ... but...' Freyja spoke hesitatingly, and her cheeks flushed. 'He's not a flasher, as he's not showing anything, and he's not a peeping Tom because he's not looking in. He just stares at the house. At the concrete.'

'Where?'

'Just there. At the bottom of the wall at the end of the rose bed,' Freyja explained. She slipped her bulging leather bag from her shoulder, putting it between her knees as she pointed at the spot in question.

'Has he done anything to you, or damaged any of your property?' Guðgeir asked.

'No,' Freyja replied quickly, and the irritation in her voice broke through. 'The guy's just there, in the garden, at night. It's really disturbing, and he has no business being there.'

'I see,' Guðgeir said, looking around at the surroundings. 'Have all three of you been aware of this man?'

'Just the two of us. Skúli wasn't home yesterday evening, so obviously he didn't see the man,' Freyja said, looping her bag's strap back over her shoulder. 'I'm going to be late for my lecture, but you have to do something. Otherwise I'm going to go crazy!'

'We'll do our best,' Guðgeir assured her. His phone rang at that moment, and he raised a hand in acknowledgement as Freyja made for the street. It was Helgi Már, letting him know that traces of blood had been found on the graveyard wall.

'It's not a lot, but it should be enough,' Helgi Már said. 'This is thanks to Elsa Guðrún.'

'Like so much else,' Guðgeir said. 'Are you still at the location?'

'Yes, we'll be here for a while yet.'

'Would you search the immediate area carefully, and look out especially for a black, pressed leather button that could have been ripped off a cardigan,' Guðgeir said. 'It could be a key item of evidence.'

'Will do,' Helgi Már said, and ended the call.

Guðgeir slid his phone into his pocket. He stood for a long moment and looked at the red house before he strolled over to his car and opened the door. He had a strong intuition that someone was watching him, so he closed the car door, looked around and saw nobody. All the same, the feeling refused to leave him. He paused in thought. He suddenly remembered the eyes of the youngster in the window of the house next door that had followed him the first time he had come to this house, Arnhildur's home. He looked up to the window of the neighbouring house. Quite right. The pale-coloured blinds moved and curious eyes followed his every movement. Guðgeir walked up to the house and pressed the button that looked likely, but there was no response. He rang the bell repeatedly, but without result. Then he tried the next one, and a moment later the door swung open. A tired-looking, thin-haired woman with a small child in her arms asked which one he had come to collect. Guðgeir didn't understand.

'Collect what?' he asked.

'Which child?' the woman replied and now Guðgeir noticed the toys scattered on the floor behind her. A little girl, somewhat younger than his own grandson, held onto the woman's leg, desperate to be picked up. When a third child appeared, howling and on unsteady feet, Guðgeir understood. The woman had to be a childminder.

'I'm not here to collect anyone. My name's Guðgeir Fransson and I'm a police officer. We're investigating a serious case and I wanted to speak to a lad in his teens who lives in this house. He hasn't done anything, but I've noticed that he pays attention to what's happening outside his window, so it occurred to me...'

Guðgeir got no further as the little girl who wanted to be held had begun to cry.

'Yeah, I understand,' the woman said quickly. She fished a phone from her back pocket and tapped rapidly with her thumb. 'I'm sending Hilmar a message and he'll open the door. His hearing isn't good and he's on a spectrum of some kind, I reckon. Just take care to face him directly when you speak so he can see your lips moving.'

'Thanks,' Guðgeir said and heard a door open somewhere up the upstairs. 'I'd like to ask if you've been aware of anyone in the gardens around here? Late in the evenings or during the night?'

The woman didn't reply right away, now that all three children were crying.

'You know, I'm out like a light long before midnight. There could be a brass band marching up and down the street and I wouldn't hear a thing. Now I need to look after these. Bye.'

She gave him a courtesy smile and the door shut practically in his face.

Hilmar waited on the landing as Guðgeir ascended the stairs. Following the childminder's advice, there was nothing difficult about communicating with Hilmar. To ensure there were no misunderstandings, Guðgeir felt it safer to tap questions into his phone and then show the screen to Hilmar, who nodded emphatically in response to mention of the mysterious man in the garden. Guðgeir wrote out the description that Freyja had given him.

'Yes, that's it,' Hilmar said. He held out his hand for the phone, and wrote '2', followed by a couple of exclamation marks.

'Not three?' Guðgeir asked, holding up three fingers to be certain.

Hilmar shook his head.

'No. Two,' he said with decision in a high-pitched monotone.

31

He'd passed a terrible night. Valthór hadn't managed to fall asleep properly until the early hours and now he was startled by the shrill ringing of the doorbell. He sought refuge under the duvet, squeezed his eyes tight shut and tried to claw back the sleep he craved. The bell rang again, more insistently this time. He stumbled from the bed, kicking as he did so a half-bottle of cognac underneath it. Valthór wasn't much of a drinker. The bottle had been a present for a birthday a few years ago, and it had remained unopened until at around four that morning when he'd tried in desperation to drink himself into unconsciousness. His throbbing head was an indicator that this had been a catastrophically unwise idea. The bell shrilled again. Who could it be? He hurried to the bathroom, found a painkiller in the cabinet and gulped it down with a glass of water. Then he snatched up the mouthwash and swigged at it to try and lose the worst of the foul taste in his mouth. He spat the blue fluid into the basin and caught sight of himself in the mirror as he stood up straight. An exhausted man in a singlet and pyjama trousers met his eyes. Now he could hear someone trying the door handle and it occurred to him that this caller might have something to do with Arnhildur. The thought was terrifying. He should never have got involved in all that mess.

Valthór splashed his face with cold water and dried himself on a towel. He would have to open the door. Not doing so would be suspicious, as his car was outside and all the lights in the flat were on, because he could no longer bear to sleep in the dark. Valthór opened a drawer, took out a brush and quickly put his hair into some kind of shape, then hurried to the door to open it for this unexpected visitor.

It was the policeman. The tall, dark one. Although this was no social call, Valthór felt relieved at the sight of him. This was a personable man.

'Hello, my name's Guðgeir, as you might remember ... I went up to Bergstaðastræti first, and of course there was nobody about. I tried to call as well,' the policeman said, as if by way of explanation. 'Are you unwell?' he asked, peering intently at Valthór.

'A friend had a party that went on well into the night,' Valthór lied. 'I've a hangover and haven't slept much,' he said, so as to add a little truth to his words.

'I understand,' Guðgeir said, stepping over the threshold. 'I won't keep you long. Just a few questions. Could we sit somewhere?' The policeman's eyes scanned the untidy apartment and Valthór realised that his manners were falling short.

'Please, come inside,' He went ahead of him. 'Can I get you anything? A glass of water?'

'That would do nicely,' Guðgeir said and took a seat by the little island unit in the kitchen while Valthór turned on the cold tap.

He took the last clean glasses from the cupboard and filled them. His hands shook noticeably as he placed them on the table. He had a terrible thirst but didn't trust himself to lift a glass. He hoped the effects of the painkiller would make themselves felt, even though his sore head was only part of his trouble, as he had barely slept for days.

'Did you call the station, identifying yourself as a medium, saying that we should look out for memory sticks and investigate a man working at an assisted living facility for disabled people?' Guðgeir asked, picking up his glass in his strong hand and taking a leisurely sip of water. Valthór could feel the sweat on his body as he stood on the far side of the island. That call had been a foolish initiative on his part, but he knew there was no point in denying it.

'Yes. That was me,' he admitted in a low voice.

'In fact, we had already come across both by the time you called, but you could hardly have known that without having inside information,' Guðgeir said. Valthór shook his head.

'No, absolutely not,' he said quickly. 'I don't know anyone there.'

'So how did you know about this?' Guðgeir asked.

'Arnhildur told me.'

Valthór's mouth was so dry that he could barely form words.

'Really? When did she do that?' Guðgeir asked with unconcealed surprise.

'The night she died,' Valthór said and felt how sweet it was to tell the truth.

'Ah. Of course. You're a medium and are in close touch with the dead.' There was a slight mocking tone to his voice and Valthór couldn't be sure if this was genuine or not. 'When you called, you mentioned a red house,' Guðgeir continued.

'Yes.'

'Why?'

'She wants...' Valthór felt his tongue sticking to the roof of his mouth. With both hands, he gripped the glass of water in front of him and gulped water.

'Who?'

'Arnhildur.'

Guðgeir rested his elbows in the worktop and rested his chin on his fists. He looked at Valthór without saying a word.

He thinks I'm crazy, Valthór thought, and felt a surge of

inner discomfort. It was as if the policeman was looking right through him – or as if he was able to see through him. Valthór made an effort to pull himself together. Now there was no question of losing his grip, he had to maintain his presence.

'Well, that's something,' Guðgeir said, and drummed his fingertips on the worktop. Each fingernail hitting the surface emitted a soft click. 'Since you mentioned the red house in your call. Did you mean Arnhildur's home?'

Valthór nodded energetically.

'Yes,' he said, fully aware of what would come next.

'Are you the man who has been going into the garden at night, staring at the house?' Guðgeir asked, his fingers continuing to drum the worktop. Valthór felt that each click dug deep into his throbbing head.

'Yes,' he whispered, his voice hoarse. 'That was me.'

'Have you also been molesting women around the graveyard?' Guðgeir asked.

'No,' Valthór replied with decision, immediately assailed by doubt. What if he hadn't remembered everything?

'All right, then. So why have you been going to the red house?' Guðgeir asked. His fingers stopped drumming, his hand went to his cheek and scratched at the dark stubble.

'Because that's where it resides. Something terribly evil.'

Valthór could feel his own voice tremble, but he knew it was for the best to be truthful.

'Well, you don't say,' Guðgeir observed, clearly doubtful.

'Arnhildur calls me. Every single night. I don't sleep at all. I have to do as I'm told, I must obey,' Valthór said. A sob threatened to choke him and he fought to form the words.

'But you were at your friend's party all last night, or what?' Guðgeir asked, gazing at him with interest.

Valthór shook his head.

'No. That was a lie.'

'I had a feeling it was,' Guðgeir said. He leaned closer,

looked intently into his eyes and spoke with emphasis, as if addressing a recalcitrant teenager. 'You have to stop this, Valthór. You're frightening the people who live downstairs. This mustn't happen again.'

Valthór looked away, again trying to avoid the intensity of the policeman's gaze.

'I will try,' he said at last. 'To tell you the truth, there is nothing I desire more than an end to this.'

'Well, good. After the séance, where were you the night Arnhildur died?'

Guðgeir's voice echoed dimly and distantly in Valthór's ears. He felt his gut twist itself into a knot of fright, and it was all he could do to tell the policeman the truth.

'Here, at home. That night she came to me the first time,' he managed to gasp before he fainted.

32

'He's seriously mentally ill, that's for certain,' Særós said when Guðgeir described his visit to Valthór. She seemed so convinced that no other explanation could be entertained. He wasn't so ready to be sure of anything relating to the medium's mental condition, but he was also aware that he couldn't allow the beliefs in the supernatural that he had grown up with to cloud his logical thinking.

'And then he just fainted?' Særós asked, after having repeated practically everything Guðgeir had said to her.

'I was about to call an ambulance when he came around. Valthór was a lot more alert once he'd had some water and a few breaths of fresh air. He was completely exhausted.'

'That's hardly a surprise if the poor man's been chasing ghosts every night. He must be worn out.' Særós shook her head. 'In this job there isn't much that takes you by surprise any longer,' she added, a mischievous smile flickering across her lips.

The working day wasn't over, and they were sitting in Særós's office. Elsa Guðrún had left half an hour before, hurrying to some shop selling cheap clothes to pick up T-shirts for her twins before collecting them from school.

'Ach, there's some pink, orange, green or striped theme at their school tomorrow and I don't remember what it's about. I need to keep better track of this,' she'd groaned, rolling her eyes. 'The boys just have track suits, won't wear anything else, so days like these are a nightmare. I don't have time to mess about borrowing clothes in this or that colour. Dressing up for Ash Wednesday and Halloween is quite enough!'

'Go on. Go and sort it out,' Særós had said, raising her hands and shaking her head once Elsa Guðrún was out of the door. 'Children are just so much trouble!'

Guðgeir pretended not to have heard her, and glanced at his phone, which showed him that it was time to call it a day. They had no evidence connecting Máni to the murder, and he'd been released – for the moment, at least. The murder weapon had still not been found. Despite a painstaking search, there was no sign of the black leather button from Markús's cardigan. Guðgeir was disappointed, and not far from giving up hope.

If this was a maze, we'd be facing a dead end, he thought, turning every possibility over in his mind as he searched for a solution.

'Did the Ministry of Foreign Affairs get anywhere with tracking down Unnur's father?' he asked, scratching his chin.

'No. No reply from them,' Særós said. She reached for her laptop and began tapping at the keyboard. 'I'll send them a reminder.'

Helgi Már appeared in the doorway.

'A shame nothing more came out of this. It would've been brilliant to have nailed Máni.'

'If he's guilty of murder, you mean,' Guðgeir said.

'Yes, of course,' Helgi Már said and glanced from one to the other and back. 'There's just the two of you left?'

'No. I'm off. See you tomorrow,' Guðgeir said, getting briskly to his feet. 'And don't even think about getting any daft ideas,' he added in an undertone as he stepped past Helgi Már.

In the car, he held his phone in his hand for a moment before punching in the name of Júlíus Jónmundsson in Stykkishólmur. Júlíus had spent many years in the police but was now retired. A few years ago, a matter concerning the police had brought their paths together.

'Yes? Hello?'

The voice was weak, and hoarse.

'Hello, Júlíus. This is Guðgeir Fransson in Reykjavík .... Remember me?'

The sound of a throat being cleared could be heard down the line, turning rapidly into a forceful cough.

'Yes, of course I remember you, comrade,' Júlíus replied when he finally caught his breath. 'I'm in bed with flu right now and I'm not at my best. Won't you call later?'

'That's a shame, as I'm fishing for information. That's to say, if you trust yourself to talk for a few minutes. Stykkishólmur's not a big place and everyone knows everyone, so I thought I'd have a word with you,' Guðgeir said.

'Let's hear it,' Júlíus wheezed, and blew his nose noisily.

'Would you know an older lady called Stella? As far as I can work out, she would be Jónsdóttir,' Guðgeir said and drummed on the steering wheel with his fingertips.

'Stella? I certainly do.'

'Well, what can you tell me about her?'

'She's lived here all her life. She worked in a shop for a while but gave that up when she found other things that were more profitable.'

Júlíus croaked with laughter that soon turned into another bout of coughing.

'Ah, what would that be?' Guðgeir asked, putting the car into gear and driving off as he saw Helgi Már leaving the police station. He had no intention of giving him an opportunity to imagine that he and Særós were conducting a secret affair and that he was outside waiting for her.

'Stella Jónsdóttir is a fortune-teller, tarot cards, tea leaves, all that kind of thing. She's always busy. They say she has a real talent,' Júlíus said, sniffing.

'They? Who are they?' Guðgeir asked.

'Well, girls. They come up here in droves, even all the way from Reykjavík, to have their fortunes told. Yep, and even a few lads as well. Hold on, I have to blow my nose again.'

Guðgeir listened to a minute of deep coughs and sneezes.

'Now then, let's hear what this is about,' Júlíus said as he returned to the phone.

'Does Stella have any children?' Guðgeir asked.

'One son.'

'Who's the father?'

'No idea. Stella brought the lad up on her own.'

'How old is the son now?' Guðgeir asked.

'Couldn't tell you. Well, yes. I reckon he'd be around forty,' Júlíus replied.

'Remember his name?'

'What was his name, now? It's a good while since he left Stykkishólmur and I'm so damned forgetful when it comes to names. Hold on, it normally comes to me if I give it a little while...'

'All right, there's no great hurry,' Guðgeir assured him. 'How's the weather up there?'

'Ach. It's been lousy pretty much since New Year,' Júlíus rasped. 'Now, listen. I remember the name. He's called Valur.'

'What's his patronymic?' Guðgeir asked, drawing a deep breath. 'Do you recall?'

'No, couldn't say. At the station we sometimes used to wonder who his father was,' Júlíus replied. 'But Stella wouldn't have taken kindly to us sticking our noses into her affairs. She's not someone to make an enemy of, y'see. There's something of the night about her, the old lady.' His laughter again dissolved into a hacking cough. 'Listen, couldn't you give me a call in a day or two? By then I might have shaken off this wretched flu,' he gasped between bouts that shook him.

'Of course,' Guðgeir said. 'Get well soon, and thanks for your help.'

33

Inga had already made coffee and there was yogurt for breakfast waiting on the dining room table when Guðgeir emerged from the shower. He went to the fridge to fetch blueberries to go with it. For as long as he could remember, he had made himself two slices of buttered toast every single morning, normally with cheese on one and cold meat on the other. But Inga had mentioned that his waistline was spreading and added in passing that cutting out carbohydrates could be a step in the right direction. Now that he'd forgone his morning toast for a few weeks, his leather belt showed him the clear difference this had made, as it was now two holes tighter than it had been.

But Guðgeir mourned the smell of freshly toasted slices of bread blended with the aroma of the first coffee of the day, and in his mind this combination was the perfect recipe for getting the day off to a good start. The thought came unbidden that he could go back to his old habits, and run or swim more to keep his waistline in shape.

He heard the pealing laughter of his namesake, who came running towards him, followed by Ólöf with a flannel in her hand. Guðgeir laughed and swept up the little boy.

'Hey, little man, don't you want to wash your face?' he asked as he planted the lad on his knee. 'Have you had breakfast?'

'We already had porridge,' Ólöf replied on his behalf. 'I was up early to get his things ready. He's going to his dad after play school today.'

Guðgeir felt a pang. Ach, Dad week for little Guðgeir Jökull. Joint custody meant that the little boy spent alternate weeks with each parent. These days the arrangement was that the parent whose week was ending took him to play school, and the other would collect him. The little boy had always cried bitterly when his father, Smári, had collected him directly from Ólöf, absolutely refusing to leave. Guðgeir didn't find this at all strange, as he'd never liked Smári even though he'd always done his best to conceal his feelings about him from Ólöf and Inga, who always said that he was being cross-grained. But he'd always had a negative feeling about Smári. There was just something about him that didn't ring true, even though he generally behaved impeccably. After Ólöf had ended the relationship for the second time, Guðgeir had pressured her for details, but she was adamant that Smári had never raised a hand to her, that he wasn't a bad man, but simply unambitious and lazy. Guðgeir had wanted to add that he was also unreliable and impetuous, but decided it was best to keep that to himself. He had no doubt that Ólöf was fully aware of all of Smári's shortcomings after having twice tried to live with him. Now that possibility had presumably been exhausted and Guðgeir couldn't help being relieved.

He hugged his grandson, and gave his teddy bear a kiss as requested, before the little boy and his mother left. Moments later, college student Pétur Andri appeared, grabbed a banana and ran for the bus, his unkempt hair unbrushed. Then Guðgeir placed a kiss on Inga's lips before the door shut behind her as well. The apartment was silent. He went back to the kitchen and poured himself more coffee. It was almost nine, so it should be all right to call.

The phone rang ten times before it was picked up.

'Is that Stella Jónsdóttir?' he asked.

'That's for sure,' a sleepy voice replied.

'Hello, my name's Guðgeir Fransson and...' he said, and got no further.

'Listen, pal. I'd better let you know that I've supported all the good causes I'm going to this year, and on top of that it's rude to call this early in the morning.'

'I'm not collecting for charity. My name's Guðgeir Fransson and I'm a detective at the central criminal investigation department of the city police force.'

'That's quite something! I almost dozed off while you reeled all that off.' Stella broke into a ripple of laughter, before it seemed to dawn on her that there might be something serious behind this call. 'Has something happened?' Now there was a note of trepidation in her voice.

'No, not at all. I'm just looking for some information,' Guðgeir explained.

'Aha. About what?'

'It's a case I'm working on at the moment,' he replied. 'Tell me ... do you have a son called Valur?'

'Yes.'

'Could you give me his full name?'

'Why are you asking me when you could talk to him?' Stella asked warily.

'I'm just looking to confirm a few things, and I couldn't get hold of him,' Guðgeir said amiably. This was a departure from the truth.

'Has he done something he shouldn't?' Stella asked suspiciously, continuing before Guðgeir could respond. 'That couldn't be, because my Valur Thór is a thoroughly honest man.'

'No, not as far as I'm aware,' Guðgeir said, making an effort to sound cheerful. 'I might be in Stykkishólmur in the next day or two. Could I drop in and see you? There's a possibility that you could help me with some aspects of this case I mentioned just now.'

'Won't you tell me what this is about?' Stella asked, her

curiosity clearly piqued. 'Is this to do with the assisted living place?'

'What do you mean?' Now it was Guðgeir's turn to be curious.

'To do with the girl. Well, she's not a girl any longer,' Stella said. 'Has someone complained?'

'Actually, no.' Guðgeir did his best to maintain a normal voice. Stella's words convinced him that he would have to meet her as soon as possible. 'I understand that you have psychic talents,' he said, and clenched his teeth as he scowled. He wasn't sure if he was doing the right thing, spinning the woman a tale, but he wasn't sure what else he could say.

Stella's laugh was full of mystery.

'I've never had such an intriguing conversation so early in the morning. Come whenever you like, my friend. I'm almost always home,' she said expectantly, and Guðgeir was quick to thank her for her time, and end the call. He had barely hung up before Elsa Guðrún called to let him know she had tracked down the art dealer who had handled the sale of the painting that had hung in Arnhildur's living room. The man had tried to dissuade her from selling it, explaining that the market was slow at the moment but there was good reason to expect it would pick up later in the year.

'But Arnhildur wouldn't be persuaded,' Elsa Guðrún said. 'The painting sold quickly, for too low a price, according to the dealer. This really was an heirloom. A work by Jóhannes Kjarval.'

'And we know where the money went,' Guðgeir said in a dry tone.

'Oh, yes,' Elsa Guðrún agreed with cold sarcasm. 'Just imagine if Arnhildur had learned something about computers, if she'd spoken only a few weeks earlier to Freyja, who was so willing to show her. She'd have been able to see through the extortion and could have gone to the police.'

'Ignorance of this kind of thing can be very dangerous, but fortunately it's rare these days,' Guðgeir said. 'Did you get anything else?'

'Yes, a patrol car was called to Markús's home last autumn because of the noise from his flat,' Elsa Guðrún replied. 'Strange sounds, groans and calls, it says in the report. Markús explained the noise by saying he'd just fitted a powerful sound bar to his television and was figuring out how it worked. He promised to keep the sound down low so as not to trouble his neighbours, and it was left at that.'

'Our grey-haired friend clearly doesn't struggle with technology,' Guðgeir said. 'Who complained?'

'A neighbour who lives in the same building,' she replied. 'I'm going to take a closer look at Markús. Are you on the way in?'

'No. I won't be coming to the station today. I need to take a drive to Stykkishólmur to have a chat with our medium's mother.'

'Really? What for?' Elsa Guðrún asked in astonishment.

'To help me get a handle on him,' Guðgeir replied. 'Her name's Stella, and when I called her just now she mentioned the assisted living facility, or that's the way it sounded to me.'

'It's a long drive. Can't you just do it over the phone?' she asked, the note of surprise still in her voice.

'You know what I'm like. I need to see people face to face,' Guðgeir said.

'I know,' Elsa Guðrún said with a piercing laugh. 'Speaking of tech, have you tried Facetime?'

'Ach, you know ... I need to get a feel for people, and I don't get that well enough through a screen,' Guðgeir said.

'Well, you always do things your way. But check the weather before you go. I heard there's a strong wind forecast under Hafnarfjall,' Elsa Guðrún said.

'I'll do that,' Guðgeir replied, a little coldly, even though deep down he appreciated her thoughtfulness.

34

The wind was blowing hard as he passed Kjalarnes and gusts battered the car on the Hafnarfjall road, which was fortunately ice-free. At Borgarnes he maintained his old habit of stopping for a coffee and a sandwich. He looked up both the met office and the roads authority websites to check there were no closures for the rest of his journey. Anything could be expected at this time of year and conditions could change very fast, but the outlook appeared to be such that he had no need to worry about the rest of the trip. Guðgeir put the last piece of sandwich in his mouth, gulped down the rest of his coffee, and then scowled to himself as he remembered that bread was supposed to be off limits.

Well, too late now, he thought to himself as he zipped his coat up to his throat, leaned into the wind and ran for the car. There was low cloud and strong winds, but he still enjoyed the drive. He was at Vatnaleið when Særós called. She sounded over-stressed and impatient.

'I've been thinking things over and feel that we ought to bring Máni back in for questioning,' she said, sounding grave.

'There's nothing new since we brought him in last,' Guðgeir said. He didn't like the sound of Særós's idea, but wasn't inclined to argue against it right away.

'Try to find something. Maybe we can dig deeper into the pictures and the extortion,' Særós suggested. 'We can't continue like this. It feels like we're floundering in the dark.'

'That's the way it usually is, as you know very well,' Guðgeir said brightly. 'If we keep going, then it's pretty certain that we'll come across something that'll take us further.'

'Yes, I know that. But I still want to bring Máni in,' she said.

'We've got everything out of him already,' Guðgeir said, digging in his heels.

'It bothers me that he was so quick to admit everything,' Særós said. 'Maybe he did that to cover up something worse.'

'Could be,' Guðgeir agreed, and his breath was taken away as the cloud lifted and he could see all the way across to the north side of Breiðafjörður. It was clearly brighter on this side of Kerlingaskarð than it was on the south side of Snæfellsnes.

'Don't you think so?' Særós asked.

'What? Yes, of course I think it's worth checking it out in more depth,' Guðgeir said. 'Máni certainly had a motive to murder Arnhildur .... But I thought we'd agreed to leave him alone and to just keep an eye on him. See what turns up...'

'Ach. I don't know,' Særós said with obvious impatience. 'We can't let this case hang about inconclusively for ever. It looks like we're not doing anything.'

'We haven't been on this for that many days and the investigation is making progress,' Guðgeir said placidly.

'Too many days,' Særós said, her irritation unmistakeable. 'Where are you, anyway? I haven't seen you so far today.'

'I'll be back at the station this afternoon, but I have to do some running around to check out a few things,' Guðgeir replied.

'Which are?' Særós asked eagerly.

SHROUDED

'Nothing solid for the moment, but you'll be the first to know if I come across anything in this darkness you were talking about just now. Can we meet in the morning? Then we can go over what I'm chasing up,' Guðgeir said. 'And maybe that other matter that we were going to discuss properly,' he added.

'Ach, yes. That. Call me if you find anything. Otherwise, I'll see you in the morning,' Særós said and ended the call abruptly.

Guðgeir cruised into Stykkishólmur. He had never been here in winter and as he drove through, he was taken by how quiet the place was. It was almost midday, but there was hardly any movement to be seen, apart from one car that drove past him as he turned into the street where Stella's house was, near the top of the older part of the town. He knocked at the white door of the green-painted wooden house, which had a diamond-shaped peephole set into it. He didn't need to wait long for the door to open. It was answered by a slim woman of average height, her hair shot with grey, although it had at one time been black. She wore a wine-red woollen dress that reached to her calves and her thick hair was held in a broad black clip. A triple string of pearls hung at her neck and Guðgeir was surprised to see someone dressed like this on an ordinary weekday.

'Hello. Are you Stella?' he asked. 'I'm...'

He got no further as she finished his sentence for him by saying his name.

'I recognised the voice that called me this morning. Why have you come all the way here?'

Her earth-brown eyes looked him up and down.

'Well, I needed to get out of the city and it seemed like a good opportunity to see you in person,' Guðgeir said.

'That's bullshit. You think I can't see through you? Nobody comes all this way on a whim,' Stella snorted. 'But come inside so I can shut the door. We don't want to catch our death.'

'True enough,' Guðgeir replied with a grin as he stepped into the hall. Many coats hung on hooks and an array of ladies' shoes were lined up on the floor, along with rubber boots. He noticed a tray of business cards on a small table and made out the name 'Stella Jónsdóttir, fortunes told'.

That's remarkable, he thought.

It was as if Stella knew what he was thinking, as she answered his unasked question.

'People need to remember what name to google for,' she said, inscrutable eyes gazing at him.

35

He had somehow imagined that Stella would live surrounded by weighty, old-fashioned furniture scattered with so many knick-knacks that there would be barely an empty space to be seen, but now he sat on a newish sofa in a living room that was practically minimalist. Stella had disappeared into the kitchen to prepare coffee. Guðgeir could hear the sound of churning, followed by a loud blast of steam that put him in mind of a huge and fiendishly expensive coffee machine.

'Do you do coffee divination as well?' Guðgeir asked once he had taken a sip of coffee so good that it would have done credit to the best restaurant, then continued without waiting for an answer. 'I remember a woman who used to come to my childhood home. She was considered to be good at it and my mother's friends used to get her to tell their fortunes. My Dad said he'd never take part in anything so idiotic, as he put it, but I know she told his fortune as well when there was nobody else around to see.' Guðgeir laughed at the memory. 'If my memory's correct, you finished your cup and then it was turned three times, sunwise and widdershins.'

'Then you need to blow the sign of the cross into it. Don't forget that,' Stella said with a good-natured laugh.

'That's it. And then let it stand upside down on a radiator. Back home there'd sometimes be a row of them, and streaks of coffee running down the radiators,' Guðgeir recalled.

'Have you come here to have your fortune told?' Stella asked, looking at him intently. 'Somehow I don't think that's what you're here for, but I can read the cards for you if you like.'

Guðgeir shook his head.

'No, thank you. I wanted to talk to you about your son, Valur Thór.'

'And?'

Stella's demeanour changed instantly to one of wariness. 'Is he called Valthór?'

'By everyone but me,' she said, fidgeting nervously with her necklace. 'But why don't you speak to him? He's a grown man.'

'I'm interested in his father,' Guðgeir said bluntly.

There was nothing artificial about Stella's astonishment. 'What on earth for?'

'You might be aware that a woman was found dead recently in the Hólavellir graveyard and all the indications are that this was murder. The deceased's name was Arnhildur Drífa Friðthjófsdóttir and I'm doing my best to gather information about her and those connected to her. Arnhildur had few relatives, and just one daughter, Unnur. She's disabled, following...'

'Yes, yes. I know all that,' Stella said. 'She had a riding accident over on the south side of Snæfellsnes. Many people around here remember this. It was talked about a lot and it was all very painful.'

'Exactly,' Guðgeir agreed, getting straight to the point. 'Do they have the same father, Unnur and your son Valur Thór?'

'Ach, I had a feeling that's what brings you here,' Stella said with a heartfelt sigh. 'Has the old woman at the assisted living place been complaining?'

'Ragna? No. Why would she do that?' Guðgeir replied.

'Well, I'm concerned that Valur Thór visits Unnur a little too frequently, and the staff there aren't aware of their connection. On the other hand, I was always aware of the girl and I got to know her mother a little...' Stella fell silent for a moment. 'Unfortunately, I must say. But that's of no importance. I suppose it must be a couple of years since Valur Thór found out the truth of the matter. There had always been just the two of us, and as far as I knew, he was happy with that. So it took me by surprise when he got caught up in this newly-discovered relationship. It hadn't occurred to me that he could take it so seriously.'

'How do you know Ragna, the facility manager?'

'I've never met this person, but Valur Thór tells me that she's starting to watch him and ask questions. It seems that Unnur confuses him sometimes with someone she went to school with. She's not all there in the head, as you're maybe aware,' Stella said, and Guðgeir nodded his agreement.

'We are trying to locate her ... their father,' he said, quickly correcting himself. 'The embassy in Germany is looking into this, but to speed things up, it would be ideal to have as much information as you can provide. Apart from that, I would ask you to tell me everything you can about the deceased. She appears to have had dealings with very few people and there's not a trace of her anywhere online. That's extremely unusual these days.'

'There are more and more people who don't want to be there,' Stella said. 'Well, I'll tell you what I know...' she kicked off her slippers and pulled her legs up beneath her. Then she reached for her cup and took a sip of coffee. 'So. Where should we begin?'

'At the beginning. Isn't that best?' Guðgeir said encouragingly.

'Hey. I could do with a liqueur with this coffee,' Stella said, and was on her feet in an instant. She went to a cabinet that stood open, displaying an array of glasses and bottles. She thought for a moment, and then poured Baileys into a balloon glass. 'Y'know, you need to have something to help you through the long winter days. You can't treat yourself to anything, can you?'

'No, of course not,' Guðgeir replied quickly. He waited in anticipation for Stella to make herself comfortable on the sofa. This promised to be interesting.

An hour and a half later he was on the way back to Reykjavík. The wind had dropped considerably while he had been in Stykkishólmur, and it was an easier drive home. As he drove, he mulled over everything Stella had told him, and listened to the recording of their conversation. Stella and Jacob had got to know each other when he'd been training horses on a farm not far from where she lived. Like many people who came to Iceland from Germany, he was captivated by Icelandic horses. Stella had been working at the town's only hotel and he went there a few times for a meal. A relationship began and before long she was pregnant with Valur Þór. The young couple lived with her parents in the house that was now Stella's, and it was cramped. Jacob was an involved father, although he was always a little distant and Stella said that the boy had become closer to his grandparents than to his own father. Jacob had wanted to move to Skagafjörður in the north of the country as he felt there were more opportunities there for him to work with horses, but Stella couldn't accept the idea of moving to a place where she knew nobody.

The boy had been four when Jacob lost his job as the farm where he had been working closed down. For a while he was unemployed, which did nothing for his mental state. Then he was offered a dream job on the south side of Snæfellsnes, where Regína and Skarphéðinn ran riding tours and a riding school. Jacob moved, although he came home regularly to begin with, but Stella quickly sensed that their relationship was high and dry. Jacob became increasingly distant and spent less and less time with the boy.

'To tell the truth, I was relieved when we called it a day. It had long been over by then. Valur Thór and I stayed here, living with my parents, and then just the two of us after they passed away. I had a few boyfriends over the years, but never anything serious. I'm sure that Jacob got to know Arnhildur through her sister Regína and Skarphéðinn. He'd have been desperate for some female company out there in the countryside by the time she came for a visit, or so I imagine things must have played out. Or else he was just drunk.'

Stella paused her narrative to laugh, and Guðgeir asked why she thought that was the way it had been.

'Ach, it wasn't that Arnhildur was unattractive, just so terribly dull. I went there once so the lad could meet his father, and she was there. Dreadfully stiff and unbending, but maybe that was what attracted Jacob to her...' Stella laughed again. 'He was a German and they like to have everything in order. But, you know, my guess is that he was just drunk when it all started, and then she got pregnant and he made up his mind to do a better job with this one than with the one before. Jacob moved to Reykjavík to live with Arnhildur. Just like me, she lived with her parents, but the difference was that there was just the mother left alive there and she died quite soon after. The three of them lived there, Jacob, Arnhildur and Unnur, until he gave up and ran for it. That came as no surprise, as the poor man was so unhappy. He came to Stykkishólmur occasionally to visit Valur Thór, but Arnhildur couldn't be allowed to know about it, so it was all very secret. It seems she was jealous of me, thought I'd take him away from her. She called me once, absolutely furious, when Jacob had been to see his son. She seemed to think I was trying to entice him back!' Stella snorted at the recollection, and added that she'd had no interest in that. 'Jacob was a good-looking man when we got to know each other, but I had the feeling that he was dull ... boring, in fact. It was as if Arnhildur had sucked all the life out of him, that's the feeling I had.'

'And you never heard from him after that?' Guðgeir asked.

'Twice. There was a postcard sent to Valur Thór, saying how much he loved him. The poor boy held on to that for years like it was an heirloom. He might well still have it.'

'Where had it been sent?'

'From the Faroes, of all places,' Stella replied. 'I don't suppose he stayed there long, as the next year there was a letter with some German marks. It was that long ago it was before euros, and I remember it was a decent amount of money. Enough to buy him clothes and a bike. That was posted from Köln, so he must have gone to Germany but I've no idea if he's still there. For all I know he could be a sheep farmer in Australia or New Zealand. But apart from that, over the years Valur Thór has become increasingly bitter towards him. I keep telling him that there's no point dwelling on old hurt and he ought to let go of all this old unpleasantness. But my Valur Thór is both emotional and over-sensitive. Fortunately, we can talk about anything, so it's been a solace to him to confide in me what's troubling him.'

'Tell me, what led Valur Thór to become a medium?' Guðgeir asked.

'He's always been very sensitive in that way, which is no surprise as it runs in the family. This is naturally something he grew up with. I started telling people's fortunes a long time ago, and that's been most of my work these last few years,' Stella said. 'But Valur Thór has been very active, and he's done some sales work as well.'

Before he left, Guðgeir asked Stella if she was aware that Arnhildur had been at the séance Valur Thór held on the evening she died. It was as if Stella's earth-brown eyes widened and darkened as she replied that of course she knew – but Guðgeir could tell she was lying.

It was getting on for evening as Guðgeir drove into the

36

city. He was stiff after the long hours behind the wheel, and he decided to try out the Lágafell swimming pool in Mosfellsbær. He hadn't been there before and it seemed an ideal opportunity to try out a new pool, since he happened to be passing. After a brisk few lengths, a couple of spells in the hot tub and then the steam bath and a long shower, he left the pool rejuvenated.

In the car he reached into the glove compartment to retrieve his phone and scanned the unread emails and messages. He put the phone aside and was about to drive off when he noticed one of the country's best-loved sportswomen walking past, with Særós. They were laughing and joking, clearly happy in each other's company. He hadn't seen Særós look so cheerful for a long time – if ever. Guðgeir put his fingertips to his forehead, covering his face with his hand as they strolled past. He was not so much concealing himself, but had the feeling that he was observing a scene he wasn't supposed to witness. There was nothing logical about this, but it was still a strong feeling. Then he saw the two women walk towards the swimming pool, watched as their hands touched, their eyes met and their fingers were entwined for a moment before they went through the doors. He sat in the car for a while before setting off. Særós had been absent-minded and out of sorts recently. Could what he had just seen be the reason? It was a long time since he had seen Særós so cheerful – even happy – as he had just now. He'd been determined to speak to her and get her to open up about her feelings, but now he wasn't sure that was the right thing to do. Her private life was nobody's business, not even his, even though they'd worked together for so long and were close enough to share confidences – or so he'd thought.

*

The following morning Guðgeir was at his desk early. He fetched strong coffee, sat at his computer and started the day with a video call to Ragna at the assisted living facility. After that he began collating all of the information that had emerged from his visit to Stella. He'd written only a few lines when Elsa Guðrún appeared in the doorway.

'Aren't we meeting in Særós's office?' she asked.

'We are,' Guðgeir replied. 'I just need to make a few notes before the meeting. I'll be with you in five minutes.'

'She isn't there. I checked,' Elsa Guðrún said. 'And it's almost nine o'clock.'

'Just take a seat. She must have nipped out of her office for a moment,' Guðgeir said, without looking up from the screen.

A few minutes later he sauntered across to Særós office, where Elsa Guðrún sat alone.

'Særós still isn't here,' she said, and it was clear from the look on her face that she was concerned. 'Should we give her a call?'

'Is that really necessary? It's still early,' Guðgeir replied and checked his phone for a message from Særós, but there was nothing to be seen.

'Now I'm going to call her. It's nine-thirty and Særós is never late. Maybe she's had an accident somewhere. She could have fallen off her bike or twisted her ankle while she was out running.'

SHROUDED

'Let's give her another five minutes,' Guðgeir said, suspecting that the reason for her absence could this time be down to something other than her passion for fitness.

'Does she do cold water swimming in winter as well?' Elsa Guðrún asked, her big blue eyes widening. 'Imagine if she had cramp in the cold and couldn't make it back to the beach.' She shuddered at the thought. 'It's awful. You lose the use of your legs as they go into spasm, terrible...' she said, then the words died on her lips as Særós appeared and strode to her desk.

She quietly apologised that for certain reasons she'd been delayed, without elaborating on what those reasons might be. Guðgeir remained expressionless, his eyes on the notes in front of him, while Elsa Guðrún watched as Særós opened her computer and scanned the more pressing messages.

'Well, anything new?' she asked as she finally looked up from the screen.

'Yes, just a bit,' Guðgeir replied, and recounted the previous day's events. 'Ragna confirmed, after seeing a picture of Valthór, that he visits Unnur at the facility where she's a resident. I informed Ragna that they're half-siblings. That certainly took her by surprise.

'She's not the only one. That hadn't occurred to me,' Særós said, her brow furrowed. 'In your notes you say that Valthór had become increasingly bitter over the years towards his father.'

'Yes, because he paid him practically no attention,' Guðgeir explained.

'Arnhildur, the new woman in his life, didn't want them to be in touch. Is that right?' Elsa Guðrún asked. 'Then a little baby was born and all the attention was on her.'

'So it's quite possible to conclude that Valthór, or Valur Thór as his real name is, could have harboured a hatred toward Arnhildur for taking his father from him?' Særós mused.

'Stella made it clear enough that their relationship was over, or as good as over, by the time Arnhildur made an appearance,' Guðgeir added.

'There's no certainty that Valthór saw things that way,' Elsa Guðrún said. 'It seems to me worth checking this in detail. He had a reason to hold a grudge...'

'But we have no evidence,' Guðgeir broke in.

'We'll find that if we keep a close enough eye on him,' Særós said firmly, adjusting her stiffly ironed collar. 'What about Valthór and Máni? Could there be a link between them?'

'I asked Ragna and she had no knowledge of any link,' Guðgeir said, pushing his glasses up his nose. 'I'll pay a visit to the Spiritualist Society and find out what they think of Valthór. I need to understand him better.'

'Don't forget that there was a book of theirs in the drawer of Arnhildur's bedside table,' Elsa Guðrún said.

'Quite right. And there was also an advert from an estate agent. I spoke to him and there was nothing conclusive. But speak to him again, Elsa Guðrún, and would you also track down the cleaner sent by the city's social services? Don't bother calling or emailing. Just go to the right places. That always works better, as you know. We're looking for a needle in a haystack here, if you know what I mean.'

Elsa Guðrún needed no prompting, leaving Guðgeir in Særós's office. She gave him an inquiring look.

'As I mentioned the other day, Særós, I don't get the impression that you've been feeling your usual self,' he said, choosing his words with care. 'To be honest, I've been genuinely concerned about you. It even occurred to me that you were struggling with some illness, but now things appear clearer and I prefer to be open. You know well that's the way I am.'

Guðgeir watched Særós for a reaction, but she sat impassively, lips pursed and her arms folded.

'So, yesterday I stopped off on the way home from

Snæfellsnes for a swim in Mosfellsbær, and I couldn't help seeing you and your friend,' he continued. 'Your personal life is of course no business of mine. But I'm very fond of you and it was particularly pleasant to see how happy you looked yesterday,' he said and paused before taking the bull by the horns. 'I know your friend is gay and I saw you were holding hands .... So I wondered if...'

'Yeah, OK. She's a well-known lesbian,' Særós interrupted.

'Like I said, your private life is your own affair, but as your longstanding colleague and friend, I can't pretend nothing's wrong when I see you're not feeling well,' Guðgeir said, and immediately felt a stab of regret at involving himself in Særós's personal life. He should have kept quiet, but it was too late now so he tried to make up for it. 'If you want to keep this to yourself, then you can consider that I've forgotten it the moment I walk out of the door. You can trust...' he said, but got no further.

'You're absolutely right, Guðgeir. It's none of your business,' Særós said. She looked angry, but her expression softened as she looked at him. 'But, thinking about it, it's probably for the best that you saw us last night. I've known this for a long time, but this is my first proper relationship...' She paused. 'Well, the only one.'

'It is something to hide?' Guðgeir asked, elated by the trust she showed in him. 'You're an adult and there's plenty in this world that's more complicated than homosexuality. It's everywhere these days and there are all sorts of people, so gay...' He stopped himself, deciding that he needed say no more as he couldn't be sure what the right reaction would be, concerned that saying the wrong thing could hurt her at a sensitive moment. 'I mean, these are feelings you've been suppressing for years.'

Særós's fingers twisted themselves into knots, and she fiddled with her rings. It was obvious that what she had kept so long to herself was not easy to talk about.

'Yes. And it was starting to do damage,' she admitted

after a moment's pause. 'I've been with men but never had the feeling it was right for me .... That was just self-deception.' She looked directly into Guðgeir's eyes and her sincerity was clear. 'This is the first time and I don't know if it will last, but I don't want to lose her. She lives overseas, she's a professional player and...'

'I hope it lasts, but maybe you ought to get to know more gay women,' said Guðgeir, who was forever focused on finding the right solutions, but now he wanted to bite off his own tongue after those last few words. He was finding this conversation increasingly uncomfortable.

'I don't know any. As you know, I'm not the most sociable of people. I work hard, work out twice a day, and occasionally meet the few relatives I can bothered to stay in touch with,' Særós said.

'There are all kinds of groups, associations...' Guðgeir began before she cut him off.

'I can't be doing with everything that comes with it ... I've looked at their websites, thousands of times, believe me, and that's simply not for me. It's too much trouble. I'm not that type.'

'What do you mean by that?' Guðgeir asked. Now he failed to understand.

'Ach, you know. The striped flag on the wall, the bracelet on your wrist. Having to turn up at Gay Pride, go to certain bars, be endlessly woke and with opinions on everything between heaven and earth. That's not me, you understand?'

'There's no need for all that,' Guðgeir told her, without being certain of his ground, but glanced at the wall where the week's aphorism still hung.

'Yes, there is. It's part of the package,' Særós assured him, shaking her immaculately coiffured head in emphasis. 'You have to define yourself as belonging in a particular box, and there are a lot of them. I'd end up in some lipstick group!'

'You don't need to do all that,' Guðgeir said earnestly.

'Who says so?'

'Society, the internet ... we live in an age of definitions. I can't be bothered with all the crap that's part of being openly queer. I'm not prepared to be pigeon-holed, given a classification, if you see what I mean. I don't want to be queer. I just want to be me, without having to discuss all this stuff with people.'

'Sure. But can't you do just that? Særós, I understand that you want to do your best in life, but you don't have to excel at everything.'

'Maybe, but then I feel I'd be betraying the whole gay community and all those who came before,' she explained in a dull tone. 'All the sacrifices and all the work that others have made.'

'Særós, it's not a world I know, but I feel that you're over-complicating things for yourself,' Guðgeir replied. 'I'm prepared to bet anything you like that in this there's no need to keep a spreadsheet of achievement and progress. Could I be right?'

'I don't know. I just want to do things well,' Særós sighed. 'Do the right thing.'

'You're not a public figure,' Guðgeir pointed out.

'True. I know I'm inclined to over-think things, and that's just the way I am,' Særós said, looking him in the eye. 'I need to take everything all the way.'

'Then it's a journey you're embarked on, and on your own terms,' Guðgeir said and placed a hand on her shoulder. 'Now it's just onwards and upwards.'

'Now you're getting poetic,' Særós told him, a shadow of a smile on her lips.

37

From behind the black curtain, Valthór watched the people as they made their way into the hall. He carefully inspected each one. He did his best to draw himself a picture of each personality based upon their manner, appearance and movements. He was a good reader of people, sensitive to both those around him and his environment. He also had the sight, as it was referred to, but unfortunately, he couldn't always trust his talents. It was difficult, and hopefully it wouldn't fail him tonight. Now they were all present, all but one, someone called Magnús who had been the last to sign up. Valthór glanced at the clock and saw that it was ten past eight, and time to get on with the routine stuff. First he would ask people to take a seat, then light the candles, say a few well-chosen words, and then fall into a trance – if he could, considering the state he was in. In that case, he'd have to wing it. He muttered a few encouraging words to himself and stepped out from behind the black curtain. They looked at him expectantly and Valthór sensed the tension in the air. Maybe it would be fine tonight. He went to the door to lock it, just as it opened abruptly and a grey-haired older man came in. Valthór felt his heart skip a beat. There was a cold aura about this man, and he had seen him before. This was Markús who had sat next to Arnhildur and then accompanied her out of the building on the last night of her life. He felt a sudden powerlessness and it was all he could do to not let show how much he'd been taken by surprise. He hurried over to Markús and whispered to him.

'You didn't sign up for this evening.'

'Yes, I did,' the grey-haired man said, glaring at him.

'I was expecting someone called Magnús.'

'That should be Markús. You must have misread the name,' the man retorted firmly and took a seat. Valthór shivered.

The meeting went badly. Valthór was unable to make any connection and felt a cold draught steal around him from every direction. He tried to tell the young man that he should choose the course of study that suited his aspirations, as that would bring him happiness, but the man replied that he'd already completed the studies in which he had an interest, and was fully satisfied on that score. Valthór heard a low sniggering around the room, which made everything even more difficult for him. After struggling for a while to overcome the insurmountable, he gave up and told the people he wasn't well. Normally he was able to keep his talents under some control, but not tonight, unfortunately. He was no doubt falling ill and meant to get himself to bed as soon as possible.

'I'll reimburse you all and you can take your envelopes on the way out,' he said, and again apologised. The people left, one by one, with the exception of the grey-haired man. Valthór again felt a discomfort at the man's presence, but acted as if nothing were amiss and pottered around putting the hall to rights.

'You don't need to wait for me,' Valthór said, forcing a smile.

'Surely that's for the best, if you're unwell,' Markús replied.

'There's absolutely no need,' Valthór assured him.

'It's not a problem,' Markús said and his expression was of sincere willingness to help.

'Well, fair enough,' Valthór said, even though it was

completely against his wishes. He pulled on his boots and put on his coat, hat and gloves, and wound a scarf carefully around his neck. The two men went out in the evening darkness.

'Does the ability often fail you at this kind of meeting?' Markús asked as they emerged onto Bergstaðastræti. Valthór shook his head.

'I wouldn't say so,' he muttered, his eyes on the ground. He could feel his own rapid heartbeat and a discomfort in his chest.

'That's just as well. It must be awkward to have promised people contact with the other side, and then there's no connection! Every line down!' Markús said and barked with unpleasant laughter.

'I never promise anything. I'm a conduit and have no control over this,' Valthór replied drily. This Markús was unbearably pushy, and he couldn't bear the man's presence a moment longer. 'Look, there's no need for you to come with me. I'm not sick. To be honest, I'd prefer to be alone.'

Markús made no reply and it occurred to Valthór that he had either not heard him, or else he was deliberately ignoring his request. He was about to repeat his words, when Markús broke the silence.

'As you're a clairvoyant, you must know what happened to the woman who was found dead after your séance?' he said, his tone bordering on belligerence.

'I've no idea,' Valthór mumbled, again wracked by a shudder.

'The two of you knew each other,' Markús stated in the same assertive tone.

Valthór shook his head vehemently.

'No,' he gasped.

'Well, hope you get better soon,' Markús sneered, and turned into a side street.

Valthór felt an almost palpable relief. He stopped, and

watched the man disappear into the distance. Then he took a deep breath and hoped that his heartbeat would settle. He counted to five every time he breathed in, and exhaled just as slowly. After repeating this exercise several times, he felt that he was again ready to continue. The cold nipped at his face and streetlamps cast a dim glow into the gloom. He saw nobody as he crossed Lækjargata, heading for the Tjörn bridge. Suddenly a bus appeared from the blackness, taking him uncomfortably by surprise. He saw that the only person on the bus was the driver, which was just as well, since his driving style would have been a danger to any passenger on board. An illustration from a well-known children's book his mother had often read for him as a boy came to mind. This was Palle, who had dreamed he was alone in the world, driving a bus. A strange feeling took hold of him as he felt he was experiencing someone else's memories. He walked along Skothúsvegur, accompanied by this odd sensation. As he approached Tjarnargata he saw a young man lock his car and run up the steps to the door of a large, white-painted house. He heard light footsteps and the low sound of a door closing. Everything was again silent.

Valthór again felt his heart beat erratically and his breathing became laboured. The events of the evening had certainly been difficult for him, and he felt a deep exhaustion take hold of him as his body was drained of energy. Each step was an effort and the snow that clung to the soles of his winter boots made them as heavy as lead. A little way along Suðurgata he had no choice but to pause and lean against the cold graveyard wall. His breath came in irregular gasps and he stared at the grey concrete wall. Surely this unearthly feeling would pass?

He heard his name whispered and lifted himself upright to see who had spoken. He peered into the faint glow from the streetlight across the road, but there was nobody to be seen. Again, he heard his name whispered, and this time he saw an indistinct outline in front of him. Valthór stood stupefied as the figure took shape.

'Come,' Arnhildur said. 'Follow me.'

His heart screamed at him to say no, and he fought back, but it was useless. Some inexplicable power forced him to allow himself to be led. Against his will, he went along the graveyard wall to the black iron gate. A piercing squeak carried through the quiet of the evening as he opened it and he went into the dark graveyard.

38

It hadn't been easy, but Elsa Guðrún had obtained the names of the two women who had cleaned Arnhildur's house at various times. The member of the city's social services staff who had dealt with Elsa Guðrún's request assured her that there had been only these two. Her conversation with the first of these two women had gone badly, as this was someone who spoke only her native language, and Elsa Guðrún had only Icelandic and English at her disposal. Speaking to the second cleaner was a better experience, as in addition to her own language, Molda spoke decent Icelandic. She was shocked into silence when Elsa Guðrún told her what had happened to Arnhildur.

'Terrible! Terrible!' Molda repeated to herself, again and again. She brushed away tears from her cheeks and Elsa Guðrún handed her a tissue. Then she waited patiently for an opportunity to ask her about Arnhildur.

'She was happy with my work but said she couldn't keep me on because she had to save money. I was very sad, because I liked cleaning Arnhildur's house. There was no rubbish lying around, but she couldn't do the cleaning herself because she had arthritis,' Molda said, holding out her hands to demonstrate where Arnhildur's pain made itself felt. As far as Elsa Guðrún could see, Molda suffered from the same complaint, as her fingers were both swollen and twisted.

'Terrible to die like that. Poor Arnhildur. I didn't think

such things happened in Iceland,' Molda continued, but wasn't able to provide any further information, so Elsa Guðrún thanked her for her time and made her way back to the car.

The estate agent was located in the western part of the city and Elsa Guðrún had arranged to meet Ívar at precisely two o'clock. When she'd spoken to him that morning, he remembered the two-storey red house clearly.

'A very promising property that we would very much like to offer for sale,' Ívar said.

The office was quiet when Elsa Guðrún arrived. A young woman sat at the reception desk, fair hair parted in the centre and pulled back into a precise ponytail. She asked Elsa Guðrún to wait for a moment and pressed a button on a machine somewhere with the tip of a long, purple gel nail.

'She's here, Dad,' she said, sounding formal and looking inquisitively at Elsa Guðrún.

'Show her in,' a voice replied through the machine.

'He'll see you now,' the young woman announced. 'It's the third door on the right.'

The door to Ívar's office was open, and he turned out to be younger than Elsa Guðrún had expected, no more than forty-five. This was a mousy-haired man of average height, with heavy dark eyebrows that she immediately longed to trim. He wore a pricy brand of jeans and a light sweater with a collar neck.

'My daughter,' he said with a grin, as he stood up and greeted Elsa Guðrún with a firm handshake. 'She decided to take a break from her studies and this is her second day working here.'

'I see,' Elsa Guðrún said, returning his smile.

Ívar offered coffee and a seat. She accepted both, making herself comfortable on a soft leather sofa.

'This house has been discussed many times here, and we've several times looked over the plans and estimated the value. Once it was actually advertised, but then it was almost immediately withdrawn,' he said. 'The owners hadn't been able to agree how to deal with this. These are two sisters, one of whom lives in the property and the other doesn't. The one who lives there is reluctant to sell. I have the feeling that this is a person who struggles to cope with change. Some people are like that, that's just the way it is. You said you were investigating a death. One of these people?'

'Yes. Arnhildur. The sister who lived in this house,' Elsa Guðrún replied. 'The one you just mentioned.'

'That's unpleasant. What on earth happened?' Ívar asked, apparently taken by surprise.

'Unfortunately, I can't tell you, and I wish I could,' Elsa Guðrún replied honestly. 'We're investigating the case.'

'I see,' Ívar said, taking a seat at his desk and turning to a computer screen of the latest type. 'Hold on, I just want to look the place up to be certain. I had no idea this was so serious, otherwise I'd have ... there must be some documentation here.'

Elsa Guðrún crossed her legs and took out her phone while Ívar searched through his database. She checked her messages for anything new, but there was nothing. The sofa was comfortable and Ívar's office was pleasantly warm. She felt how tired she was and longed to close her eyes for a little while. Her boys had needed to catch up on homework, and it hadn't been easy to keep these energetic lads focused. Once they were asleep, after a demanding tussle with mathematics, she'd still been up long after midnight cleaning and tidying.

'Yes, yes, quite right,' Ívar muttered. 'More than I thought.'

'How so?' Elsa Guðrún asked, startled from her dozy thoughts.

'Arnhildur owned a sixty percent share of the property, while the other forty percent is owned by her sister and brother-in-law. The house had previously been owned by the sisters' parents, so I don't understand why they didn't have equal shares, but I suppose there must be some explanation for that. The couple wanted to sell, but the sister living in the house didn't. Relations between these two parties were very strained. I tried to convince Arnhildur to sell just the lower storey, which came to slightly more than forty per cent of the property, so she could hold on to the upper floor and the space in the basement that hadn't been fitted out. That would have sorted out the issue and she would have been free of this endless arguing, but she wouldn't have it. She wouldn't even discuss it.'

Ívar shook his head, and a look of frustration flashed across his face.

'When was this?' Elsa Guðrún asked, wide awake, with any thoughts of closing her eyes banished.

'Regína and Skarphéðinn last came to see me around a year ago. At their request, I called Arnhildur several times, but she wouldn't budge.'

'Had they been in touch with you before?'

'Yes, at least three or four times. But at quite long intervals,' Ívar replied.

'But you didn't recall these people right away when I asked,' Elsa Guðrún said, fixing the estate agent with an inquiring look as he calmly leaned back in his chair.

'You know, I'd have a superhuman memory if I were able to remember every single person who had come here or been in touch,' he laughed.

'Yes, but all this unpleasantness between them...'

'How many apartments and houses do you imagine I sell that are subject to some kind of divorce or inheritance dispute? If only you knew ... it's unbelievable how nuts people can be. You see, as soon a sale has been concluded, then I clear everything to do with it from my mind.'

'But this was one that wasn't concluded,' Elsa Guðrún

pointed out, realising that now she was being more pushy than necessary.

'No, because it never came to anything. There isn't even a folder for this on the computer, just a few notes,' Ívar replied, and was now beginning to look less comfortable in his chair.

'There was an advertisement, a flyer, from this estate agency found at the home of the deceased. Your name had been underlined. Do you have any explanation for that?' Elsa Guðrún persisted.

Up to now, all of Ívar's answers had been quick, but this time he hesitated.

'No, I don't. I've never set foot inside this apartment. The advertisement was prepared around two years ago, in three different versions. That's for visual media, radio, and the flyer that you can see here, and which was put through people's letter boxes around the city, including in the western part. I suppose it must have come through Arnhildur's door at that time?'

Elsa Guðrún was mentally forming her next question when her phone pinged an alert. This was from Guðgeir, asking her to call, or come to the station right away. She thanked Ívar for his helpfulness, and left. As soon as the door closed behind her, she called Guðgeir, who told her that his attention had been drawn to something that had come up overnight.

'This could have passed us by, as it was a new recruit who took the statement,' Guðgeir said. 'Someone who isn't aware of what we're working on.'

'What statement are you talking about?' Elsa Guðrún asked impatiently.

'Valthór's statement. He was picked up during the night at Arnhildur's house,' Guðgeir replied. 'The three of them who rent the basement flat were all at home and this time they were quick and managed to get pictures of him. They even went out into the garden and spoke to him, but he was deep in a conversation with some invisible being. It seems that Skúli was very agitated, accused Valthór of threatening behaviour, and wanted to make a formal complaint.'

'Skúli, that's the hairdresser?' Elsa Guðrún asked.

'That's him,' Guðgeir confirmed. 'I've just finished reading the statement Valthór gave last night, and it's very bizarre. His answers are more or less nuts.'

'Was he under the influence?'

'No. He was tested, and had consumed neither alcohol nor drugs.'

'And where is he now?' Elsa Guðrún asked. 'Was he released?'

'Yes. He had simply not done anything illegal, so he's presumably at his home, getting some rest after the night's adventures,' Guðgeir said.

'It didn't occur to them to take him to hospital?' Elsa Guðrún asked.

'I don't know about that ... at any rate, it's not mentioned in the report.'

'Did you get anything out of the Spiritualist Society?'

'Yes, they said Valthór had no longer been able to pay for the use of their facilities, so his membership lapsed automatically. They said he'd received excellent training from them, and for the first few years he did well, but then he did less well and his popularity dropped off.'

'What was it that didn't work out for him?' Elsa Guðrún asked.

'According to what the Spiritualist Society told me, his séances became poorer, and he could no longer cope with one-to-one sessions,' Guðgeir said. 'But they maintain that he has talent as a medium, it's just that he doesn't cope well enough with his own capabilities. He was all over the place, unstable, to use their own words.'

'Ha! Exactly!' Elsa Guðrún said sardonically. 'People can be so crazy.'

'Agreed,' Guðgeir said, placing no emphasis on the word. 'Are you far away?'

'No, on the way,' she replied.

'Good. I'll be waiting when you get here,' Guðgeir said. 'I feel we need to pay the medium a visit, as soon as possible.'

39

Valthór had managed to sleep for around three hours in the morning, after having spent half the night at the police station, where he had done his best to answer some schoolboy of a policeman's idiotic questions. To begin with, he'd tried to explain what he'd been doing late at night in the garden of the red house, that forces beyond his understanding had drawn him there, but then the boy in uniform's questions had become so ridiculous that he replied with random answers, or simply laughed like a madman. By that point his nerves were stretched so taut that this was all he was capable of. But now he felt better. He'd slept a little, taken a shower and ordered a pizza, since the fridge was bare. Once he'd eaten something and relaxed properly, he'd go and see his old colleagues at the Spiritualist Society. Since this last incident, he was determined to take the step he'd been seriously considering ever since Arnhildur's death. It was clear to him that this couldn't continue, that he no longer had any control over his own capabilities. He would have to shut himself away and completely end any work as a medium. Now that the decision had been taken, he was hoping that matters could be concluded as promptly as possible.

The doorbell rang, and he picked up his phone so he could pay the pizza delivery at the door. He pulled the door briskly open, asking 'how much?' as he did so. Then he was startled by the sight of two police officers. He instantly recognised the tall, calm man with the dark complexion who had not only visited him before, but who had also gone to see his mother in Stykkishólmur. This was Guðgeir Fransson. Valthór recalled having seen the woman before, but couldn't bring her name to mind, which was disconcerting as he'd always been able to trust his memory perfectly.

'What are you looking for now?' he groaned, feeling overwhelmed. His heart hammered and he felt ready to faint with fear. Had this Markús spoken to the police?

'Just a chat. Could we come in?' the woman asked, giving him a smile. She was on the petite side, with a broad face and eyes as blue as the sky. Her thick brown hair was drawn loosely into ponytail.

There was clearly no point refusing, so he mumbled his agreement, standing aside so they could pass through the narrow hallway. He was about to shut the door behind them when the delivery guy arrived, with a piping hot sixteen-inch pizza in his hands. The man looked at the three of them in surprise, handed Valthór his pizza and held out the payment terminal, a suspicious look on his face. Valthór paid without a word, shut the door and gestured for the police officers to go in.

'Please, go ahead and eat while we talk,' the woman said, and now Valthór remembered that her name was Elsa Guðrún. He placed the box on the island unit, opened it and pulled free a large slice. He'd been looking forward to this, but now his appetite had vanished and he forced himself to take a bite. He needed the energy and had to appear normal.

'Would you like some?' he said quietly, wiping his hands on a serviette.

'No, thanks,' they replied, almost in unison, and sat down on the only sofa in the living room. Guðgeir took his spectacle case from a pocket, opened it and began painstakingly polishing the lenses, while Elsa Guðrún sat still, watching him eat.

This is so awkward, Valthór thought, chewing as if his life depended on it. The pizza base was tough, the olives were tasteless and the pepperoni stuck to his teeth.

'What do you want to talk about?' Valthór asked when he had forced down a whole slice of pizza. Guðgeir put on his glasses and looked at him with interest before speaking.

'I gave a statement last night, and promised not to go near the house again,' Valthór said. 'As far as I'm able to control my own movements.'

'What do you mean by that?' Elsa Guðrún asked.

'I could walk in my sleep,' Valthór replied.

'You're a sleepwalker?' she said.

Valthór wasn't sure what answer to give. If he were to say yes, then that would be a plausible explanation of his night-time wanderings that only those with no understanding of the unpalpable would take as fully valid. He decided to take the more difficult choice and tell the truth.

'The times I've been to the red house, I've been between sleep and wakefulness. It's a terrible waking nightmare, and I've been led there by Arnhildur,' he said, and noticed that Elsa Guðrún looked quickly down, taking hold of her ponytail and running her hand down it repeatedly as if smoothing the hair, although Valthór knew she was doing this to hide the smile on her face.

'So she comes to you,' Guðgeir said, his note neutral. 'Aside from that, we are now aware that there are closer connections between you and the late Arnhildur that you hadn't mentioned, as her daughter Unnur is your half-sister. Why didn't you tell us that right away?' he asked, and Valthór felt the weight of the policeman's gaze on him. He decided that it was best to not say anything.

'That's correct, isn't it?' Guðgeir reiterated.

'Ye-es,' Valthór muttered.

'We're also aware that you've had money problems, which is something you and Arnhildur had in common.'

Guðgeir sat up straight on the sofa, and leaned forward. His gaze remained fixed on Valthór. 'Could you have found a way out of your own difficulties by abusing your relationship with your sister?'

'What do you mean?' Valthór could hear the tremor in his own voice.

'The two of you were in this together. You and Máni Sölvason, former employee at the assisted living facility,' Elsa Guðrún said. 'You got Unnur to carry out sexual acts, and the two of you took photos and videos.'

'No! Absolutely not! What is this bullshit?' Valthór said in distress, his voice rising. 'How on earth can you imagine such a thing? I would never do anything to harm Unnur!'

'You haven't known each other long, have you?' Guðgeir asked. 'But long enough for you to know that nobody would believe her if she were to speak up, because she frequently confuses fiction with reality.'

Valthór was at a loss. These cops had found the pictures and had totally misunderstood. How could this have happened? This had all been twisted around and he'd completely lost control of events. He felt the tears trickle down his cheeks and tasted the saltiness as he opened his mouth to try and explain.

'You're jealous of her?' Elsa Guðrún suggested, before he'd been able to say a word, staring at him with those bright blue eyes. Valthór could sense that at some point something bad had happened to her. He also had a strong feeling that she would do everything in her power to prevent the same thing happening to anyone else.

'No!'

'And her mother? Arnhildur? Were you jealous of her?' Elsa Guðrún rasped.

'Maybe, but only back when I was a child,' he replied honestly.

Elsa Guðrún asked no more questions. They were both silent, watching him. Valthór held his head in his hands and looked down at the floor. It would be as well to make a clean breast of it. He no longer had anything to lose, and in any case he'd decided to shut all this down and have nothing to do with the otherworld sorcery. Valthór the medium was gone, his last séance had been held. Now he needed help to deal with his experiences and then get onto the job market.

It was time to put his cards on the table and he began to tell them the whole thing – everything – how he had visited Unnur at the assisted living facility, forged a connection with her and became deeply fond of her. After all, with the exception of his mother, she was his closest relative. Then Arnhildur had heard about these visits and contacted him. She hadn't objected to his visiting Unnur, as it wasn't as if she had many visitors, and made sure to protect her. One day Arnhildur asked him to meet her. She had been deeply depressed, in a very bad way, and she told him about she was the victim of extortion but wouldn't say who was behind it. Arnhildur told him that if she didn't pay a certain amount on five or six occasions, then revolting pictures of Unnur would be distributed on the internet. She'd already been through her entire savings, had sold a painting and the car was about to be sold. The news shocked Valthór, especially that Arnhildur was forced to sell the car, as Unnur particularly enjoyed being taken out for a drive. He'd wanted to do everything he could to help her.

'Didn't it occur to you to go to the police?' Guðgeir asked, looking grave.

'No. Arnhildur was adamant. Not least because of my sister Unnur's disability. It's bad enough for a fully healthy person to go through that kind of experience, let alone someone with a serious disability who sometimes gets fiction mixed up with reality,' Valthór said and fell silent, staring at his hands.

'What happened next?' Guðgeir asked, and now his deep voice was soothingly mild.

'At first I felt there was nothing I could do, as I was broke myself, but after thinking things over it occurred to me to ask Arnhildur to attend a séance...' Valthór said and paused. The sobs rising in his throat prevented him from continuing.

'Tell us the whole story,' Elsa Guðrún said, gazing at him sympathetically.

'I hadn't been doing well and my séances had become pretty uneventful. Spirits weren't coming through and people weren't satisfied. I explained to Arnhildur and after a while she agreed to come to liven things up.' Valthór drew a shuddering breath. 'It only needed one time for things to start doing better and for attendance to increase. Of course, Arnhildur didn't come to every session, but we had done this a few times. She tried to dress and do her hair differently each time, which wasn't easy for her as she was so deeply set in her ways. But I have to admit, she had some talent for acting. We were about to stop this when she died. We were determined to find some other way to bring in money, as we couldn't afford to try this trick too often in such a small place, and then...' Valthór said, unable to continue.

'Arnhildur was murdered on the way home from one of your séances?' Guðgeir said, finishing his sentence for him.

'Yes. And since then she hasn't left me in peace,' he said, wiping beads of sweat from his forehead.

'What do you mean?' Elsa Guðrún asked.

'She comes to me practically every night and demands that I go with her,' Valthór said. His voice quavered and he looked at them beseechingly. He noticed that Elsa Guðrún discreetly rolled her eyes. 'You have to believe me,' he added feebly.

'What does she want from you?' Guðgeir asked, and Valthór sensed his sincerity.

'Arnhildur leads me to the place where she died, and

then to the red house. She stands close to it, where the shrubs are, points and says something I'm not able to discern, but I know it's something evil. She talks constantly and her hands are animated. Arnhildur has a purple aura, which I interpret as guilt. I have the feeling she wants to make amends, to fix something. I feel terrible when Arnhildur comes and wants me to accompany her. I push back, but she has great power, prevents me from sleeping and takes away my own will. So I have no choice but to follow in her footsteps and experience what she went through. Over the last few days I've genuinely been wondering if I'm losing my mind,' Valthór said and looked up to see that both of them appeared to be taking him seriously.

'This was an idiotic idea of mine to add a little spice to séances that had become pretty dull. It didn't make much money, but it was still something towards helping Arnhildur, who was in despair. So it was Máni who abused Unnur? Her mother would never give me the person's name, just said it was a man.'

'He's admitted it and can expect to be prosecuted,' Guðgeir replied. 'We found several memory sticks in Arnhildur's home, and from that point it was straightforward.'

'Memory sticks? What do you mean?' Valthór asked in confusion.

'Arnhildur had very little understanding of technology. Máni showed her some pictures and then put them onto a memory stick. She bought those from him, in the belief that she was paying for the pictures to not fall into anyone else's hands.'

'I don't understand any of this!' Valthór wailed.

'That's understandable,' Guðgeir replied. 'I'll try to explain. Look, your mother Stella no doubt took pictures of you with a camera and then sent the film to be developed. Maybe twelve pictures, which then went into an album.'

'Yes, of course I remember. I'm not that young,' Valthór said, making an effort to smile.

'If the film was destroyed, then it wasn't possible to produce more pictures. As we understand it, Arnhildur was under the impression that once a picture had been put onto a memory stick, then it was no longer on the computer, which was a complete misunderstanding and for her it was an expensive misunderstanding,' Guðgeir said.

Valthór could hardly speak and felt a wave of anger sweep through every nerve in his body. Just how much of an idiot could that old fool of a woman have been to let herself be tricked like that?

'I don't know what to say …. I was certain that the pictures … I'd never have got involved if I'd known.' Valthór shook his head and he felt suddenly hot. How could she have been so stupid?

'Not so much stupid, as fixed in her ways and conservative, but the day before her death she discovered exactly this,' Elsa Guðrún said.

Valthór glanced from one to the other.

'But she still came to the séance,' he said.

'It's possible that she wanted to keep to what she had agreed, or that she wanted to help you out as you'd been prepared to help her,' Guðgeir said. 'That's what comes to mind, although we can't know. It's just a possibility.'

'This Máni who abused Unnur and extorted money from Arnhildur … is he the one who assaulted her in the graveyard?' Valthór felt himself compelled to ask, although he had no expectation of a clear answer.

'He was expecting more money from her and there's no evidence in that respect, but we aren't excluding anything,' Guðgeir said as he got to his feet. 'Any more than you, who don't have a cast-iron alibi.'

'I would never do anyone harm…' Valthór said, and Guðgeir interrupted him.

'Let's say that Arnhildur told you that evening about the

lie concerning the memory sticks, and on top of that announced that she was going to the police. In that case, that would also have brought the deception at the séances into the open. Your face would have been on the front pages of every media and you would be known as the fake medium. Nobody would have believed that you just wanted to add a little excitement to your gatherings. No, your reputation would have been wrecked, immediately, and would never recover.'

Valthór felt himself shrivel up. He looked up at Guðgeir, standing in front of him with his hands on his hips, eyes fixed on him, seeing him as a giant figure holding his life in his hands.

'I'm innocent of everything except some minor deception,' he stammered. 'But you should look at the grey-haired man who calls himself Markús or Magnús.'

'Do you have grounds to suspect him?' Elsa Guðrún asked.

'He came to a second séance, and I had the feeling that afterwards he led me towards the old graveyard.'

'Had the feeling? What do you mean by that?'

'I can't explain, but Arnhildur was waiting for me there,' Valthór replied, with all the conviction he could muster, and the two of them looked into each other's eyes.

'Well, let's call it a day,' Guðgeir said after a moment's heavy silence, and went to the hall. 'We'll be in touch.'

'Try and get some sleep. Long-term insomnia can lead to problems with mental health, so maybe you ought to see a doctor and get some help,' Elsa Guðrún said, giving him a warm smile as she stepped out of the door.

40

Later that day they sat in the car outside the Nes church. Arnhildur's funeral was taking place inside and it wouldn't be long before the doors would open. Their interest was in those attending, and whether or not any of them could cast a little light on the mystery. The church bell rang out, without anything else happening, although the casket would surely be carried out before long. The hearse waited in front of the church. Guðgeir jabbed Elsa Guðrún with his elbow as the church doors suddenly opened and immediately closed again. Valthór stood on the steps, looking around. He zipped his coat up to the throat and jogged through the falling snow towards a car that waited for him, and Guðgeir was sure he could see Stella at the wheel. She hadn't been present at the funeral, which was no surprise. Then everything was again quiet as there was no sign of any others attending the funeral.

'There must be a reception in the church hall, and since nobody else is coming out, it must be attached to the church so people can go straight there,' Guðgeir said. 'Arnhildur was such a loner that I hadn't expected there to be a funeral reception. Her daughter Unnur can hardly be up to organising anything like that.'

'There's her sister, and family on that side,' Elsa Guðrún said.

'True, but relations between them have been anything but friendly, as we know,' Guðgeir said. 'Shall we take a look inside?'

Without waiting for a reply, he got out of the car.

He was right. The refectory adjoined the church, and in the lobby between the two stood a simple white coffin on wooden trestles. There were few people present, so their arrival attracted attention. Regína stood up and came over to them. Her light grey hair had clearly been freshly styled and her face was made up. She wore a black suit and her only jewellery was an understated string of pearls. Skarphéðinn hurried behind her, and it was obvious how uncomfortable he was in a suit. His face was flushed, as if his tie was strangling him.

'We felt we had to offer people some hospitality,' Regína said apologetically. 'I know Arnhildur would have done the same for me, even though our relationship has been difficult over the last few years. Her ashes will be interred in the cremation plot alongside those of our parents.'

'It's beautiful there,' Guðgeir said, wondering what else to say.

'It is. But the geese crap everywhere there during the summer,' Regína replied. 'Is there anything new?'

'Not a great deal,' Guðgeir said, and now it was his turn to be apologetic. 'Unfortunately.'

'Hopefully it'll be resolved as soon as possible. But please have something to eat, now that you're here,' Regína said, wringing her hands. Despite her immaculate make-up, she came across as stressed and tired.

They did as she asked, and stood for a few minutes in a corner, watching those present. They helped themselves to flatbread with slices of smoked meat and tiny twisted doughnuts, while taking sips from the cups of coffee they placed on chairs, relieved to be able to put them down where nobody was sitting. At the far end of the room, a group of older women stood talking.

'I'm going to have a word with those ladies,' Elsa Guðrún decided. She swallowed the last of her doughnut and set off across the room, leaving Guðgeir to watch her from the corner of his eye, making the acquaintance of one woman after another. It wasn't long before the group was deep in conversation, and he smiled to himself. Elsa Guðrún was always quick to connect to people when she wanted to, and this had often been an advantage in investigations. Then he noticed a grey-haired man who came up the stairs that led down to the cloakroom in the basement. He recognised Markús. Guðgeir kept an eye on him as he walked, straight-backed, into the room and made for the table of refreshments. He kept him in sight, and wondered what Markús was doing at the funeral of a woman he'd met only once.

Guðgeir set off in his direction and at the same moment, Markús noticed the policeman and immediately turned on his heel and made for the stairs. He had a foot on the first step when Guðgeir's hand landed lightly on his shoulder.

'Hello, there. I didn't expect to run into you here,' he said cheerfully. Markús looked around, and the pained expression on his face made it clear that he didn't appreciate such an encounter. He shook his head. 'Did you know Arnhildur better than you let on the other day?' Guðgeir continued.

'No. I met her that one time,' Markús replied. His tone was dry and he appeared to feel like a cornered beast.

'You make a habit of attending the funerals of people you've met just once?' Guðgeir asked, unable to resist a sly dig. 'You're hardly going to get much else done on a weekday.'

Markús's hand tightened on the banister and he sighed.

'I'm simply the type that has an interest in people, I'm curious by nature and because of the circumstances of her death I have a particular interest. To my mind, there's nothing extraordinary about that. I wanted to see how the funeral would be conducted. Since I retired, I come here often for various services and events, and after my wife died...' he fell silent as Guðgeir raised a hand and told him that there was no need for him to make excuses. It went without saying that people were free to do what they liked with their own free time. Clearly relieved, Markús quickly said good-bye and hurried down the stairs. A few minutes later he reappeared in a dark coat, the collar turned up, and hurried to the door.

Guðgeir didn't take his eyes off him, and the guilty look on Markús's face showed that he was aware of being watched. It was a known phenomenon that killers would attend the funerals of their victims, and Guðgeir wondered if this was the case.

Elsa Guðrún was still talking with the group of women, so Guðgeir sauntered over to the table of refreshments and helped himself to another doughnut – in spite of his carbohydrate ban. There could hardly be much flour in these tiny morsels, and he was hungry. From the corner of his eye he could see Unnur and Ragna sitting together on a chair by the wall. They held hands tightly. Regína went to speak to them, but Unnur barely looked up. Skarphéðinn stood nearby, speaking to someone. Guðgeir considered going across and joining the conversation, and then Elsa Guðrún came over to him.

'Most of these women I was speaking to worked with Arnhildur at the lottery, over varying lengths of time. One of them,' she said and pointed discreetly. 'Her name's Sigrún and she worked with Arnhildur for almost forty years. I got her phone number and it wouldn't do any harm to speak to her again later, considering we have so little to go on.'

'Good work,' Guðgeir said encouragingly. 'What were they talking about?'

'All sorts of things. For example, Arnhildur always had the same thing for lunch in all the years she worked at the lottery. Three pieces of crispbread with shrimp spread, every day for forty years, thanks very much! They went on a staff trip to Germany at one point, and she took two packs of crispbread with her, but had to eat foreign spread, as the Icelandic one she took with her went bad on her. They told quite a few stories about her, maybe not all that pleasant, some of them, but she was certainly a memorable character.'

'Markús, the guy with the grey hair, was here just now, but he left,' Guðgeir said, gazing meaningfully at Elsa Guðrún.

'What the hell was he doing here?' she asked in clear astonishment.

'I don't know. He seems to be everywhere,' Guðgeir replied, and nudged Elsa Guðrún. 'Look. Unnur's sitting over there with Ragna.'

'Are you going to speak to her?'

'I think it's best to leave her alone. She must have enough to worry about taking all this in. Shall we call it a day and take ourselves off?'

41

He'd been dreading the funeral, and he knew he had to get out. He had been the last to arrive and was the first to leave. The church was half empty and he found a place to sit at the back. A group of women on the pew in front of him whispered to each other. He found it distasteful, hearing them blathering about Arnhildur. He noticed flowers arranged in vases by the altar, and the coffin between them. It was draped with the Icelandic flag and no wreath lay on it.

Valthór closed his eyes and concentrated all the energy he had on the person lying in the coffin. He pleaded for tranquillity for her, as well as for himself. If she could be at peace, then so could he. He was faintly aware of the funeral service and took care to stand when others did. Those present intoned the Lord's Prayer so that the church echoed and sunbeams broke through the stained-glass windows to illuminate the coffin. When the first notes of *Allt eins og blómstrið eina* could be heard, those present rose to their feet. The coffin was carried out, and his eyes followed Unnur, who wept and clung to Ragna. He joined the line, made the sign of the cross over the coffin, and then made for the door. He could breathe more easily. This was over.

Back home, he lay exhausted in bed and fell asleep. Certain that he was free, he slept dreamlessly, until Arnhildur woke him. He rose up quickly, hoping that it had been nothing more than a bad dream, but she was back. The black mist again hung in the corner of the room, demanding that he accompany her. He protested, begged for mercy, was determined to not go with her, but finally he gave up. He pulled on his winter boots, put on his coat, hat, gloves and wound his scarf carefully around his neck. Once again he set off on this walk that he couldn't escape.

He was scratching at the window set in the wall just above ground level, trying to get in, when he came to his senses, on all fours on the wet ground. He stared down at his bloodied, muddy hands. What the hell was going on? Had he been trying to get into the house? His breath came in heavy gasps and he could hear the hoarseness in his own airway, trying to haul himself from the mud and think clearly. He had to get away before the people living in the house noticed him and called the police. Valthór put his muddy fingers to his head while he tried to regain his bearings. Now he would have to leave as quickly as he could, without anyone seeing him. The damp of the ground seeped through his clothes as he crawled as rapidly as he could away from the house. After a few metres he got carefully to his feet and bent over, running for the street, to the light. Until a man suddenly appeared in front of him.

'Where are you going, my friend?' the man asked and Valthór sensed a spicy aroma about him.

'Home,' he gasped, struggling for breath.

'You're lost,' the man said and Valthór made out the outline of a slim, tall man in the darkness. A wave of discomfort swept through him as he slipped past and made for home.

Spring

42

It was May, and Máni Sölvason had been prosecuted on a number of counts related to his offences against Unnur Jacobsdóttir, but little progress had been made on the murder investigation. They had amassed more information about the grey-haired man, Markús, who for some reason seemed often to be present at events connected to Arnhildur.

Around three years ago, his neighbours had complained that he had a powerful telescope in his apartment. The suspicion was that he was spying on nearby houses, and a few instances were described. His neighbours had begun to keep their curtains drawn, even during the day. The police had knocked on Markús's door and spoken to him, but there was nothing that could be done and, since no formal complaint was ever made, the matter went quiet. Nothing else of interest came to light, and it seemed that Markús was simply very curious about the doings of other people – and also very lonely.

New assignments cropped up constantly and dealing with these ate up the days. Guðgeir longed to be able to concentrate on the mystery of Arnhildur's death, but not only were they a small team, there was also a distinct lack of any solid evidence to work on. Guðgeir was convinced that if he were given the flexibility to investigate every possible angle, then they would eventually find the truth. But as things stood, the expectation was that this would languish on the list of unsolved crimes. He and Elsa Guðrún talked it over occasionally, and at one point she hinted that the investigation would have been given more resources if this had been the murder of someone other than a woman of seventy.

'What people, especially women, have in common with cars is that their value drops dramatically as they get older,' she said sarcastically, although Guðgeir found himself unable to agree. He suggested that she should speak to Særós, who bore responsibility for allocating the department's resources. He couldn't see that Arnhildur's age or gender had anything to do with it, although the suspicion remained at the back of his mind.

As far as Guðgeir was aware, Valur Thór Jacobsson, otherwise known as Valthór, had held no further meetings with the dead since admitting how he and Arnhildur had deceived people. All the same, Guðgeir had some dealings with Valur Thór, as the tenants in the red house called several times and complained about his behaviour. They had been informed as clearly as was possible that the man suffered nightmares, and that they had no reason to fear him. Now that the bright nights of May were here, the hope was that the fear would disappear with the darkness. But then they called to report a disturbance, as Valur Thór appeared to be drunk, beating the wall of the house with a piece of wood and yelling confusedly. After one such incident he was arrested and brought to the police station, where a breath test showed him to be completely sober.

Guðgeir visited Valur Thór and talked things over with him, explaining that he was causing not only inconvenience but considerable discomfort. It was frightening for the tenants in the house to know that he could be there whenever they returned home late or looked out of the windows. Valur Thór's response was simply that he had no control over this behaviour. He had no choice but to obey and do as he was told. Guðgeir encouraged him to seek medical help, but Valur Thór repeatedly refused, saying that there was nothing wrong with him except that his spirit channels had remained open. He said that this was his burden and he longed for nothing more than to be free of it. Guðgeir didn't understand completely what he was talking about, but gathered that this concerned ending his capabilities as a medium, or at least his supposed talent, as Valur Thór had admitted to having deceived people. It was sad to see what had become of the unfortunate man. What had previously been a neat and tidy apartment was now grubby, and the same could be said of its owner.

Guðgeir had discussed the matter with Ísgerður, who considered that Valur Thór could be suffering from schizophrenia, as he claimed to hear voices and was clearly plagued by visions. He would need treatment as soon as possible. Guðgeir even called the man's mother, Stella, who dismissed the idea that her son might be unwell. According to her, he was a picture of health and had hardly ever suffered a day's illness. This left Guðgeir with no further options, as he had already gone further than his responsibilities required.

Now it appeared that the problem of the red house would resolve itself, as it was now in Regína's and Skarphéðinn's hands. They had mortgaged the place, given the tenants notice and were about to embark on extensive renovation work. The intention was to then sell the house and to pay Unnur her share.

'It's expensive to be disabled, and she could use the money,' Regína told Guðgeir during one of their conversations. She called regularly to ask about progress on the case, and Guðgeir invariably found it difficult to have to inform her that her sister's murderer was still free.

There were no witnesses who had seen anyone that night, and the only camera that covered that area turned out to be out of service. All the samples that had been identified at the scene had been tested and were the victim's, and the murder weapon still hadn't been found. It was difficult to identify who might have had a motive for wanting Arnhildur dead. As far as the police had been able to establish, there was nothing about her life that gave anyone a reason for doing her harm...

'Except Máni,' Regína said, cutting him off.

'Yes, but as you know there's nothing that indicates he committed the murder, even though he's guilty of other things,' Guðgeir said and added that there was a strong suspicion that this had been an attempted mugging that had gone badly wrong.

Sadly, there were more and more such unfortunates and this was the speech Guðgeir gave Regína every time she called, and never failed to feel a nagging guilt.

He wasn't satisfied – he was a long way from being satisfied.

43

Follow me. Follow me.
The voice echoed in his subconscious.
It's a dream, a nightmare, he reminded himself as his mind floated to the surface. That thought lasted no more than a moment before he sank quickly back.
Follow me, follow me, the beguiling female voice continued to demand, and he put all the energy he could muster into resisting.
'No, get away! Get out of here!' he yelled. 'Away with you!'
'Guðgeir, what's the matter? Bad dreams?' Inga's voice blended with that of the woman who wanted her to come with him. He told that woman to be off, pushing her away, but then he sank even deeper and his surroundings changed into a thick, clinging fluid. He had the sensation of slipping down a narrow, slimy tube, his face covered by something revolting that prevented him from breathing. A vast purple hand stretched out from the darkness, pulling him free of the viscous ooze. A face he recognised swam into focus...
'Guðgeir! Wake up!'
He felt a finger prodding his shoulder.
'Get away, I don't want to ... leave me alone,' he mumbled, but sensed that reality was gaining the upper hand in his mind.
He opened his eyes in confusion and saw Inga. She sat on

the bed, hair wet and wrapped in a towel. It took him a moment to get his bearings. He stared at her with his eyes wide, then at the bedside table where the novel he'd been reading the night before lay half-open, and finally at the familiar pictures on the walls. Inga tenderly stroked his forehead.

'You're bathed in sweat,' she said, her voice heavy with concern. 'I was just getting out of the shower when I heard you shout.' Inga leaned close and used a corner of the towel to wipe the sweat from his forehead. 'What on earth were you dreaming?' she asked gently, giving him a kiss.

'Ach, something incredibly stupid,' Guðgeir replied, still shaken by the nightmare. 'It felt like the woman who was found dead in the Hólavellir graveyard had come and wanted me to accompany her. It was as if she was dragging me down into the depths.'

'It's horrible to have that kind of dream,' Inga said. 'Maybe it's because you're not satisfied that the case still isn't resolved? Worries can stack up in your subconscious and their outlet comes in the form of nightmares.' Inga stood up and dried her wet hair with the towel. 'Unless Arnhildur was giving you a reminder? Could be?'

She stood up and went to the window to draw the curtains. Beams of spring sunshine stretched out across the floor and up the walls.

Guðgeir put a hand over his eyes as the brightness stung.

'Don't, please. How about you come over here?' he said and lifted up the duvet. Inga smiled, let the damp towel drop to the floor and slipped under the bedclothes.

The pleasure of the morning was uppermost in his mind, the nightmare suppressed, as he set off to work, and when Elsa Guðrún dropped in to see him at midday, his thoughts were far away.

'Weren't you informed?' she asked eagerly, her feet shuffling as she stood in the doorway.

'No. What?' Guðgeir looked up from the screen. His intention had been to deal with of all kinds of dull paperwork that had piled up recently.

'Some bones have been discovered at Arnhildur's house. I was just speaking to Helgi Már and he's sure these are human remains,' Elsa Guðrún said. 'Shouldn't we get over there?'

Guðgeir was on his feet and on his way before she even finished speaking. A little later they parked in exactly the same spot as they had the day Arnhildur's body had been found. The forensic team were again at work, this time examining more than just the deceased woman's apartment. The scene had been fenced off and a shelter had been erected over a large hole and a pile of earth by the wall of the building. Beside this stood a mini digger, which had also been meticulously taped off. The forensic staff were at work, while Leifur, Helgi Már and an older man in overalls stood outside the taped-off area.

'Looks to me like Skarphéðinn, Regína's husband,' Guðgeir said in a low voice to Elsa Guðrún as they got out of the car.

'He's clearly been working on the house,' she observed.

'Good morning,' Leifur said as they approached. 'We've unearthed more bones and have to work very cautiously.'

'How did this happen?' Guðgeir asked, hands on his hips as he looked around at the scene.

'This chap, Skarphéðinn, was digging and... Look, it's best he tells you himself,' Leifur replied.

Guðgeir looked questioningly at Skarphéðinn, who wiped his muddy fingers on his overall. It was clear from his expression that he was in shock.

'I ... Regína and I ... are getting on with fixing the house up. I rented this digger and was digging a trench for a new drain ... and we were going to renew the sewage pipes as well ... and...' Skarphéðinn stammered.

'And these bones?' Guðgeir asked. He could hear the

irritation and impatience in his own voice, and he had an odd feeling. It occurred to him that last night's bad dreams had been a precursor to all this. If Valur Þór had suffered anything close to what he had experienced last night, then the man must have been through pure hell – again and again.

'Tell us what happened, Skarphéðinn,' Elsa Guðrún said mildly, giving him an encouraging smile.

'Well, I was hard at work and then I noticed a bone sticking up out of the earth. At first I thought it had to be an old dog or a cat that someone had buried there by the wall, not that I recall my parents-in-law who lived here ever had any pets. But I thought nothing of it and got on with the job. Then I noticed another bone and jumped down to take a closer look, and then...' Skarphéðinn fell silent and ran a trembling hand over his bald head. He was clearly deeply upset by what had happened. 'So I realised these looked like the bones of a hand and could hardly believe my eyes, so I got the little one there,' he said, gesturing to a small spade leaning against the wall. 'And dug out a bit more, and saw there are holes in the foundations. I must have hit the wall hard, or else the concrete must have been so poor. It's horrible, I'm still shaking. Look!' He held out his hand and it shook so much that he couldn't have held a cup without spilling the contents. 'Look at those bushes I'd started to take out. I reckon you'd best take a close look, because the bones were under there.'

Leifur gestured to Helgi Már, who went straight to the spot.

'How old do you think these bones are?' Skarphéðinn asked in a voice loaded with dread as he looked from one face to another. 'Shouldn't we call someone from the National Museum? I mean, get an archaeologist to look at them?'

'These bones aren't that old. We'll soon have an idea of

how long they've been there,' Leifur replied.

'How do you know that?' Skarphéðinn asked uneasily. 'Don't you need a specialist to examine them?'

'That goes without saying, but years of experience gives me a rough idea of their age,' Leifur replied calmly and went over to speak to Helgi Már. Skarphéðinn's hand stroked his bald head repeatedly. This beefy man was obviously weighed down with fatigue as his shoulders slumped. Dark bags hung under his eyes, extending down his cheeks. His thin lips trembled and his eyes flickered back and forth.

'Who could it be?' he asked in a voice that shook.

'Identifying this person could be complicated, but hopefully it'll be resolved before long,' Guðgeir said, having regained his calm demeanour. But the nightmare that had stolen away his night's sleep was still clear in his mind. This could hardly be a coincidence and he was certain that Arnhildur had come to him with a message. Then a new idea occurred to him.

'Tell me, Skarphéðinn. This wall you were digging alongside, what's on the other side of it?'

Skarphéðinn thought for a moment, and pointed.

'The laundry room comes to about there,' he said, waving a hand to show how far it extended. 'Then there's the little cold storeroom, like people had in the old days. The rest is a space that's never been used for anything and there was still an earth floor in there as far as I know. There was a plan to make it into a small apartment, but that never happened...' Skarphéðinn said, and fell suddenly silent.

The blood drained from his face, and Guðgeir suspected what unpleasant thought had just come to him. The same thing had occurred to him.

'This is the area that Arnhildur would never allow to be finished so it could be rented out?' Guðgeir asked, running fingers through his dark hair.

'Yes,' Skarphéðinn said in a low voice. 'They were about to lay a concrete floor in there just when Jacob left the country.'

'When he disappeared, you mean,' Guðgeir said with quiet emphasis.

'She was so upset that she'd never go in there, said it reminded her of him,' Skarphéðinn said slowly. 'Do you really think this could be Jacob Winter?'

Guðgeir didn't reply, but went over to Leifur to tell him that there was a strong likelihood that the owner of these bones had been buried inside the wall of the house. Then he spoke to Helgi Már, and asked him to request DNA samples from Valthór and Unnur.

'You'll have to be cautious with her. I'll speak to Ragna who manages the place where Unnur's a resident and let her know.'

Helgi Már nodded.

'It shouldn't take long to get confirmation. This will get top priority.'

'We have to go to the station,' Guðgeir said as he returned to where Skarphéðinn and Elsa Guðrún stood. 'I'll have to take your statement. If you go in your car, Elsa Guðrún and I will meet you there.'

Skarphéðinn burst suddenly into tears, this brawny man shaken by sobs that he struggled to contain. Elsa Guðrún and Guðgeir instinctively looked away. This was a painful sight to witness. Finally, Elsa Guðrún could stand it no more, and stepped over to him. The slightly-built woman took the rawboned man in her arms to comfort him.

'I was so fond of Jacob. It wasn't just that we were married to sisters, we were good friends,' Skarphéðinn said, swallowing, his voice shaking with emotion. 'He'd given up on Arnhildur and was planning to leave. He told me that himself. For years I was aggrieved that he never said goodbye, or got in touch. And now I know that hurt was for a dead man.'

'It's still not certain this is Jacob,' Guðgeir said and felt how his voice was devoid of any conviction. 'We can't be sure of anything until we know more. On top of that, we don't know how this individual's death occurred, or exactly how old these bones are.'

Skarphéðinn disengaged himself from Elsa Guðrún and straightened his back. He ran the grubby back of his hand over his cheeks, leaving them grimy. Then he coughed hard and began to apologise for his emotional reactions.

'It's a shock, something like this, you see. I rented this digger and had just made a start getting to work. It's been a hard winter, as you know. Something like this hits you hard...' He drew a deep breath and exhaled loudly.

'All right, we understand. Nothing to worry about,' Guðgeir assured him, patting his shoulder.

'Elsa Guðrún and I will go over to your car with you, and you can follow us. It won't take long to take a statement, and after that you're free to go home to Hveragerði and take it easy. There's no chance that you'll be working on this drain for the next few days or weeks. Every inch of this ground will be gone over and checked, but let me have the receipt for the digger rental and I'll make sure it's collected.'

They waited while Skarphéðinn collected items from the digger and then walked with him over to his van.

'You're going to be all right, aren't you? Do you trust yourself to drive?' Guðgeir asked as Skarphéðinn opened the back of his van where the receipt lay on top of a large toolbox.

'Here's the paperwork, and don't worry about me. I'll be fine,' Skarphéðinn said. 'I'll be right behind you.'

'Fair enough,' Guðgeir said, looking around with the feeling that they were being watched. The street was deserted, apart from the police presence. He looked over at the next house. A pair of youthful eyes stared at him from the upper floor window. As always, Hilmar made sure that nothing happening in the street escaped his notice. Guðgeir raised a hand and waved to him.

44

They held a meeting with Særós once Skarphéðinn was on his way home to Hveragerði. The forensic team was still at work inside and outside the red house, along with the pathologist and his assistant. This was painstaking work that demanded extreme caution and endless patience. By now it was clear that the remains of a man had been found, and an initial analysis indicated that they had been there not more than thirty years.

'It seems to me overwhelmingly likely that Jacob Winter has shown up,' Særós said, voicing what they had all been thinking.

'And that he had intended to leave, but that was as far as he got,' Guðgeir said.

'You're suggesting that Arnhildur murdered him?' Elsa Guðrún said. 'You believe she would have preferred him dead than to let him leave her?'

'We have no evidence for that, and we mustn't allow imagination to run away with us,' Særós said. 'This investigation is still at an early stage.'

'Skarphéðinn said that the cellar had been poorly finished when they took over the house from the parents of the sisters. There was a thin layer of gravel beneath the floorboards, and under that there was just earth. He remembered this clearly because he helped Arnhildur and Jacob take up the floor in the laundry room and the storeroom, and they started concreting a new floor in that part of the basement. The two of them were going to finish it off,' Guðgeir said.

'So if Arnhildur committed the crime, then she must have buried the body in the unfinished part and after that day nobody was ever allowed in there. Her sister and brother-in-law believed that this was for emotional reasons, and for those same reasons she didn't want to sell,' Særós said. 'If your reasoning stands up, then the picture looks very different.'

'Quite apart from the fact that we haven't identified the deceased, Stella who had a child with Jacob told me that Valthór had been sent a card from his father, and some time later a wad of banknotes,' Guðgeir said. 'The card was from the Faroes, and the money was posted from Germany.'

'You remember the women we spoke to at the funeral reception?' Elsa Guðrún said animatedly, her eyes alight with excitement. 'They talked about a staff trip to Germany...'

'Do you think...?' Særós asked, looking at them in turn.

'I have a phone number for one of them,' Elsa Guðrún said quickly.

'What are you waiting for? Call!' Særós said. 'Guðgeir, will you speak to Stella?'

'Of course,' he replied, already on his feet and on his way to his desk.

It wasn't long before Elsa Guðrún returned with confirmation that the staff of the lottery had normally gone on an overseas trip every second year, and that Arnhildur had twice gone with them. Both times were after she had become a single parent, and her former colleague recalled that little Unnur had been looked after by her sister and brother-in-law. The trips Arnhildur had gone on had been to the Faroes, and to Germany. The woman was sure of her facts, and even offered to show them the album of pictures, each one carefully captioned.

Guðgeir had managed to get hold of Stella, but her recollections were less precise than those of Arnhildur's former colleague at the lottery. Stella thought that Valur Thór could still have the postcard in his possession. She recalled that the postcard had been a pretty picture of Tórshavn, and that the boy had been of roughly confirmation age when it had arrived. It was less easy to pin a date to the arrival of the bundle of marks, but Stella felt it likely that the boy could have been a year older by then. She remembered being surprised that such a large amount had been sent through the post like any other letter, and not by recorded delivery. It had taken her by surprise that this gift came so late, and decided that maybe in Germany children were confirmed later than in Iceland.

'The timeline fits, more or less, and it shouldn't be too much of a problem to confirm all this,' Elsa Guðrún said.

'Don't you want to call on Valur Thór and ask about the postcard?' Særós asked.

'No, let's wait,' Guðgeir said. He wasn't sure why he didn't want to go right away, but instinct told him that this was the right decision.

'Maybe he's not so crazy after all,' Elsa Guðrún said. 'The woman he claims forced him to go to the house could have been Arnhildur.'

'You mean that for decades she's done everything she can to keep all this hidden away, and chooses to draw attention to it after her death?' Særós said, her voice sharply dismissive. 'Isn't that too far-fetched? No. I've the feeling that this Valthór is quite simply not right in the head.'

'Don't you remember, Guðgeir, when Valthór said that Arnhildur had a purple aura, which he considered was a symbol of guilt?' Elsa Guðrún said earnestly, while Særós rolled her eyes and shook her head.

Guðgeir took out his phone and found a search engine.

'According to Christian theory, this colour can signify

healing, cleansing, suffering, remorse, atonement...' he said, and fell suddenly silent as the purple hand from last night's dream came to mind. Surely Arnhildur's guilt couldn't run so deep that...? Guðgeir hardly dared follow that train of thought, let alone mention it out loud or catch Elsa Guðrún's eye.

'Hey, come on. No bullshit,' the ever down-to-earth Særós instructed. 'The two of you are talking crap now. Let's stop speculating and wait for scientific conclusions from the investigation.'

45

Guðgeir felt drained by the day's events and felt an inner disquiet as he left the station at the end of the day. Behind the wheel of his car, he sat in thought for a long time without starting the engine. Finally, he reversed out of his parking space and went direct to Valthór's home, fully aware that he wasn't doing things strictly by the book.

The Valthór who opened the door bore no resemblance to the man he and Elsa Guðrún had visited just a few days before. The furtive glances that had been so apparent the last time they met were gone, and now he didn't hesitate to look Guðgeir in the eye.

A vacuum cleaner lay in the middle of the living room floor and Valthór pushed it aside with one foot.

'I got round to cleaning and tidying the place up,' he said apologetically.

'I can see you're feeling better,' Guðgeir said, looking around. Efforts had clearly been made and the apartment was much tidier than it had been. 'Are you able to sleep now?'

'Yes, slept well last night, and had a nap this afternoon. Slept like a baby for more than two hours.'

'So the woman who had been troubling you has left you alone?' Guðgeir asked in a gentle tone.

Valthór looked at him for a long moment, as if weighing up whether the question was being asked in all seriousness, or simply to needle him.

'Yes. And she won't trouble me any more. Arnhildur is gone,' he replied gravely. 'For good,' he added.

Valthór gazed into Guðgeir's eyes, and he had the feeling that the medium sensed the nightmare that had come to him during his sleep. He tried to suppress that thought.

'Human remains have been found at Arnhildur's house,' he said. 'In exactly the spot you used to stare at during your night time walks.'

The news appeared to take Valthór by surprise. He swallowed rapidly, so that his Adam's apple bobbed up and down. His hand went to his mouth, as if instinctively, and he didn't reply immediately. The furtive look that had gone reappeared in his eye.

'No, but I didn't know what was there,' he stammered. 'I swear it! But I felt a huge relief this morning, and I'm not exaggerating when I say it was as if a burden had been lifted from my shoulders. I suspected that something big had happened.'

'It certainly has. Arnhildur's brother-in-law Skarphéðinn was digging a trench for a new drain when he came across human remains. Our initial analysis suggests that this is a man, and it seems likely that he hasn't been there more than thirty years,' Guðgeir said. 'Have you been requested to supply a DNA sample?'

'No... or yes, it's possible,' Valthór replied, and stared at Guðgeir. The possibility that his father had been lying there under the foundations of the house appeared to be just dawning on him.

'You don't know?' Guðgeir asked in surprise.

'Someone rang the doorbell, but I didn't answer it and went back to sleep, and the phone was switched off. I didn't want to be disturbed once I finally managed to relax enough to get some sleep,' Valthór gabbled.

'You must have wondered why the woman took you repeatedly to that spot,' Guðgeir said in a low voice, without taking his eyes from Valthór.

'You have to understand that I was caught in a nightmare and it had its origins in pain and guilt,' Valthór said in a voice full of hurt. 'That's all I knew.'

'I see,' Guðgeir said, with no particular emphasis on his words. He went over to the living room window and gazed out. The grass was green, the trees were sprouting leaves and a few brave flowers had lifted their heads. He stood still for a moment, and then turned.

'Valthór, I'd like to ask you to do one thing for me, and after that I'll leave you alone,' he said.

'My name's Valur Thór, and I'd prefer you to call me by that name.'

Guðgeir lifted one eyebrow.

'Valur Thór or Valthór, it makes no difference to me. I'd like you to walk with me the route that Arnhildur took after your last séance.'

'What on earth for?' Valur Thór asked. He stared in confusion at Guðgeir, and seemed to be trying to work out what was being asked of him, and why.

'We often do this as part of an investigation. It can help in establishing where events took place.'

'All right. I understand,' Valur Thór said. He fetched a jacket, and his body language indicated that this was not to his liking. 'Is this really necessary?' he asked, with one arm in the jacket. 'To be honest with you, I've had more than enough of all this and thought I was free.'

Interesting choice of words, Guðgeir thought.

'Let's just say you're doing your duty to society by assisting the police. After that you should be free to return to putting your flat to rights.'

Few words were spoken during the short walk from Valur Thór's home to the hall on Bergstaðastræti.

'Let's start here,' Guðgeir said.

'I don't know what you're hoping to achieve, but conditions are nothing like they were then,' Valur Thór said. 'That was in February when it was cold and there was snow on the ground. Now spring's in the air. There's even a scent of freshly mown grass.'

'Arnhildur forced you to walk this way many times and now that she's gone, I'd like to accompany you along the route. Just this once,' Guðgeir said with firmness.

'You mean, you believe me?' Valur Thór said.

'I do indeed,' Guðgeir assured him.

'Good,' Valur Thór replied. 'Let's go.'

They walked quickly side by side to the end of Bergstaðastræti, where Valur Thór paused.

'This is where Markús turns to go along a side street,' he said unexpectedly. Guðgeir nodded and tried not to show his astonishment as Valur Thór seemed to be under some kind of autopilot control. They took the next corner and walked in the direction of the lake. 'This is where a bus goes past, and we feel like poor Palle, alone in the world,' Valur Thór added as they crossed Lækjargata and went along Skothúsvegur. 'Soon there's a young man running up the steps of a white house.'

Guðgeir drew a deep breath. This was uncanny in the extreme. He could see neither a bus nor a young man, but just people about their usual business. They turned to the right into Suðurgata and followed the graveyard wall as far as the iron gate.

'I feel a weight in my chest as I reach this point,' Valur Thór said. 'And it gets worse, to the point that I can barely breathe, and with it there's a terrible headache. You wouldn't believe how terrible I've been feeling.'

Guðgeir pushed open the iron gate and they walked together into the graveyard.

'It's worst here,' Valur Thór said, pointing.

'This is precisely the spot where Arnhildur was found,' Guðgeir said. He had a strange feeling, and this was certainly a unique experience. 'What next?' he asked.

'The pain fades and I'm filled with this desperation, and it's so overwhelmingly strong that I feel I'm about to burst.

I know it sounds weird, but I had the feeling that Arnhildur was pulling me towards the house. There's no point trying to resist. I have to go. There's no human power than can hold me back.'

'Let's go that way,' Guðgeir said quietly.

They continued without a word spoken, all the way to Arnhildur's house and stopped by the garden fence. Yellow tapes were strung around the excavation.

'What was the feeling here?' Guðgeir asked.

'It's not a feeling I can describe, except that it was unbelievably bad,' Valur Thór said.

'Was it hatred?' Guðgeir asked.

'Maybe. But blended with suffering and regret,' replied Valur Thór, who now seemed to have reverted to his usual self. 'These weren't my feelings, but I could sense them.'

'So you sensed Arnhildur's feelings and through your capability as a medium, you experienced her pain,' Guðgeir said.

'Yes,' Valur Thór said. 'You could put it like that.'

'Your mother told me that you always blamed Arnhildur for your father leaving,' Guðgeir said. 'Is that correct?'

'You could say that,' he replied quietly, his eyes drawn to the excavation.

'But she also told me that he hadn't had much time for you before he took up with her,' Guðgeir said.

'That's true. I realised that later,' Valur Thór said. 'Love and hatred are powerful emotions. When one disappears, the other can take its place. I was hurt that he wasn't there with me any longer and I used to dream that he'd turn up one day. I saw him like any other hero. Ach, those were just childhood dreams that he'd show up one day, really cool, with a fantastic motorbike for me so all the other boys would be envious. I used to imagine that he was rich and he'd come and set me and Mum free of all the troubles we went through in those years. I pictured the three of us moving together to Germany where I had a wonderful big family living in some kind of palace. It was all rather silly ... the dreams of a fatherless child.'

'You realise that there's a strong suspicion that those are your father's remains that were unearthed today,' Guðgeir said.

'I'd already put two and two together,' Valur Thór said. 'A few years ago, when I got to know Unnur, I realised that he had neglected not only me but her as well. All those years I had envied her, and then I felt guilty and so sympathetic to her, as she'd not only been abandoned by her father but had also suffered such a terrible injury.' Valur Thór fell silent, and his fingers gripped the fence. 'Now I'm facing the bizarre thought that maybe he didn't leave but was murdered. Who knows what would have happened if he had lived?'

'Although we aren't able to prove it, there's every reason to believe that Arnhildur caused his death,' Guðgeir said. 'That would explain much about the way she lived.'

'That's the way it was, and that's why she had no peace,' Valur Thór murmured.

'Does she get peace while her own murder is unexplained?' Guðgeir asked.

'Yes. Her own death is an absolution of her sins,' Valur Thór said in a determined, clear voice.

Then he turned away from the red house and walked away.

Guðgeir stood in silence. He would need to regain his equilibrium after this experience, and he would have to work out the meaning of what he had heard. A large raindrop landed on his head, soon followed by another, but Guðgeir remained motionless. It wasn't until the pile of earth was about to become mud that he moved, almost from habit looking up to Hilmar's window to give him a wave.

46

Guðgeir kept his visit to Valur Thór strictly to himself. The following days passed with little progress as those involved in the case waited for the results of the DNA comparison of the remains that had been unearthed in the garden of the red house to samples provided by Unnur and Valur Thór.

When the big day came, a case meeting was called for everyone who worked on the investigation. The results were clear. There was a definite connection between the half-siblings and the bones. Jacob Winter had never left the country, but his remains had lain for decades in a shallow grave in the foundations of the house. Trauma to the back and front of the skull showed definite indications of injury caused by an implement such as a hammer or a jemmy.

The case meeting took time and had gone through every detail. Now Guðgeir and Elsa Guðrún talked things over in Særós's office.

'It must be a dreadful feeling for Valur Thór to know that he conspired to trick people with the woman who murdered his father,' Elsa Guðrún said, and Guðgeir murmured his agreement.

'Doesn't it serve that fake medium right?' Særós said. 'I loathe people who take advantage of others' misfortune, lying to sick and bereaved people.'

'He seems to have had some genuine psychic talent,

considering he stood so often by the red house,' Elsa Guðrún said.

'I'm not convinced, since he hadn't managed to find out what happened to his father. He had no more notion of that than his witch of a mother did,' Særós said with ice-cold decision.

'Maybe it doesn't work like that,' Elsa Guðrún said.

'She was quite something, this Arnhildur. Jacob was going to leave her so she just bumped him off,' Særós said. She leaned back in her chair, clasped her hands behind her neck and sighed.

'She must have done it in a fit of panic,' said Guðgeir, who had been sitting in silence up to this point.

'It must be horrific to spend your life with that on your conscience,' Elsa Guðrún said. 'And after that she couldn't move or sell the house. She was stuck where she was, with her beloved buried in the basement.'

'We don't know if she had such a thing as a conscience,' Særós snapped.

'Yes, of course she did. Arnhildur did everything she could for her daughter. We don't know what this Jacob was like. For all we know, she could have done it in self defence,' Elsa Guðrún pointed out.

'That's quite true. And there are all kinds of things we're never going to find out,' Særós agreed. 'Imagine if she hadn't been in this fix she could have had that unfinished space fitted out and either sold it or rented it out to pay Máni off.'

'Whatever Arnhildur should or shouldn't have done, or whatever opinions we may have about the way she lived, that doesn't change the fact that her murderer still hasn't been identified,' Guðgeir said.

'That's right, and we need to get back on the case,' Særós said.

'It occurs to me,' Elsa Guðrún said, 'that much of this needn't have happened if notice had been taken of people, if they'd been listened to.'

'What do you mean?' Guðgeir asked.

'Such as Unnur. Several times she tried to tell people what had been happening to her, but nobody took any notice,' she replied.

'Well, yes. That's because she has brain damage,' Særós said in her usual blunt style, about to continue as Elsa Guðrún interrupted.

'That's certainly true, but it doesn't mean that anything Unnur says should be disregarded, just because she likes stories,' she said firmly, her eyes darkening.

'Hold on, yes. That's absolutely right. Unnur tried to raise the alarm. More than once,' Guðgeir said, turning to Elsa Guðrún. 'Was there anything else you had in mind?'

'Yes, and I'm not saying that I believe in mediums and all that kind of stuff, but Valthór or Valur Thór, or whatever his name is, has repeatedly pointed us to Jacob's grave. We've received plenty of complaints about him, and the story was always the same, that he stood still, staring at that particular point. Why didn't we do anything about it?'

'Such as what?' Særós said, palms up as she spread her hands wide.

'We could have investigated that spot. Stuck a spade in the ground,' Elsa Guðrún said animatedly.

'That's damage to private property,' Særós said.

'The owner was dead, more than likely murdered, and of course we could have got permission from her family members. We should have taken notice,' she said with deep conviction.

'It's easy to be wise with the benefit of hindsight,' Særós said, an eyebrow arching as she looked at Guðgeir, who'd stayed out of the conversation and was tapping at his phone. 'What do you think?'

'I think there's a lot in what Elsa Guðrún says, and I'm afraid I'm as guilty of the same thing,' Guðgeir said as he

looked up. He'd found what he had been looking for.
'What's that?'
'Something I need to check out. I'll let you know if it comes to anything,' he said, and was already on his way out of the room.

47

Furniture was being carried out of the red house and loaded onto a flatbed. Freyja and Skúli carried the kitchen table between them, with Hafdís hurrying behind, clutching a pink kitchen blender in her arms. Guðgeir got out of the car and went over to them.

'Weren't you supposed to have the flat until the end of the month?' he asked.

'Yeah, but no way we can stay here ... it's way too creepy,' Freyja said, and shafts of sunlight glittered on her tight curls.

'And there are people snooping around the place,' Skúli added. 'The media types are just lapping this up.'

'I see,' Guðgeir said, and his eyes went to the next house. A pair of young eyes in the window followed every movement.

'Did you want to talk to us?' Freyja asked when the table had been put on the flatbed. She leaned against the truck and angled her face to take in the sun's rays, while Skúli went back inside to fetch more of their belongings.

'Not as such, just a courtesy call,' Guðgeir said. 'Did you find another flat?'

'I've rented a room. Hafdís is going to her parents and Skúli's going to be staying with a friend for a while,' Freyja explained. 'They've split up.'

'I see,' Guðgeir said, his thoughts elsewhere as he gazed at the house next door.

'He's fallen for someone younger in the hairdressing business. The girl who found Arnhildur's body. Don't you think that's a bit creepy?' Freyja asked and shuddered in spite of the summer warmth.

Guðgeir shrugged.

'I've come to see Hilmar, your neighbour. Maybe you know him?'

Freyja shook her head.

'Don't know who that is,' she replied.

'No, of course. I hope the move goes well,' Guðgeir said. He lifted a hand in a wave and walked over to the next house.

Hilmar answered the video doorbell immediately and let him in. Guðgeir went up the steps slowly, past the childminder's door, and up. Hilmar waited for him on the landing.

'May I come in?' he asked, taking care to look directly at the youngster as he spoke.

'No,' Hilmar replied. 'Mum and Dad aren't home and I'm not to let anyone in.'

'That's all right. Then let's sit here on the steps,' Guðgeir said and sat down, while Hilmar stood still and watched him.

'I know your name and when you were born, and your wife and children and your grandchild.'

'Is that so?'

'Yes, of course,' Hilmar replied and Guðgeir listened in astonishment as without a pause the boy reeled off the names and dates of birth of the whole family.

'That's brilliant!' he said, delighted, almost clapping his hands. 'You have a fantastic memory. Maybe even unique!'

'Yes,' Hilmar said. 'I know.'

'You remember when I asked if you had seen this man before?' Guðgeir said and took out his phone to show Hilmar the picture of Valur Thór.

'Yes.'

'You wrote '2' on my phone, look,' Guðgeir said and handed it to him.

'Yes,' Hilmar replied.

'And I said 'not three?'

He held up three fingers to be absolutely clear.

'No. You don't understand. It wasn't three times I saw this man,' Hilmar said and pointed at Valur Thór's picture. 'Two men. First there was another man. He had some papers and he went into the house. I saw from the window that he was arguing with Arnhildur, the woman who died. He was very angry. Then they went out and she walked away. The man sat in his car and then he got out of it and followed her. His car was here, and he came back very late, and drove away.'

'Do you remember what his car looked like?' Guðgeir asked, making an effort to not push this along too fast.

'Yes. He was here a few days ago. This man was digging by the house and he was working with a digger and his car was parked in the space on the street,' Hilmar answered clearly.

Guðgeir's jaw dropped and he stared.

'You're certain?' he asked when he could finally speak.

'Yes, of course,' Hilmar said. 'I remember everything.'

'Thank you, that's a great help,' Guðgeir said gratefully. 'Do you feel able to come to the station and make a statement about what you witnessed?'

'When Mum and Dad are back. I can't go anywhere until they're home,' Hilmar said with finality.

'That's fine, and I understand. You have such a strong memory. Do you remember if the man was holding anything when he came back that night?' Guðgeir asked.

'I saw him take something from his coat and put it in the car,' Hilmar replied. 'But I couldn't see what it was.'

Guðgeir felt almost faint. He rested his chin on his balled fists, elbows on his knees as he calmed down. He had a vision of the advertisement on Arnhildur's living room table, and the heavy hammer from Skarphéðinn's tool bag.

'Thank you, Hilmar. You've been unbelievably helpful. I'll go now, but I'm sure I'll see you again later today or tomorrow.'

Guðgeir called Særós as soon as he was out of the house. Shortly after that patrol cars left the central police station, heading for Hveragerði.

48

Guðgeir was tired. This case had taken a mental toll in a way that most others didn't, and it hadn't helped that he'd barely slept more than a few hours after what had been an exceptionally eventful day. A broken man had awaited their arrival at the little house in Hveragerði that afternoon. He admitted immediately that he had caused the death of Arnhildur Drífa Friðthjófsdóttir on a dark night around four months ago.

'You've beaten me to it,' Skarphéðinn had said as he extended his hands for the cuffs to be snapped around his wrists. 'There were only two options left, as I couldn't live with this on my conscience any longer.'

Guðgeir had a suspicion of what the other option might be, and made sure a careful watch was kept on Skarphéðinn, who now sat in a cell. Guðgeir stood up from working on the statement, sauntered over to the machine and prepared a double espresso. He'd just taken a first sip when Bogga bustled along the corridor toward him.

'There's a woman waiting for you,' she said. 'She says her name's Regína Friðthjófsdóttir and I think she's...'

'Yes, quite right. Would you show her in?' Guðgeir said quickly and hurried into his office, the cup in his hand.

A moment later Regína was standing in the doorway. There was no mistaking the exhaustion on this tall woman's face and she appeared to have aged dramatically. Her usually neat hair was tangled and her eyes were puffed and red. The life force in her seemed to have been snuffed out.

'Please, take a seat,' Guðgeir said, shaking her hand. 'Can I get you some coffee, or water?'

'No, thank you,' Regína said as she sat down. 'I don't need anything.'

'What can I do for you?' Guðgeir asked. He made himself comfortable and took off his glasses.

'I want to tell you my side of the story,' Regína said, a beseeching look on her face.

'Yes?'

'This is important to me,' Regína said.

'In that case I'd like Elsa Guðrún to join us,' Guðgeir said, reaching for the phone. 'Do you have any objection?'

'No. The more, the merrier,' Regína replied, her face blank.

'Fine. She'll be right with us. Do you mind if I record this conversation?'

'Yes, do what you like, but I'm not being questioned or making a statement. I just want to give you my side of the story,' Regína said, twisting her gnarled fingers together.

'Certainly,' Guðgeir said amiably. 'Hello, and thank you for coming,' he said as Elsa Guðrún appeared, greeted Regína and took a seat. 'So, what would you like to tell us?'

'I know my husband has confessed and now it's my turn to do the same. That Tuesday night in February he didn't come home until three in the morning. I opened my eyes and noticed the time on the clock,' Regína said, and pursed her lips. Guðgeir felt his cheeks flush hot and he stiffened. He put a hand over his mouth and rubbed the dark stubble with his fingertips. He caught Elsa Guðrún's eye. Like him, she was completely alert.

'You know I had no part in any of this,' Regína said, looking pleadingly at the two of them in turn.

'But you lied to the police and obstructed the investigation for many months. I'm sure you appreciate that comes with consequences,' Elsa Guðrún said with emphasis.

'He smelt of booze and I assumed he'd forgotten the time and had been glugging beer in the garage after he'd finished dealing with that greenhouse. It happens sometimes, and it didn't occur to me that he could have anything bad on his conscience. Since then I've thought this over again and again, and that I shouldn't have gone out that evening,' Regína said, and the effort she was making to speak was clear. 'If I hadn't gone on that course, my sister would be alive today and my husband would be at home.'

'Thinking like that serves no purpose other than to harm yourself. You can't control the actions of others,' Elsa Guðrún murmured.

'I knew something was troubling Skarphéðinn because he's been in such a state ever since Arnhildur died. Of course, I asked him, asked if they'd been in contact ... it never occurred to me that ... imagined that at the worst they could have argued ... but it wasn't until Jacob's remains were discovered that he'd say anything. That hit him hard, and it broke him. He got drunk and told me the whole story, that the hatred had grown inside him like a serpent, and he repeated it again and again. It was terrible to hear this. In reality, we both bear the responsibility for this.' Regína straightened her back and quickly glanced at them both in turn. 'When he'd hit her once, he had to do it again. He was overwhelmed with terror, that this had gone so far ... because she recognised him. He was petrified, and knew what the consequences would be .... Which would naturally have been so much milder than this... this horror. It all happened in a rage, Skarphéðinn had been to speak to her so many times over the years to try to persuade her to sell the house. He was desperate, and it was practically all he could think about...' Regína said and fell silent.

'Would you like a glass of water?' Elsa Guðrún said, glancing at Guðgeir. They were both thinking along the same lines. Regína was presenting a picture of the state Skarphéðinn had been at the time, but none of this could alter the fact that he had taken a hammer with him to meet Arnhildur.

'No, thank you. I'll speak while I still have the courage to do so. You ought to be aware that Skarphéðinn has been on medication for many months, and suddenly stopped taking the tablets. He was a contractor, and there had been complaints. Quick-tempered, they said. He grabbed a tourist who was about to wade into the water at the Reynisfjara beach. It was a woman and her shoulder was dislocated, which is bad, but he was trying to prevent her from getting into real danger, and there were other minor incidents. But the whole legal process because of the accident, Arnhildur's constant accusations that he was responsible for Unnur's disability, losing the farm that had been in his family for generations, our business and the riding school, has been such a burden. We're in debt, getting old, and we're tired. In fact, we're worn out. Skarphéðinn could never understand why Arnhildur refused to sell the house, and neither could I. He saw my sister as his tormentor. He blamed her for everything. We naturally had no idea that there was such a terrible secret buried under the house, but now I can see why Arnhildur couldn't sell. She was a prisoner of the house. Nobody could go down into the unfinished basement, because that was the grave of the husband she loved so jealously that she murdered him rather than allow him to leave her.'

'The murder of Jacob Winter could have been committed while she was in a state of mental turmoil,' Guðgeir said. 'We don't know the circumstances.'

'Well, that sounds likely. My sister wasn't a person inclined to violence, but she was besotted with that man,' Regína said, her voice quavering. 'I just want you to know that Skarphéðinn wasn't like that, not before all this happened. Arnhildur was also a good person. She was perfectly ordinary as a girl, except for her lack of self-confidence. Jacob thought of himself as quite something, not that he was anything special, but he was good-looking and he could turn on the charm. He and Skarphéðinn were good friends, and he said that she'd threatened to commit suicide if he ever left her. But instead of killing herself, she murdered him. After that, her life revolved around two things, concealing her crime and bringing up their daughter. After the accident, the pressure was incredible. Skarphéðinn tried to get her to sell the house,' Regína said and got to her feet, her sad eyes on Guðgeir. 'Arnhildur gave herself a life sentence. She was in her own personal prison from the moment she murdered Jacob. I'm not trying to justify what she did, because you can never justify murder, but I feel myself compelled to sympathise with the misery that must have gnawed at her soul every single day. My husband, Skarphéðinn, has also had his share of suffering. We lost everything and he hasn't had a single happy hour since the accident. Such a promising girl who'd been part of our lives from the day she was born. We loved her with all our hearts and for years Skarphéðinn has been plagued with guilt. If he hadn't given in to her being so obnoxious, if he'd put her on a more placid horse that day, if he'd encouraged her to stay at home that day because she'd been complaining of flu symptoms, if, if, if. All this has plagued him endlessly. This eternal if kept him from me, our children and our grandchildren. We saw Unnur just once after that. It was a month after the accident and Arnhildur wouldn't allow us to see her until then. It was horrible! She could barely walk or talk, she behaved like a toddler. I could hardly look at her.'

'You don't have to be afraid of that now. Unnur's therapy has helped her make some huge progress, even though the damage was considerable,' Guðgeir said, but his words hardly reached Regína, who was on her way out of the room, her hands to her mouth to stifle her sobs.

Summer

49

Unnur sat on the bench in the garden, headphones clamped to her ears. There had to be something pleasant coming from them, as she lay back smiling, her eyes closed, and sunbeams played over her fair hair. Valur Thór gently laid a hand on her shoulder.

'Hi,' he said, sounding happy.

Unnur looked up, her smile broadened and she pulled the earphones down so they hung around her neck.

'Hi,' she responded.

'How are you?'

'Fine,' she said. 'Ulla is crazy. She's always doing something silly, but she's always funny. Hold on, I'll pause the story.'

She pressed her finger to her phone.

'Is that the new manager?' he asked.

'No! You're getting confused again!' Unnur said, pointing at her headphones. 'Ulla is in here, but the new one's called Margrét.'

'Of course. What was I thinking?' He laughed, leaned down and plucked a couple of flowering weeds that had poked their heads up through the green patch of grass. 'For you,' he announced with a courtly flourish, handing them to her. A little sap seeped from the stems to stain Unnur's fingers.

'Look what you've done,' she scolded, throwing the flowers aside.

'Calm down. That'll wash off easily enough,' he said lightly. 'Can I sit with you?'

'Sure,' she said, and moved along the bench.

'How are you feeling in your heart,' he asked, looking her up and down.

'Better now,' she replied. 'But it still hurts.'

'I understand,' Valur Thór said, his voice warm. He reached for her hand and squeezed it gently. 'It's always difficult to lose a loved one, but you can be sure that I won't leave you.'

'People can die all of a sudden, just like Mum,' she said in a low tone.

'Not in my case,' Valur Thór said. 'I'll have to wait for death. I'll be as old as the hills and sick by the time I finally get to die.'

'How do you know that?' she asked in all sincerity, but he didn't reply.

They sat for a while in silence, side by side, holding hands while they let the sun's warmth play over their faces. Valur Thór felt a tranquillity. His eyelids became heavy and he felt at ease. Suddenly Unnur pulled herself away from him and picked up the weeds she had only just thrown aside. He opened his eyes and watched her split the stems, rubbing them over her hands. Dark stains began to appear on her fair skin.

'What are you doing that for?' he asked. 'You'll be covered in black patches.'

Unnur stopped, and stood motionless as she stared at him.

'They were always arguing,' she said at last.

'Who?'

'Mum and Dad. I wanted them to stop and didn't know he was standing at the top of the stairs when I pushed him. It was an accident.'

Valur Thór gaped in shock.

SHROUDED

'Unnur, please don't ... don't,' he managed to gasp before she broke in.

'Mum told me that if I said anything, they'd take me away from her, so I was always really careful. After the accident when my head was damaged, I didn't say anything, but Mum was always frightened I would.'

Valur Thór felt the tears coming, and blinked rapidly to hold them back, but he still felt them flowing down his cheeks. As fast as they appeared, he wiped them away with the back of his hand. For a moment he was unable to speak, but he took a firm grip of his sister's hand and gazed with determination into her eyes.

'Unnur, my love. You've been saying some crazy nonsense, just like Ulla does in the story you were listening to. Understand?'

She gazed back, her eyes barely present, fiddled with her fringe to straighten it and nodded as she put her headphones on again.